Brave Girl, Quiet Girl

Also by Catherine Ryan Hyde

Stay

Have You Seen Luis Velez?

Just After Midnight

Heaven Adjacent

The Wake Up

Allie and Bea

Say Goodbye for Now

Leaving Blythe River

Ask Him Why

Worthy

The Language of Hoofbeats

Pay It Forward: Young Readers Edition

Take Me with You

Paw It Forward

365 Days of Gratitude: Photos from a Beautiful World

Where We Belong

Subway Dancer and Other Stories

Walk Me Home

Always Chloe and Other Stories

The Long, Steep Path: Everyday Inspiration from the Author of Pay It Forward

How to Be a Writer in the E-Age: A Self-Help Guide

When You Were Older

Don't Let Me Go

Jumpstart the World

Second Hand Heart

When I Found You

Diary of a Witness

The Day I Killed James

Chasing Windmills

The Year of My Miraculous Reappearance

Love in the Present Tense

Becoming Chloe

Walter's Purple Heart

Electric God/The Hardest Part of Love

Pay It Forward

Earthquake Weather and Other Stories

Funerals for Horses

Brave Girl, Quiet Girl

A Novel

Catherine Ryan Hyde

LAKE UNION
PUBLISHING

Published by Lake Union Publishing, Seattle

www.apub.com

Amazon, the Amazon logo, and Lake Union Publishing are trademarks of Amazon.com, Inc., or its affiliates.

ISBN-13: 9781542010054 (paperback)
ISBN-10: 1542010055 (paperback)

ISBN-13: 9781542017831 (hardcover)
ISBN-10: 1542017831 (hardcover)

Cover design by Shasti O'Leary Soudant

Printed in the United States of America

Brave Girl, Quiet Girl

Chapter One

Brooke: Shattered

It started that day with just the normal levels of my mother driving me crazy. Which, don't get me wrong, is plenty bad enough. And some left-over feelings from the odd conversation I'd had with the young woman at my daughter's new day care might have factored in.

I'd picked Etta up at day care after my work, at about five thirty, and it was the first time I'd seen the place. It was only my baby's third day there.

My mother had been taking her in and picking her up, at least for the first two and a half days. But then she'd started complaining that it was too much for her "old bones."

I guess it sounds strange that I hadn't checked the place out first with my own eyes. But I was dealing with a stress fracture to my psyche, thanks to my mother, that sprang up midweek. And three entirely unrelated people had recommended this as the best place in the city. And my phone and internet experience with them was stellar. Also, my mother would have been the first to point it out if the place wasn't up to snuff. It's not like me to fall back on her judgment. But if there's one thing I can trust her to do, it's judge.

The yard of the place was on the side of a hill, shaded by trees. Terraced, so the kids had nice flat areas to play, with steps in between. On different levels I saw giant sandbox complexes, swing sets, riding toys. A building pad where two boys were constructing a small city of giant blocks.

It was late in the season, so nearly dark outside, a heavy dusk, but the yard was well lit.

My eyes flew directly to my daughter. She was sitting on one of the riding toys, a bright red plastic horse with a black "flowing" plastic mane. It wasn't a rocking horse, exactly. It was attached by springs to a solid metal frame. It had handhold pegs below each ear, and nice wide platforms for little feet where the stirrups would be. She could bounce up and down on it, or rock it back and forth just a few inches, imitating the gait of a galloping horse.

Etta was doing the latter.

I had dressed her that morning in red tights—almost exactly the color of her horse—and a striped tunic. A light wind was blowing the curly brown hair off her face. And she was lost in utter concentration. She hadn't even noticed me yet. I wondered how real the ride felt in her head. If her horse was galloping along a sandy beach or down a grassy hillside.

She was so beautiful it hurt to look at her. But I did anyway. In fact, I couldn't stop.

The young staff member came up behind me. I didn't notice her until she spoke, so it startled me a little.

"I like the way you look at her," she said.

I smiled a little. At least, I think I smiled. I meant to. I said, "Don't all mothers look at their kids that way?"

"Ha!" she said. "I wish."

Then we watched the girl in perfect silence for a time.

"Etta is very attached to the bouncy horse," she said. "Almost to the point where it's become a problem for her. It's very hard for her to let the other kids take their turn. The good news is, she will. She's not the least bit bullying or unfair about it. But it hurts her. You can tell. She mopes. She seems brokenhearted."

"Oh good heavens," I said, "I'll end up having to buy her a pony. Number three hundred and thirty-four on the list of things I want for her but can't afford."

She laughed. But it hadn't really been a joke. It had been a genuine worry about the future.

"She did very well with her big-girl pull-up pants and the potty today. No accidents."

"That's good to hear."

"We were glad to see you come in instead of your mother." That just sat in the air for a moment. Awkwardly, like a thing looking for a place to hide. I could feel that it had been a mistake on her part. A slip that she was now inwardly scrambling to cover. "I'm sorry. That came out wrong."

"Not really," I said. "It sounded about right to me."

Despite my dismissal of her words, it was an odd thing for a woman at a day care center to say. Then again, you never know what a person might say. People step over lines of propriety every day.

"I didn't mean to . . ."

"Look. I know my mother. And now so do you. It's actually a relief to me when other people see the problems, too. Makes me feel a little tiny bit vindicated. I'm not proud of that, but it's true."

"She just seems to have a big cloud of negativity surrounding her. And that's hard on a kid."

"Tell me about it," I said.

She took a moment to appear deeply embarrassed before speaking.

"Right. Sorry. You grew up with her. But it's good that you seem to be more positive. That's all I meant to say."

"Well, you know how it is. We either grow up to be our mother or we make a solemn vow to the universe to be her polar opposite. Doesn't work every minute of every day, though."

Etta noticed me for the first time. Her face lit up. But she didn't run to me. Just waved with vast enthusiasm and went back to riding her horse. More stridently, though, as if riding took on a whole new meaning with me watching.

"I can't tell you how hard it's been," I said, "going back to living in her house. After the divorce my finances had me over a barrel. But I've been watching how my mother behaves around Etta and how it affects her. And this week I just got to a breaking point with it and put her in day care. But I'm creating a vicious cycle, because my salary doesn't cover much more than the day care. So I'm not entirely sure how to break this cycle I've gotten myself into." I glanced at the woman's face and wondered what she was thinking. I regretted going into such detail. "I'm sorry," I said. "This is more than you needed to know."

"No, it's okay. I must admit, I wondered."

She walked up the steps to the second terraced level, where Ella rode her bright red steed.

She tried to gently steer the girl off the horse, but Ella only fussed, just at the edge of a tantrum. She was clearly tired, which didn't help.

I walked up to them, thinking I could do better.

"Honey," I said. "We need to go home to Grandma's."

Then I regretted bringing up Grandma. Who would want to go home to that? Even a two-year-old knows better than to want that. Hell, a two-year-old probably knows better than anybody.

"Horsey," she said, and started to cry.

"Honey, we'll see the horsey again tomorrow. I promise."

I shouldn't have promised.

Be careful what you promise your kids. We ask them to believe that the world is a deeply predictable place, and you can always know where you'll be tomorrow. But how sure are we?

—

We were closed into our room as a way of steering clear of my mother.

She had the TV on far too loud. She doesn't have trouble with her hearing. I have no idea what she thinks she's doing with that—what need it fills in her. My personal theory? I think she's trying to drive all the thoughts out of her head. Keep her own mind at bay. Then again, it's just a theory.

As though that din weren't bad enough, she kept yelling in to where Etta and I were hiding in our room. And of course she had to shout at the top of her lungs to be heard over the blare of the TV.

I don't know what she was watching, but something with a laugh track. And that was getting under my skin. It was beginning to feel like the worst, most irritating moments of my life came with amused onlookers.

It felt like the ultimate insult that any of this could be considered funny, even if the laughter was mostly in my head.

"Brooke?" she bellowed into our room. She always started with my name, though there was really no one else she could have been talking to. These were not statements one would make to a two-year-old.

I squeezed my eyes closed and sighed.

She kept yelling.

"You need to take Etta out more."

I sighed again. Walked to the bedroom door.

Etta was sitting on the circular rag rug, playing with some blocks. Well, banging them against each other more than anything else, but I guess for her that's a kind of play.

I opened the door a crack to give my mother half a chance of hearing me over the TV.

"I'm tired, Mom. I'm on my feet all day."

"But your daughter's been without you all day. She needs to get out. She needs to spend time with you."

"Why do you think I'm spending all that money on day care? So she can be out all day."

My mother was in poor physical condition. Hugely overweight and out of shape, with bad knees, hips, and feet. She couldn't be expected to get Etta outdoors, which was another brick in the wall of my expensive day care decision.

"That's not spending time with *you*," she barked.

"I *am* spending time with her," I shouted. "Right now! We're playing!"

I don't mean shouted as in yelled at her in anger. More like shouted as in attempted to be heard. I tried to be civil to my mother whenever possible. Two uncivil parties in that household would have been unlivable. It was so close to unlivable as it stood.

Besides, it *was* her house. And I *was* fortunate to have it as a place to land, uncomfortable a landing as it may have been.

"But she needs to go out. You torture that girl. She likes to go out."

I almost blew my stack at that. At the pronouncement that I "torture" my beautiful little daughter. Instead I closed my eyes. Breathed. Literally counted to ten in my head.

"She's been out all day!" I said, and left it at that.

"But not with you!"

"It's dark, Mom. Where am I supposed to take her in the dark?"

It was only six something in the afternoon, but it was nearing winter. And it was dark.

"They have lights in the playground, you know."

I closed the bedroom door.

My mother continued to yell in to me, but I did my best to ignore what she was saying. I could vaguely hear that it was the long story about my cousin's little boy, and how a doctor finally intervened and said the kid wasn't getting enough sunshine. I had heard the story before.

It wasn't worth asking where she thought I would find sunshine at that hour. Or why she thought the day care center didn't have any. It would only cause her complaints to veer off down a different, barely related path. You couldn't stop her once she got on a tear like this. Only send her in new directions. Ones I had learned I wouldn't like any better.

I picked up my phone. Opened the web browser and looked at the website for the movie theater down on the boulevard. I had seen on their marquee that they were playing a kids' movie. The one about the talking cartoon lizards.

I did not do this because I thought my mother was right. Etta loved to sit quietly on the rug with me and play. I did it because being in the same house with the woman was driving me crazy.

I could still hear the drone of her voice—if a full-throated shout could be called droning.

There was a 7:00 showing.

"Etta," I said. "Do you want to go to a movie?"

She turned her huge brown eyes up to me, full of questions. Her brown curls spilled onto her forehead.

She was gorgeous, if I do say so myself. She was also too young to know what I was proposing.

I did a quick internet search and brought up the movie trailer. And played it for her. The phone was turned away from me and toward her, so I don't know exactly what she was seeing, but she shrieked with laughter, waving her arms up and down.

"Okay," I said. "We'll go."

———

"Mom," I said. "Mom!" I had to raise my voice to be heard, even though I was standing right behind her chair.

"What? I'm watching this."

For a woman who interrupted my every thought, she had precious little tolerance for any kind of interruption.

I walked around to the footstool of her chair and grabbed the remote, muting the TV. The silence was stunning. I'd had no idea how utterly punishing the noise had been until it stopped. It felt as though someone had been driving a spike into my ear with a mallet. I felt the absence of that pain as a wash of relief.

"Hey! I just said I was watching that!"

"Etta and I are going to a movie."

"A *movie*?" From the tone of her voice you'd have thought I'd said I was going to run my daughter through a car wash or toss her off a cliff. "Who takes a child her age to a *movie*?"

"It's a kids' movie. She'll like it. It's funny."

"So you want to take her from a dark, cramped house to a dark, cramped movie theater."

I counted to ten again before speaking.

"Mom," I said. Calmly, but it was an artificial calm. "This house is over six thousand square feet. She's not cramped."

"I just think you don't know what kids need. You haven't been a mother long enough."

"I think I'm doing a good job raising her, Mom. Please don't suggest otherwise. It really bothers me when you take that away from me."

She sighed, and I knew she at least would stop attacking me on that particular front. A sigh was a good sign from her. It was a complaint over the fact that she couldn't keep jabbing.

"Take my car," she said. "It's safer."

"My car is fine."

"Your car is a total disaster. What if it breaks down in a bad neighborhood?"

"We don't live in a bad neighborhood, Mom. We live in a nice part of West LA. And the theater is in the same nice part of West LA. I'm not going to purposely detour through a bad neighborhood. I don't know what you're thinking."

"All of LA is a bad neighborhood. The whole world is dangerous. Not like when I was a girl."

"Funny. And yet you just said you wanted us to go to the playground in the dark."

"Don't speak disrespectfully to me."

"Then don't treat me as if I were a child. I'm not a child. I'm thirty-nine years old."

She drew back an arrow and hit me right between the eyes.

"Well, you wouldn't know it to look at you," she said. "Back living at home with your mother like a little girl."

I knew counting to ten would not do it. Not that time. So I just picked up my daughter and left.

"Wear your seat belt!" she shouted to me as we walked out the door.

I normally wear my seat belt, and I always, always buckle Etta into her car seat, in the back, rear facing. Just the way you're supposed to do it. But one time—one damn time—my mother saw me leave the driveway without buckling myself into my own seat belt, and she just wouldn't let it die. "Wear your seat belt, wear your seat belt, wear your seat belt." It became a mantra. An ad slogan that goes through your head so many times you begin to push back against it. My mother can take even a good thing and make it into something I need to flat out refuse to do.

Then the din of the TV drowned out everything again.

—

I buckled Etta securely into her car seat in the back of my mother's car. But I left my own seat belt undone, just out of spite.

I suppose it was a tiny act of rebellion.

—

Etta fell asleep in the first fifteen minutes of the movie. But it was okay. We were together.

The movie was cute and funny, and the laughter of the older children was improving my mood. Tired as I was, I had discovered that being home with my mother was far more tiring than going out and finding a moment of peace.

I draped my arm around my little girl's shoulders, and I could feel the slight vibration of her snoring.

Every now and then my love for that child hit me so hard I felt bowled over. Like a turtle knocked upside down onto its shell, unable to right itself. This was one of those moments.

I watched the rest of the movie and savored that small feeling of everyday joy. Or maybe it wasn't small at all. Maybe it was everything.

Or, most likely of all, maybe it was small and everything at exactly the same moment.

—

My plan was to put on my seat belt to drive home.

I had Etta strapped into her car seat, still snoring like a miniature soprano buzz saw. I was sitting in the driver's seat of my mom's Mercedes, trying to get my own belt done. Sounds easy enough, but I was wearing a big, long sweater, and the folds of it kept getting in the way.

I go back to this moment a lot.

It wasn't much of a struggle before I gave up. It wasn't *that* frustrating. Which makes it even harder to explain after the fact. To myself or anyone else.

As best I can figure after the fact, it was this: In that moment, I was happy. I was out in the world with my child, enjoying one of those perfect moments made perfect by the simple fact that I had her. I was in a state of joy, which felt increasingly rare.

When that moment of slight frustration arose, I didn't want to spoil anything.

I drove away with my seat belt undone.

—

I was stopped at a red light when it happened. And the best I can say to describe the ordeal is the most trite statement of all: it happened very fast. What I'm about to describe in some flawed detail happened in a matter of seconds. Single-digit seconds. Six or seven, tops.

A whole life changed in six or seven seconds.

I saw the shape of a person moving fast toward my car window. Purposefully. It startled me, because it was clear that he was coming right for my driver's side window.

He pulled his arm back as though he was about to throw a punch. I swear he looked as though he would punch the car window, except he was a couple of steps too far away for that.

The arm came forward again.

I saw a small object sail toward the window. Toward my head.

But it was so small. I didn't know what it was at the time, but it seemed too small to be afraid of. Too small to do me much harm. And yet I was instantly afraid, because of the violent intention behind someone hurling a small object at me.

The window shattered. And I do mean shattered. In slow motion.

The window turned from solid glass to a sea of glass pebbles. And just for a flash of a second, they didn't fall. They just hung there in the air between me and the outside world.

I realize that's not entirely possible. But it's what I saw.

Then all at once the pebbles were bouncing all over my lap. All around my feet.

My brain felt frozen. My gut felt frozen. The sudden fear had taken me outside of myself somehow. I felt as though I were watching this violent moment play out from a short distance away, both physically and emotionally.

I punched hard on the gas pedal to get out of there.

I knew as I did it that it would send the Mercedes out into the intersection, and I had no idea if a car might be coming. But I had to do something. There was an arm reaching into my car. A strange, dangerous arm. I instinctively felt that anything I did would be better than doing nothing at all.

The gloved hand on the end of that arm grabbed the steering wheel and pulled hard, and the car veered around in a half circle.

Then the hand opened my door from the inside.

I was still punching the gas pedal in my panic. But the guy was not getting left behind. He was staying with the car. Part of me was mystified. Another part of me could see that he was simply bracing his armpit over the top of the door and he had one foot braced on the bottom of it.

He was riding along.

I looked once at his face before it was all over. I had a distant, detached thought that said I should see his face. To be able to describe it. All I saw was a dark ski mask.

The driver's door was fully open by then, and that was the end of that.

If only I had been wearing my seat belt. If only I had taken that extra minute to put on the seat belt. I could have stayed with the car. It would have been hard to pull me out of the car.

I felt my foot come off the accelerator.

I felt myself out in the air of the night.

I landed on my hip on the tarmac.

I looked up.

The driverless car had slowed, but not stopped. The door was still yawning open. The dark shape of a man was jumping in.

I heard the tires scream on the pavement as he roared away.

I sat up in the middle of the street.

In my peripheral vision, I saw a car stop for me, its driver step out and run in my direction. But I didn't look. I just watched my mother's Mercedes speed off.

I was having this thought, this feeling. Noting that I was alive. That I continued to exist beyond that desperate moment.

The car was just a car. It was a thing. Only a thing. My life was a life, and I was alive. It would be hard to tell my mother I'd lost it, but—

And then it was there. In my head. In every part of me. Fully there, and it seemed unimaginable that it had taken even that split second to arrive.

Next thing I knew I was on my feet, but with no memory of standing up. And I was chasing the car down the dark street. Through an intersection, where my ears were assaulted by the blaring horns of cars that almost hit me. Almost ended my life in that moment.

But they sounded far away.

My chest caught fire, but I just kept running. The Mercedes was moving ten times faster than I was, its red taillights fading into the distance. But I couldn't stop running. I couldn't bring myself to stop.

To admit that it was over.

And I was screaming at the top of my lungs. I knew because my throat was strained and sore. But my voice sounded distant and small to me.

I was screaming, "Etta!" Over and over and over.

Chapter Two

Molly: Because of a Banana

I just wanted a damn banana and I just had this feeling like it was not too much to ask from my life. Like life owed me one little stinking banana after everything else it gave me.

It was dark, but I didn't know how late it was—just that it was dark, and I was walking back from the recycling place—but I only had one dollar and forty-two cents. That's it. From a whole day of going around picking up bottles and cans. One dollar and forty-two cents. It just wasn't a very good day recycling-wise.

I stopped at the corner store, and I was looking at everything they had to eat, and it was all the same crap I ate every day. Well. Every day I was lucky enough to eat.

Chips. Jerky, but that's expensive. Nuts, but they're so salty. But at least they're pretty cheap and they have some protein.

I looked up at the guy behind the counter, who made me nervous. I sort of knew him, but not in a good way, because he used to offer me food and say he would trade me. I kept saying I had nothing to trade and he would only laugh this creepy laugh and he would never tell me straight out what he meant.

After a while it was my friend Bodhi who told me what it meant. Bodhi wanted to help me so he went in and told the guy he was my boyfriend and threatened to beat him up, and after that the guy was mostly just mean and rude to me.

Bodhi was not my boyfriend. He just said that to try to help.

Anyway, the corner store guy still made me nervous. He was old and bald—literally old not just old compared to me like everybody is—seventy, maybe, so it was extra creepy when you thought about it.

On the counter in front of him was a plastic container of bananas. They had never been there before—at least, not that I'd ever noticed. They actually looked kind of disgusting, because they were completely green, but all of a sudden none of the other food in that place looked like food to me at all. It all sounded salty and dry and old and not fresh and not something I wanted. Not even anything I could bring myself to choke down.

I think I hadn't had a single fruit or vegetable since I left Utah with Bodhi.

I walked up to the counter but I never took my eyes off the guy because he made me nervous. And he never took his eyes off me— believe me when I tell you that—but for different reasons.

"How much?" I said, and pointed at the green bananas.

"Dollar fifty."

"*A dollar fifty?* For one banana? It's too much!"

"Then don't buy one."

But by then I wanted one so bad that it was more like I needed it. You know how that can happen? How all of a sudden a thing gets to be more than just the thing it is, and then all of a sudden it feels like everything that's wrong in your life? Not having bananas felt like everything that'd gone wrong in my life since I had to leave home, and, let me tell you, that's a whole big bag of wrong.

He opened his mouth to say more and I knew what he was going to say so I walked out before he could. I have to be worth more than the price of a banana, even a too-expensive one, and the day I lose that I think I'd rather just be gone from this world.

I decided to walk to the all-night market.

Problem was, it was kind of a stupid idea, because all of a sudden I was feeling it in every cell of my body how I'd been eating nothing but junk food—empty calories, my mom would say—and feeling like I needed actual nutrition that my body could use for actual health. Full calories. But at the same time I knew it was a long walk to the all-night market and by the time I got there and back I would've walked off the calories two or three times over. But by then it was a thing I couldn't let go of in my head. I don't know how to explain it any better than that.

So I got into the market and right off the bat this older lady in a company polo shirt and apron started following me around, and not on the sly, either. Real obvious, like "Here I am, you little punk kid, and I'm watching everything you do." But I wasn't doing anything, so it made me mad—I was just walking over to the produce section to look at their bananas, and there's no law against doing that as far as I know.

I found the bananas and looked at them, and they looked really nice—nice and yellow and ripe but not with brown spots yet—but I wasn't sure if it was okay to take one off the bunch. I turned around and that lady was still staring at me with her hands on her hips, her face set hard like she hated me. How can you do that to a person? Hate them when they haven't even done anything to you?

"I'm not going to steal," I said to her, real nice and loud. There was nobody else in the store to crane their necks around and wonder what we were fighting about—at least, not that I could see. "It really sucks that you've already decided I'm going to steal and you don't even know me. That sucks, you know? I would never do that to you—or, actually, I'd never do it to anybody."

She didn't bother to answer, just stared at me with her hands on her hips, which also sucked.

They do this to you when they can tell you're on the street. The younger and dirtier you are, the more you get this everywhere you go. And I'm always thinking, *Damn it, I'm the same person I was when I lived at home with my parents like a regular kid, like everybody else,* but I can't show them that, and they'll never see it, and the whole thing just sucks.

And, by the way, I didn't ever steal. Bodhi stole when he needed to, but I never ate anything he stole, because it wouldn't have been right.

I took my money out of my pocket, the dollar bill, and the forty-two cents in change, and I held it out for her to see, even though she was a pretty long way away.

"I have enough for a banana," I said, "and I'm going to buy it, I'm not going to steal it, and I just need to know if it's okay to take one off the bunch and just buy the one."

I probably should have gone ahead and done it and not even stopped to ask, because I couldn't afford a whole bunch, and if she said no I would've walked all that way for nothing.

"There are some loose ones there in the corner," she said, and pointed over to the left-hand side of the bin where the bananas were sitting.

I found a real nice one, and weighed it, and looked at the price per pound, and did the math in my head, and figured out I could afford an apple, too, and picked one out. And the whole time she never stopped staring at me. I got a Fuji, because that's my favorite kind. I hadn't had a Fuji apple since I left Utah with Bodhi.

I took them both to the checkout counter, and the woman took my money and asked me if I wanted a bag, but I said no because I figured they wouldn't last that long and it was just another thing to throw away. Just more trash on the street in LA, and I felt like I was living in a world overflowing with trash.

Just as she handed me back my eighteen cents change, kind of dropping it into my hand so her clean hand didn't touch my dirty one, she said, "Sorry, hon."

Which I guess was nice.

I said, "That's okay," but it wasn't completely true. I mean, it was and it wasn't, but I figured it was better than if she hadn't said that.

I ate the banana on the long walk back. I could never bring myself to call that place Bodhi and I had been living "home" because that would've been ridiculous. It was never anybody's home and never could be. It was just a place to hide at night. It was good—the banana, I mean—but it didn't last long enough, and when it was gone I wasn't sure it had been worth everything I'd gone through to get it.

I dropped the peel into a trash bin on a corner because I don't like to litter. Not that one more piece of trash would make much difference around where we'd been living, but it was just a thing that mattered to me.

I decided to save the apple, so I put it in the pocket of my pants, which was sort of a weird and bad thing, because there shouldn't have been room for an apple in my pants pocket. When I left Utah I would've had to mash an apple up into applesauce to get it to fit in the pocket of those pants.

Then I looked up, and on the sidewalk on the next block I saw something, but I didn't know what kind of a thing it was. It was under the streetlight, and it didn't look like trash.

I walked closer, and kept looking at it, and when I got closer it started to look like a kid's car seat, like the kind my mom used to use with my little sisters to strap them proper into the car. I guess she used one with me, too, but I was little so I don't really remember.

Anyway, here's the thing: It wasn't trash—or, at least, it didn't look like trash. It looked like a nice, new one that nobody in their right mind would throw away, but I figured when I got closer I would see a strap that got broken, or some other thing that would explain why somebody pitched it. But this other little voice in my head said, *No, maybe it's fine, maybe it's a real find and maybe I could sell it. Take it to a pawnshop or something, and Bodhi and I could have the best meal we've ever had since we've known each other.*

I didn't know Bodhi when I had a family and a house.

Sometimes Bodhi came back with money at night but we never spent much of it on food. He was saving it up so we could get a real place to live. I knew probably it would never happen but anyway that was the plan, and it gave us a way to not be completely hopeless about everything.

It was faced away from me, the car seat, so I was looking at the back of it, and that made it hard to know if it was a good find or not.

Then I went to that place in my head where I got kind of frozen up inside, which I pretty much always did when I thought something good was about to happen, because once you let yourself believe something good is about to happen, it can also not happen. Any idiot knows that.

I got up to it, and I looked down, and I was still kind of nervous because I was about to see if I'd found something worth real money or not.

And then, when I looked, I was shocked by what I saw. Really shocked.

This little girl was looking up at me with these huge brown eyes. She was being real quiet, but you could see she'd been crying. Her eyes were red and puffy and her nose was all snotty right down to her lip, but she wasn't crying anymore. Just sitting real quiet.

She looked up at me, and she didn't really look scared of me. She didn't really look happy to see me, either, though. She just looked confused, like she couldn't figure out the world at all in that minute, and, let me tell you, I really know how that feels.

I said, "What are you doing out here all by yourself?" but it was kind of a stupid thing to say, because she was just a baby. I mean, not a *baby* baby, not a little baby, probably old enough to toddle around on her feet, but not the age of a kid who would answer me back in a full sentence.

She just stared at me with those big eyes.

"Where's your mommy?"

"Mommy," she said, and wrinkled up her face like she was going to start crying again.

"Oh, no, baby, don't cry. Don't cry, little girl. We'll find her. We'll find your mommy."

She looked up at me with those big eyes again, and her face straightened out like she could maybe stop crying and believe me. Trouble was, I didn't know if what I'd just told her was true or not.

"First let's get you all unstrapped here," I said to her, because I had a feeling she might've been strapped in there for a while. I can't say for a fact why I thought I knew it, other than the way you could tell she'd been crying for a long time with nobody wiping her nose. "I know all about little girls," I told her while I unclipped her, "because I've got two little sisters. They're a lot bigger than you now, but they weren't always. They used to be just about your size and I used to help take care of them a lot and right now I just miss them so damn much I could . . ."

The word I was heading for was "cry." But I looked down at those huge brown eyes and I figured I'd better not do it—I'd better not even say it—because she was looking to me for reasons to stay calm, so all I said was "Sorry for the cussing. Don't repeat stuff like that."

But she had no idea what I was saying, I could tell.

I pulled her up into my arms and she accepted me right away. Just like that. Sometimes a little kid her age won't want to go to a stranger. They'll fuss and try to get back to their mom. Of course that's a different situation because it means their mom is right there to go back to. This little girl had been strapped in a car seat on an empty sidewalk in the dark, so if she hadn't decided to be okay with going to me, what better choices did I figure she had?

I got kind of panicky, just all of a sudden, because it came over me in a big way that I *had her* now, and she was my responsibility. I couldn't just put her down and walk away, so what was I going to do?

I walked around in circles calling stuff out into the dark.

"Hello? *Hello-o?* Mom of this little girl? Parents of this little girl? Are you around here? Somewhere? Anywhere?"

I had to ask, because I couldn't just walk away with her. What if they'd only set her there for a second to get something out of the car or go into a building? Well, the answer to that, of course, was they would be terrible parents to do it, but I still couldn't walk away with their kid.

But I stood there with her, her cheek down on my shoulder and her little fingers holding tight to the back of my shirt, and just listened for an answer, and let me tell you, there was nothing and nobody out there. This was a pretty industrial part of the city. Not literally downtown, where the office buildings are, because that's nicer, but definitely a business-y part of the city, mostly machine shops and warehouses, and nobody actually lives here except people who're on the street. We live everywhere, especially places where other people don't, because that way there's nobody to call the cops on us to drive us out of the neighborhood. And it's not a place you really want to be at night, so it's not like there were people walking by or anything.

I just stood there in the middle of the sidewalk for a minute, holding her, and I got this spooky feeling like in those movies where the star character realizes they're the only person left alive on the earth.

"Okay," I said to the little girl. "Next idea. We have to find a phone and call the police and report you missing. Or . . . found, I guess I mean. Report you found."

But, finding a phone . . . that was not nearly as easy around here as I'd just made it sound, and I so completely knew it.

—

I bombed out on finding a phone.

I went to the corner store, but the guy had already closed it up for the night. He didn't keep what you might call regular hours, just gave up and went home when there was nobody coming in. And there were no pay phones around there. There were probably no pay phones anywhere in the city, because who needed them? Everybody had a cell phone except Bodhi and me.

I didn't want to walk back to the all-night market, because I had the girl on my hip, with her head on my shoulder, and the car seat hanging from one hand, and it was too heavy. It was too much for me. Plus there was an even more important reason. It was a bad neighborhood and it was only getting later, and I was willing to risk myself by walking down the streets here, but I wasn't willing to risk somebody else's little baby girl.

I took her back to where Bodhi and I had been hiding at night. It was a huge wooden shipping crate in the far corner of a vacant lot full of trash, made up of slats with a tiny bit of room in between, that you could've seen the stars through if you could see the stars in the city. But it was handy for seeing if anybody was coming, and the empty slots were too narrow for them to see us. When I say it was huge, I mean for a crate. For a place to stay it was pretty damn small, but Bodhi and I slept wrapped around each other anyway. But only because it got a little bit cold. We didn't like each other like that.

I left the car seat outside because there was no room for it and sat inside with the girl and waited for Bodhi to come back. Sometimes he would come back too late and with too much money—a scary amount of money, like forty dollars—and I would be worried about where he got so much.

I held her tight in my arms and said, "Come back, Bodhi, come back, Bodhi, come back, Bodhi," over and over and over.

And the little girl said "Mommy" and "Horsey," in no particular order, and I never did know which one she was about to say next.

—

Bodhi got back probably an hour later.

He stuck his head in and looked at me and looked at the girl, and got this strange expression on his face, like life was just so completely surprising and he couldn't decide if he should like that about life or not.

He had this way of tilting his head like a curious dog if something struck him strange, and he did that.

He was experimenting with different ways to have a beard, which meant he had to find a way to shave every day or two, but I guess it was worth it to him. Right now it was a little square soul patch under his bottom lip, but with the rest of his beard poking out around it because it was near the end of the day. But it was all kind of wispy and light, his beard hair, because he was young, too. Not as young as me. I think he was around nineteen but I never asked.

"Well," he said, and his voice was super familiar so it made me feel better. "Who. Is. This?" He made his voice kind of high and light on the last word, which was nice, because it made the baby less scared of him.

"You need to go find a phone," I said. "Maybe run down to the all-night market and ask the lady there to call the police. Tell her we found a baby just all by herself on the street and they have to come get her and figure out who her mother is and how to get her home."

He frowned, and the baby fussed a little because it scared her.

"And what if her mother dumped her on purpose?"

I actually hadn't even thought of that, and then I was wishing I didn't have to think of it now.

"The police still need to come and get her. You know. And get her a foster home or something. Whatever they do with kids."

But then I got worried because I didn't really know what they do with kids, and if what they do is okay for the kid, and the weird thing was that I already cared what happened to this one, even though it had only been an hour or two. But there was nothing I could do about it. She wasn't my baby and I had to turn her over to the police, and there was just no other answer to a question like that one.

"The police," he said. Like the words tasted bad in his mouth when he said them. "I kind of hate to call the police. I just now finished out-running a couple of them."

"Again?"

I said it like I was mad, but really it scared me, because if Bodhi got arrested then what would I do?

"Gotta make a living," he said.

"You can get lost before the police show up."

"Hate to bring them here," he said. "Might be the end of our good hiding place."

"Just tell them we'll meet them on the corner. When I hear a car pull up or voices or whatever, I'll come out. They won't see where I came from behind all the junk."

For a minute he didn't do anything at all. Just froze there with his head in the crate and his body out, like he was thinking about things. Then he gave us a little salute like an army man, and his face was gone.

The whole Bodhi was gone.

———

He got back maybe half an hour later, but time is a weird thing to try to judge, especially at a time like that when you're scared and nervous and wanting it to go by fast.

"Bad news," he said. "We have to move."

"Move? You mean permanently?"

"No, maybe not permanently. But as long as you have that kid. You know those three guys who call themselves the Three Musketeers?"

I knew them all right—well enough that my blood got a little bit colder thinking about them—and he knew I knew them. It was just the way you start a sentence, not a serious question. They were on the street like us, but also *not* like us because they were meaner. They lived in the basement of an abandoned building three or four blocks over, and everybody avoided that block because they were bad news.

"What about them?"

"They were in the store trying to steal some candy, but the lady wouldn't take her eyes off them. She was following them around with I think a gun in the pocket of her apron. And when I asked her to call the cops and told her why, they heard me. I didn't think they would hear me. But then I was outside a minute later and I heard them say they want the kid."

My blood went from cool to frozen, just really fast like that. I could see the sky past Bodhi's head, and I actually could see a couple of the brightest stars.

"That doesn't make any sense. Why would they want her?"

My voice was real quiet, like a scratchy whisper, like they were right outside the crate listening and maybe hearing everything I said.

"They figure she's worth a lot of money because her parents'll want her back. They want to try to ransom her back to her parents. And I'm pretty sure they know where we hide. So we need to move. Like, now."

"Wait. No. That's stupid. They don't even know who her parents are."

"Well, they're going to try to find out. Watch for an Amber Alert or find something in the paper about it or something like that. Anyway, they're going to take her now and figure that out later, so we need to move."

But after he said that I was so scared I almost couldn't move. But I did move, anyway, because anything else, anything that wasn't getting out in time, would've been just too awful to think about.

"Get the car seat," I said as we rushed out of our crate.

But I didn't say it because it was worth money. That didn't matter anymore. I said it because I didn't want to leave anything behind that they could use to see where we'd been. I figured it was better if they felt like we could be just about anywhere. I figured it would only get their mouths watering too much to see a sign that they'd just missed us.

We hurried down the street together, but I had no idea where we were going, and he couldn't have either, and it was a really lost feeling.

I would've told you, just before that happened, that I couldn't possibly have felt more lost in this big, crazy world but I would've been wrong.

———

Bodhi found us a place to hide under a freeway overpass. There was this really steep hill going up under it, and then the hill kind of flattened out at the top. And it was sort of cave-like under the iron structure of the bridge, getting smaller and smaller at the back.

In a way it scared me because if they found us here we'd be pretty cornered, but it was a good hiding place, too.

There were all these sheets of flattened cardboard, like big cartons flattened out, and a hollow space under them that could make it look like they were lying flat with nobody underneath them. I wondered if somebody had hidden there before. You know, like dug it out as a place to hide. In this city it was a pretty good bet.

I hoped nobody was about to come back and claim the spot.

"Here," Bodhi said, and handed me a bottle of apple juice. A round, squatty glass bottle. "I forgot. I stole this for her. And this. I thought maybe she was hungry. I don't know how much she's on solid food, but . . ."

He held up a box of goldfish crackers and I saw the baby reach out for the box. I don't know if she knew what they were by the picture, or if she was just hungry and figured it was a box of food.

"Thanks," I said. And I took the crackers, even though I never, ever took anything he stole, because it was stolen. But it was different this time because it was for the baby and not for me. "How are you going to find a phone where nobody can overhear you?"

"Not sure," he said. "Maybe my best bet is to flag down a car and get somebody to call on their cell. Anyway, you stay right here." He covered us up with a sheet of cardboard and the whole world got very dark. "I'll be right back."

But he wasn't right back. In fact, he never came back at all.

That was the last time I saw my friend Bodhi for a really, really long time.

Chapter Three

Brooke: Chop Shops

The door of the police station opened. In came . . . my mother.

I think I said, "No, not that. Don't do that to me."

I think I said it out loud.

I did not say those words *to* my mother, and they were not said loudly enough for her to hear. I think I was talking to some entity or power larger than myself. But that was odd, too, because I've never managed to define such a thing in my life. Then again, we all know the old saying about atheists in foxholes.

She moved across the room in a sort of . . . I'm tempted to say *waddle*, but I'm resisting the word because it seems derogatory. I swear I don't mean it that way. Just . . . it feels like the only word that really catches the thing right. Let's say she teetered from one bad knee to the other, pushing her great bulk forward. Toward me. She still hadn't looked up.

When she did finally look into my face, I looked away.

I got that feeling again. Like I was falling down a well. A very deep well. Maybe a bottomless one. I'd been wrestling with it for hours. Ever since that damned Mercedes drove away without me.

For the first three hours or so, I'd been too much in shock to feel like I was falling. Instead I'd felt empty. Numb. As though everything around me were a movie or a play. An unconvincing one at that.

Now it was beginning to catch up. The truth was just at the edge of catching me. Every time it arrived, such as when I looked at my mother's face, I found myself losing my grip. On something. Hard to know what. And the feeling that followed was that of a terrifying free fall.

I scrambled desperately to reclaim my denial.

This was not happening. This could not be happening.

She rushed toward me—as best she could rush—and threw her arms around me. It was alarming. Normally she was not big on any kind of touch. Then again, these were not normal times.

Heaven help me, I found the soft bulk of her strangely comforting.

"Any news?" she asked near my ear.

I dropped my face against her shoulder and shook my head.

When I looked up again, I noticed that the few officers in attendance were watching us, their faces warm. As though witnessing a touching scene. It struck me strange, knowing everything I knew about my fraught relationship with my mother. Well . . . I don't literally mean I thought it was strange. What could they be expected to know? It just caught me off guard. A surprise.

It was the middle of the night. The population of the place had thinned out considerably. There were maybe thirty desks in that huge room, and only five of them were occupied.

The policewoman who had been helping me all night was moving in our direction. And I dreaded her arrival. Because I worried she was going to tell me to go home. I didn't want to go home. I felt like the police station was the closest I could get to my daughter.

She was strangely tall, the officer. Well over six feet. Reed-thin and elongated, as though someone had stretched her out. Her white-blonde hair was very short. Like a cut a man's barber would do. She was probably close to fifty, but looked good for it.

Her name was Grace Beatty. She had told me so. Her name tag said "Officer G. Beatty."

"Now that your mother's here . . . ," she said.

I knew where we were going with this. I'd known all along.

I opened my mouth to object, but she talked me down.

"I get it," she said. "I really do. But you have to give a thought to yourself in a moment like this. It's important for you, it helps us, it helps your daughter if there's a sudden development. You need rest. We need you to rest. The whole world needs you to rest right now, Brooke. An actual emotional breakdown is a real possibility in a situation like this, and the best way I know to ward it off is rest and food. And staying hydrated. I know pacing around the precinct feels right, but it's not really serving any purpose except to wear you down. Go home. Really, Brooke. Go home. We'll call you the split second we know anything more. That's a promise."

Again, I opened my mouth in my own defense. This time my mother beat me to it.

"You don't have any children," she said to Grace Beatty. It was not a question. But she made it one. By adding the following throwaway tag. "*Do* you?"

"I have four," the officer said, her face soft.

That stopped all the words for a few moments.

"We have the Amber Alert up on all the freeways," Grace Beatty said. "Just like we said we would. The guys are arranging raids on any known chop shops between here and the Mexican border—"

"I don't know what a chop shop is," my mother said. Interrupting. She sounded aggravated. As if the officer had no right to use a phrase that wasn't understandable to her on its surface.

She had let go of me by then. She'd tried to keep one hand on my shoulder, but I'd just ducked out from under it. Now that she was talking, my ability to view her as a comforting figure was evaporating fast.

It irked me, what she'd said. Because *I did* know what a chop shop was. I'd had it explained to me earlier that night. And it bothered me that she was forcing the proceedings to slow down because *she* wasn't caught up.

"People who jack cars sometimes take them to a warehouse or a garage," Grace Beatty said. The model of pasted-on patience. Or maybe it was real patience. Maybe it would need to have been pasted on only if it were me. "They take them to these places to break them down, or repaint them, or otherwise disguise them before shipping them somewhere else. They usually file off the VIN number. I mean, this is not the case with every carjacking, of course. Sometimes an individual is just desperate for a car. But the fact that it was a high-end model . . . well, it's hard to know."

"Why would you let these shops stay in business?" my mother asked, her voice hard. She had begun speaking to the policewoman as if she were her own daughter. Heaven help us all. "I mean, if you know where they are, why didn't you shut them down a long time ago?"

"Mom," I said.

But Grace Beatty waved me off. "No, it's fine. We keep on top of them as best we can, ma'am. When a thing like this happens, we try to get some information on the street as to where new ones might've sprung up, so we can get a fast bead on where the car might've gone. It doesn't always work. But it's something we can do, and we're doing everything we can."

I got that sickening feeling again. The falling. This time I couldn't scramble back to denial. I was too tired even to try. I just let myself fall. I let my entire existence hit rock bottom.

"When a thing like this happens?" my mother parroted back, emphasizing that the words were not believable to her. "You're telling me a thing like this has happened before?"

"Oh yes," Grace Beatty said. "Carjackings tend to happen fast, and it's not all that unusual for a child or a pet to go unnoticed in the back seat. Of course, the children are more helpless. We actually like it a lot when a jacker finds out the hard way that there's a big German shepherd or pit bull in the car. We think of that as help dispensing our justice." She stopped talking. Scanned our faces. Seemed to realize she'd pulled the conversation off track. That her story was the wrong mood for the wrong audience. "But in cases like this . . ."

"If it's happened before," my mother asked, interrupting again, her voice thin and almost whiny, "what did they do with the children?"

"Three times out of four they just put them out of the car when they discover them. The fourth time they might try to ransom them back to the parent. They can usually find a registration in the glove compartment. They know how to get in touch."

It struck me, with a panic I felt in my throat and lower intestines at the same time, that the phone was unmanned at home. Also that my child, my baby, the love of my life, might be out on the street at night alone. Or in the hands of a ransoming criminal. I had no idea which felt worse.

But my mother was still grilling the officer.

"And if it was just a crazed individual needing a car?" I heard her ask. As if far away. As if I were hearing her voice echo down a long tunnel. "And if he never takes it to one of those chopper places? And if he never calls us wanting money to give her back? Then what?"

"Well, then we really have to earn our paychecks," Officer Beatty said. "But let's try to be optimistic and believe we'll get a good, clear early break."

And, with that, I fell even deeper. Past the false bottom of my first well. To a whole new depth. One I'd never even known existed in the world.

———

"We have to call a cab," my mother said as we walked out the door together.

"You didn't drive my car here?"

"Oh my goodness, no! I would never drive your car. I'd be thinking the whole way that it was just about to explode."

I let it go by. I was too tired. Too far down the well.

"If we need to make a phone call," I said, "why are we walking out onto the street?"

"You don't have your phone with you?"

"No."

"Why didn't you bring your phone with you?"

"I did."

"Well, where is it now?"

I experienced a sudden flash of anger. It surprised me. I hadn't felt it coming. "If I knew *that*, Mom, we wouldn't have a problem!" I shouted at her.

I watched her rock back a step. Her eyes looked as though I might actually have hurt her. I saw her try on the idea of shouting back. Saw her anger rise up, then fall away again. She was experiencing a rare moment of humanity. This disaster was bringing out the best side she had.

"I'm sorry," I said. "I didn't mean that the way it came out. It was sitting in the console of your car."

"Oh," she said. Quietly. Then, "I see."

We stood on the dark street together. Not talking. The mood seemed to sink further. I think it was coming down on both of us. The fact that we were somehow supposed to move forward from this moment. Draw a post-disaster breath.

"I'll go inside and ask that nice policewoman to call us a cab," she said.

I watched her move her huge, fragile body back to the police station door. It surprised me to hear that she thought Grace Beatty was nice. She hadn't treated her as though she thought so.

I looked up and saw actual stars. And I was angry at them. For shining. As though nothing had happened. I was angry at life for going on. They say it always does, but this seemed like too extreme an example.

"Just one thing," I heard my mother's voice say. She was standing at the door to the station, one hand on the door pull. "I still don't get how he could drag you out of the car. You had your seat belt on."

I pulled a big breath. The blank denial came back to save me. For a minute, anyway.

"It just all happened really fast," I said.

"But you did have your seat belt on."

"Yes."

To this very day I haven't corrected the lie. To this very day, I feel guilty and uncomfortable about the lie. But in that moment, I couldn't. I just couldn't.

———

The most astonishing part of later that night is the fact I slept. Even briefly. It might only have been a minute or two, but it still amazes me.

I hadn't meant to. There was nothing purposeful about it.

I'd just been lying on the bed. I'd brought the kitchen phone into my room and plugged it in. There was an old-fashioned phone jack in there, but I'd never used it. Because I had my cell.

I thought I was awake the whole time. But when the phone rang, it startled me out of a dream. Just as well. It was a terrible dream. I was thrashing through water that was jet black and felt as thick as quicksand. Every minute or two I'd get a quick glimpse of my baby's car seat. I'd push desperately in that direction, but the blackness of the waters would close in again and it would be gone. I could barely move through the stuff.

The ringing sent my heart up into my throat. I guess that's kind of an old cliché, but in that moment I really understood what it meant. I felt it.

I grabbed up the phone, my mind filling with horrible ideas. Not really visual images. More like concepts. This growly, deep-voiced monster would tell me he had Etta. He might threaten to hurt her. I'd hear her crying in the background. And die inside.

By the time I got the phone to my ear, my heart was pounding so hard I could hardly breathe. I couldn't speak.

"Brooke?" I heard on the line.

It was the voice of Grace Beatty.

All that breath rushed out of me at once. Too much breath to have held in those poor lungs of mine, by all rights. Those horrid images of the monster who was about to own my life, my heart and soul—they flowed out of me. I felt like nothing without them. They had taken me with them as they exited. There was nothing left.

I tried to speak. But what came out was more of an unintelligible grunt.

"We didn't find her. I didn't call to say that. I know it's best to say that right up front, as fast as possible."

The bedroom door flew open. So hard it swung back and hit the wall. I jumped. My mother stood in the open doorway, panting. She looked into my eyes and asked a direct question with her own.

I shook my head.

She began to cry.

I don't think I'd ever seen my mother cry. I don't think I'd ever gotten the impression that she cared that deeply about anything. In retrospect, I guess I should have known better.

Then I burst into tears, too.

I think I hadn't cried yet, though I had been so numbed by shock as to not trust my own memory. I think I'd been so overwhelmed with fear that it had drowned out the sorrow underneath.

But when my mother cried, there was no holding it in anymore.

Meanwhile Grace Beatty was talking. And I was only half hearing her.

". . . so they raided this chop shop in San Diego. Not far from the border. And we recovered your mother's car. They were already halfway through repainting it, but they hadn't filed off the VIN yet, so we got them dead to rights. The San Diego PD has them in for questioning, but the guys running the shop seemed surprised to hear about a child. Could be an act, but our colleagues down there don't think so. They think whoever dropped the car off didn't share much. Just got his money and left. So we have the car. And we're still doing all we can to find your daughter, I swear. But I'm afraid this development doesn't put us any closer. But of course I had to call and tell you."

I was falling again. And every one of her sentences was echoing down the well to me. From farther and farther away.

"Of course," I said. "Thank you."

And it was amazing, because I said it like a real person speaks in a normal situation. I have no idea how that happened.

"Are you doing okay?"

"I don't know," I said. "Probably not."

It was the most honest answer I could find.

"If you have a doctor, you can call. I'm sure you could get a prescription for some kind of sedative."

"Okay," I said.

But only because I wanted the conversation to be over. Only because I wanted anything that required anything from me to stop. I had nothing to give to the world in that moment. Literally nothing. Couldn't everybody see that?

I knew I would not call the doctor or take any sedatives. What if my baby needed me?

"Okay," the officer said. "Well . . ."

"I know you're doing all you can," I said. Or somebody said. It didn't really sound like me. Or feel like me. But it was my lips and my breath, so who else could it have been?

"Stay by the phone. We'll be in touch."

"Bye."

I gently hung up.

I purposely didn't look at my mother. But at the edge of my vision I saw her rush across the room to me. She lowered herself onto the edge of my bed and wrapped me up in her huge arms. I didn't resist. I had nothing in me to mount a resistance. Even if I'd wanted to.

I mostly didn't want to.

"They'll find her, Brooke," she said. "It's their job, and they're good at it. It's what they do."

It may have been their job. They may have been good at it. But they don't find every child who goes missing. And we both knew it.

We just couldn't bring ourselves to say it out loud.

—

About an hour later I crawled out onto the slant of roof outside my bedroom window. The way I used to do when I was a child.

I sat with my knees up tight to my chest, my arms wrapped around them.

I spoke a few words out loud.

It wasn't praying, exactly. Because I wasn't sure if I believed in God or not, or what kind of God I believed in if I did. But more importantly than that, God just wasn't who I was talking to in that moment.

I said a few words into the night to whoever had her. Whoever was with her. If in fact anybody was with her.

I said, "Please be gentle with her. Please don't hurt her. Please comfort her when she cries. Please don't let her be too scared. She's a good girl. She's totally innocent. She doesn't deserve anything bad from anybody. Please take good care of her and get her back to me."

Then I sat still, as if listening. As if waiting for the night to say something in reply.

Nothing came back to me except silence.

Chapter Four

Molly: Brave Girl, Quiet Girl

It took me a long time to figure out that Bodhi might not be coming back right away like I expected. I don't really exactly know how long it took me, because I didn't have a watch—and if I'd ever had one, I'd have sold it for food a long time ago—but it might have been hours. Literally hours. Because you know how there are these situations where time stretches out? Like, ridiculously long? It was that sort of a thing, and so no matter how much time went by I kept thinking maybe it wasn't as much time as it seemed like it was.

Or maybe I just really didn't want to know what was right there to know.

I gave the baby about half the apple juice and a handful of the crackers. I was thinking it was too bad Bodhi stole apple juice, because I had an apple in my pocket, and I could've given her some of that, but now what was the point? It was just apple and more apple, and the only difference was whether she had to chew it up or not. Something different with a different kind of nutrient for her would've been better, but it wasn't his fault, because he didn't know. The crackers I knew would keep her happy but they were mostly empty calories.

Then she started to cry again, because it was dark in there, in that dirt hole under the flat cardboard boxes, and it was getting cold. And the cars that went by on the freeway over our heads were making these weird loud thumping noises, and it was scary. It was scary even to me, and I'm mostly grown.

So I started telling her she was a brave girl. I said, "Brave girl, brave girl," over and over, and then after a while I sort of started to sing it. Two notes, the first one higher than the other.

At first it didn't seem to make any difference to her. She was probably too young to understand what it even meant to be a brave girl. But still, I think if you repeat something over and over to a baby, especially in that singsongy kind of a voice, it soothes them. I think it's almost hypnotizing for a kid.

So after about a hundred "brave girls" she stopped crying and fell asleep.

I stayed awake for a long time, even though it was the middle of the night and I was drop-dead tired. I was so tired that all the muscles in my arms and legs felt like they were buzzing, like with electricity, and my stomach felt all rocky and bad, and my eyes felt like they were full of sand.

I stayed awake and held her tight and rocked her just the tiniest little bit, even though she was asleep, because I didn't want her to be scared. Even in her sleep, I didn't want her to be scared. You can be scared in your sleep—believe me, I know.

I started thinking about how Bodhi told me he had just finished outrunning a couple of cops, and then I started worrying about what if they saw him again while he was walking around looking for a phone. After you run away from the cops you really want to keep your head down, at least until after their shift changes, and here I'd sent him out to make a call. What was I thinking? I mean, that's no way to treat your best friend, except for the fact that I'd had absolutely no choice but to ask him to go.

I started thinking how scared I would be if he never came back, which it was starting to dawn on me might be happening. I don't mean it like I was thinking of myself and not him, because that would make me a lousy friend, and because if he'd been arrested, then it sucked much worse to be him that night. I thought of that first—of him first—and then after that I thought of how much it would suck for me, too.

I mean, going forward it would be the worst, because he was my only friend since we'd left Utah, and I'd never lived one full day on the street without him, and I wasn't even sure I knew how. But even more, it was the worst just in that moment because I didn't dare come out of hiding with the little girl, because I didn't want those three horrible guys to get her, but there was no phone in here, and I started getting panicky not knowing what to do. She would get more and more scared, and her diaper would get dirty, and she had nobody to depend on but me.

It was too much responsibility but there was nothing I could do about it by then because it was already too late. I was all she had, and there was no way I was going to let her down—I mean, if I could help it. But at the same time I knew my hands were more or less tied because she was just a baby and she needed so many things and I had nothing for her. I had not one thing this little girl needed to be okay.

Well, that's not completely true—I had two things she needed. I had a bottle of apple juice and some goldfish crackers, and I knew how to comfort a little kid.

—

The most amazing and hard-to-believe part of the whole night—for me, anyway—was how I fell asleep. I would've bet you money that I never would, not even for a second, because I was too cold and rattled and scared, and the responsibility of this tiny little perfect life was sitting too hard on my head and keeping me awake.

And, you know, I have no idea—maybe I was only asleep for a second. All I know is that when I heard the first one of their voices it scared me up out of a weird dream.

I was sitting in a tree outside my family's house in Utah—in the dream, I mean—and I was some kind of big bird. Like an eagle or a hawk, just looking down on them living their lives, and I guess I was thinking it was sad how they were just going on without me like nothing much had changed. Like I was a number in a math problem and they could just subtract me and get a different total and move on. Why I was a bird, I have no idea, but you know how dreams are.

Then I heard it.

"Yoo-hoo." The words were drawn out real long, like singing. But let me tell you, it's a song I never wanted to hear again as long as I lived. If I ever turned on the radio and heard a thing like that, I'd be gone. I'd run screaming out into the night.

Well, I was out in the night all right, but there was no place to run.

I jumped when I heard it, and that woke the baby, because we were all wrapped around each other, cuddled really close together to keep her warm and not so scared. But when she felt me jump like that, she not only woke up, but she woke up scared to death again, and she started to cry. She started kind of slow, but I could tell the crying was going places, because kids can build up a lot of steam behind a thing like that, and if she got too loud then I knew it was all over. But it made me scared to know that, and she could feel it, being so close and all, so that didn't help.

I started whispering in her ear, but so quiet. It was so quiet I wasn't sure she could even hear me. It was more like making the words with my lips against her ear, but then just this tiny breath of air that was the sound.

I said, "Brave girl, quiet girl."

The noise of the cars on the freeway going over our heads was a good thing, because if we only made little noises, then the thumping of their tires on—actually I have no idea what the tires were thumping on—would drown us out.

She said it back to me, just as quiet, which really surprised me. She stopped her run-up to that big cry and whispered back to me, "Brave girl, kiet girl," right in my ear. She didn't really get the *kw* sound in *quiet*—I think she was too young to have gotten the hang of that sound—but anyway I knew what she meant so what difference did it make?

Then I heard "Molly," also real long and singy, and then "Bodhi. Where are you?"

I knew the voice and I knew it was one of the wild boys, the Musketeers. The one who was really smart and actually had a lot of schooling and wanted to make sure you knew it.

"Brave girl, quiet girl," I whispered again.

"Brave girl, kiet girl," she whispered back, and I was so proud of her it almost made my chest explode. Because I knew she was doing more than just imitating the words like a parrot, she was really working hard to be brave, just like I was asking her to do.

It hit me in that minute that I would have to give her over to the police as soon as I could—unless those boys took her away from me, which was too awful to think about—and then I'd be alone. No Bodhi, no little girl, and already I knew I would miss her, which was weird because it'd only been a couple of hours, but I could feel how it *was* that way whether I *wanted* it to be or not.

"We're going to *find* you," I heard one of them say, the dumber one. He wasn't singing. He meant business. But the good news was that his voice came from a little farther down the block, like they had already passed us.

It was a good hiding place Bodhi had found for us—at least, I hoped it was—but then I wondered how much of a sitting duck I would be if I didn't have him to figure out stuff like this for both of us.

I heard some banging noises at the end of the block, so I lifted up the flattened cardboard, but just the tiniest bit you can possibly imagine. Like an inch, like just enough to see under it with one eye. Two of them were crossing the empty street to the next block, and the one I thought was dumb was already across, and he had a big stick that he was banging against a row of dumpsters. Then he flipped their lids open and shouted "Ha!" each time, but of course we weren't in there.

There was a billboard on the other side of the freeway that I could see through that little slit, and it had this really nice expensive luxury car on it that probably cost like a million dollars. Well, not really, but you know what I mean. Just a whole lot. There was a light aimed up at the billboard so people could see it in the night, but it kept flickering on and off.

It's weird, I know, but when I look back on that night, I always think of that car, and see it behind my eyes. Like, it's there, it's gone, it's there, it's gone. I think I was stunned by the idea that all over this city—hell, all over the world—people have so much money that you can just show them a picture of a pretty thing like that and they'll run out and spend a million dollars on it. I mean, somebody must, or they wouldn't keep putting up the billboards, because they're not free to put up. I wondered how it would feel to see a thing like that and just go out and buy one, and whether I would ever know how that felt, even once in my whole life.

The boys turned the corner, and I breathed out a big bunch of air I must've been holding in. I waited a minute or two just to be safe, and then I started talking to the little girl.

"Is your diaper wet?" I asked her, not really expecting she would answer me. It was more like talking to myself.

But she understood me, and she shook her head no.

I thought it was kind of amazing that she could hold it so long, but I guess looking back that's kind of a weird thought because I had no idea how long it had been. I had no idea how long she'd been sitting in that car seat, or how long it had been since I found her there. But a few hours at least.

"You want some more apple juice?"

Then I wished I hadn't asked her that, because the more apple juice I gave her, the more she was going to need to go. But you have to give a kid stuff to drink, because the littler they are, the more you can't let them be dehydrated. I knew that from the time one of my little sisters was throwing up and had diarrhea. The doctor said it's really important not to let them get dehydrated, so I figured diaper rash was less dangerous than that.

She reached right out, and I opened the bottle again, but I had to sort of turn her over so she was more facedown, because you don't want that juice going down into her lungs and choking her. Well, not choking, exactly, because she could breathe around it, but it would make her cough something fierce. And coughing is loud, but also it wouldn't be good for her.

She took about three sips and then we both heard it. We heard those boys coming back, retracing their steps along this avenue under the freeway bridge.

I could feel her gather her breath in, like gearing up to cry, and I almost panicked and put my hand over her mouth, but I didn't.

Because I remembered a story we read in school.

It's actually weird how much of it I *couldn't* remember, like I didn't know if it was a true story or fiction, and I didn't remember if it was from a war, like World War II. I think it was World War II, and I think the people who were hiding were Jewish and hiding from the Nazis, but it could have been a lot of different wars and a lot of different kinds of people, because a lot of bad stuff has happened in this world, let me tell you.

I just remembered this lady, this young mother, covering her baby's mouth with her hand so she couldn't cry and give them away. And then when the soldiers were gone she saw that she had suffocated her own baby, which I thought was just the saddest thing I'd ever heard in my whole life.

But the thing I think is weirdest to not be able to remember was whether it was a total accident or not. I mean, did she know the baby couldn't breathe? Maybe in her panic she didn't know that. But the really scary thing is that maybe she knew full well what she was doing but it was still better than the other way around, because maybe her baby dying on her lap, in her hands, was better than what would have happened if the soldiers had found them.

Anyway, I know I'm getting off track, but I just had to say that I remembered that awful story, and that's why I didn't put my hand anywhere near that baby's mouth.

Instead I just held up one finger and put it to her lips, because everyone knows that means "shhh," even a baby.

I whispered, barely with any sound at all, "Brave girl, quiet girl."

And she whispered back, "Brave girl, kiet girl," and I swear it was even quieter than when I said it, which I didn't think was possible.

They were talking to each other a lot down there, just passing under the freeway bridge again, right near where we were hiding. I figured that was good that they wouldn't shut up for even a split second, because the more noise they made, the less likely they were to hear us.

"The problem is," the dumb one said, "there are just too many *places*. In a city like this we just sort of have a problem with the number of *places*. You know what I mean?"

The smart guy said, "I never know what you mean. Not once that I can remember in all the time I've known you. And that's such a long time it's depressing just to think about it."

There was also a quiet one, but he didn't say anything—why do you think I call him the quiet one?—but I swear he was the most dangerous one of all.

"There're too many places in the city where someone would hide and we wouldn't think to look. It's like they go on forever. There's a word for that, but I can't think of it. I can't think what it is. What's that word I'm trying to think of? When there's no end to something?"

"Don't try to use big words, idiot. They don't suit you. Just say there's no end to it."

"But now I can't think of that word, and it's driving me crazy."

"Ubiquitous," the smart one said.

"What?"

"I think the word you're looking for is *ubiquitous*."

"No," the dumb one said. "I don't think it is."

"Infinite," the quiet one said.

Which was weird, because I'd literally never heard his voice before. The only reason I'm saying I thought it was him is because I could tell it wasn't either of the other two.

"No," the dumb one said. "That's not it either. This is driving me cra—"

"Hey," the smart guy said. I wish I knew their names to talk about them, but I never did. "We didn't look behind that box."

My blood turned right away to ice, and my gut, too—this really fast, sudden deep freeze, because I figured they were talking about the flattened box we were hiding under.

"Go up and look," the smart guy said.

But I don't know who he said it to.

"Me?" the idiot said. "Why should *I* go?"

"It's steep, and my shoes are bad."

"*Your* shoes? *Your* shoes are bad? Your shoes are heaven compared to my shoes. I would trade you in a heartbeat if your feet weren't so small."

"I'll go," the quiet guy said.

You could tell by the way he said it that he was sick of both of them. Just sick of the whole thing.

Then nobody said anything, and I figured he was coming up. And he was really the last one of the three of them I would want finding us.

My blood got even colder, and my heart started pounding so hard that I could hear it and feel it in my ears, and it actually hurt a little because it was throbbing so hard. And it made a lot of noise in my ears, but I could still hear the little girl suck in her breath to cry, so I pressed a finger to her lips again and said, "Brave girl, quiet girl," with barely any sound, partly just to be quiet and partly because I barely had any breath.

And she said, "Brave girl, kiet girl" back to me.

And that was when I knew I couldn't just sit there any longer. I wanted to, but I couldn't. If he was coming, I had to know. I had to know the exact moment he was about to get there, so I could fight him. Maybe I could use surprise to beat him, even though he was big, because he wasn't expecting somebody to jump out and knock him over backwards on that steep hill.

But then a second later I'd have all three of them on us and I would lose. I already knew I would lose, because I can't beat three older guys who are all bigger than I am, no matter how important it is to try to win.

But I still had to do it. I couldn't just sit there and do nothing and wait for them to come take her away from me. I had to try. Maybe after I bought some time by knocking him down the hill, I could climb up onto the freeway and flag down a car. I'd been thinking about it anyway, earlier that night—climbing up the high side of that bridge onto the freeway, but I didn't think I could do it with the baby in my arms, and besides, it would've been dangerous to take her on the freeway. What if there was hardly any shoulder to stand on? And nobody was going to stop for us anyway, because it was the freeway, and they would only get crashed into from behind if they tried, and how did I know the person who stopped for us wouldn't be even worse than what we were running from?

But I had to do something, even if it was something dangerous, because what was headed our way was too dangerous for me to just sit there and let it catch up.

I decided I had to look out and see how close he was, so I could surprise him and not the other way around.

So I lifted that cardboard again, only about an inch, so one eye could look out. And what I saw made all the air rush out of me at once, with a sound. But it didn't matter.

He was on the other side.

He was climbing the hill on the other side of the street. There was a big cardboard box sitting under the other side of the freeway bridge, but not flattened—a regular set-up box, and that was what they wanted to look behind. They must not ever have seen the flattened boxes we were hiding under.

I let our cardboard cover back down and put a finger to the little girl's lips again, but maybe I didn't even need to bother, because she could tell I wasn't as scared anymore.

A second later we heard a big *whap* sound that I figured was the boy hitting or kicking the cardboard box, and it made us both jump, but we didn't make a sound, because we knew what we needed to do by then.

Then a minute later I heard their voices again, down on the street, and it sounded like they were going away, because I could hear their words getting quieter as they walked off.

"I'm tired," the dumb guy said. "I just want to go back."

"Go back? Go back? Do you have any idea how much money this could be? We could buy a car. Maybe even a house. And you just want to go back and rest? What's wrong with you? After tonight we can do nothing but rest for our whole lives. And you want to give that up because you're tired? Fine, go back, idiot. I'll keep the money."

"No. I'm still in, I want the money, too. But I'm just not sure how we're supposed to get it."

"Well, you saw that Amber Alert up on the freeway. So you know the parents want her back."

"But we don't know who the parents are."

I was starting to think the dumb guy was not as dumb as everybody thought. But I only had one quick second to think about that because I had just heard something really important. There was an Amber Alert, which meant she hadn't been dumped by her parents. They wanted her back.

They were still talking, but in a minute they would be too far away to hear.

"Well, the police know who they are," the smart guy—who I figured was not as smart as he made himself sound—was saying.

"That's the dumbest thing I ever heard in my life! You think we're gonna call the police and tell them we got the kid and then . . . what? You think they'll tell us who to call? I just don't know how . . ."

But they were pretty far down the block by then, and I wasn't sure what it was he didn't know. It was too quiet to hear, but still I had a pretty good idea of everything they didn't know, which was a whole lot.

———

About ten or fifteen minutes later, when I was really, really sure they weren't coming back, I asked the little girl, "Do you need to go?"

She nodded really fast and really hard.

I know it sounds weird to say, but I sort of fell in love with her in that second, like she was my own daughter or my own baby sister, because I knew she'd been purposely holding it all that time, which was a totally amazing thing for a kid that young to do.

I lifted up the back of our cardboard cover, the side away from the street, and helped her out of our little hole, and we worked together and found the best spot where the pee wouldn't roll right back into our hiding place. I held up the cardboard with my back so we were still invisible from the avenue, and I helped her take down her red leggings and her little ducky pull-up pants—they had ducks on them—and held her hands while she squatted down so she wouldn't lose her balance and roll down the hill. She peed a lot. She'd been holding it for a long time, poor little girl.

I didn't have anything to wipe her with, but I figured it didn't matter, because the pull-up pants were absorbent like a diaper. I figured she'd be okay.

Then I helped her back into the hole and we just hunkered down in there for a long time. How long, I really have no clue. I was trying like hell to come up with a plan, but every idea just turned into a dead end. I could flag down anybody I saw walking down the street, but at this hour the streets in this neighborhood were completely deserted. And there was no way I could climb up onto that freeway with her in my arms, and no way I was leaving her alone to do it by myself.

And I couldn't just wander out with her and go in search of help, because those boys were still around somewhere, looking for us, and I had no idea where they were or how not to run into them.

We really had no choice—at least, not a damned thing I could see—except to lie there and hold each other tight and wait for some kind of safe chance to come along and find us, almost by, like . . . sheer luck.

Chapter Five

Brooke: Twenty-Four Hours

Morning came and found me still out on the roof.

I almost fell asleep. I came close to falling off—losing my balance and tumbling down the slope. Then I caught myself and decided to go back to the police station.

No real solid reason except that I couldn't prevent myself from doing it. I had to stay as close to the inner workings of the search as possible. It was an obsession.

My mother was downstairs in the kitchen fussing over a pot of coffee. Sounds like an odd description, but, believe me, she was fussing. She kept swaying back and forth like some kind of neurotic robot, reaching for something and then changing her mind. Or simply losing the thread of the action.

Toward the stack of filters on the counter. Back toward the pot without picking up a filter. Reaching for the faucet. Back toward the filters.

"Mom," I said, and she jumped the proverbial mile.

"Brooke," she said, one hand on her heart. Too dramatically, I thought. "Don't sneak up on a body like that. You scared the living daylights out of me."

"Sorry. I'm going back to the police station."

"They'll call if they know anything."

"Don't argue with me about this. Please."

I made it clear by my tone that my nerves were currently existing along a very thin thread, and were not to be disturbed. For about the hundredth time since the incident, I resented the fact that people didn't make these observations about me on their own.

"Well," she began, "take my ca—" She stopped before the *r* sound in car had made it out of her mouth, and just stood there looking sheepish and more than a little bit sad. "Call a cab," she said.

I could not contain my irritation.

"I'm not going to call a cab, Mom. I have a car. And I'm not made of money."

"I'll pay for the cab."

"I have a car. I intend to drive my car."

"But your car is so dangerous. See, you never believe me when I tell you the world is dangerous, but now you see."

I lost it. Granted, I was on a thin thread to begin with. But this sort of twisted My-Mother logic set me off every time.

"*See?* What do I *see*, Mom? What would you have me see? I didn't get into a dangerous situation in *my* car. I got into it in *your* car. You convinced me your car was safer. But you were wrong, weren't you? For once in your life can you just admit you were wrong? Turns out my car would have been safer because *no one would want it!*"

The last few words came up to a full-throated shout.

My mother's defenses crumbled before my eyes. She stumbled over to the kitchen table. Sank down into a chair. Dissolved into tears.

Then, of course, I felt like eighteen different kinds of human trash.

I settled next to her.

"I'm sorry," I said. "I didn't mean to yell. I'm just so . . ."

"No, we might as well get it all out. You think it's my fault."

"I don't think it's your fault."

She raised her eyes to mine. A scary sob escaped her. Something that just took over her whole body.

"But it *is* my fault," she said.

Then she set her face down on her forearm and cried it out.

"It's not your fault, Mom. It's not your fault that criminals take nice cars right out from under you and sell them to illegal chop shops. It's only the fault of the guy who took it."

She waved me away without raising her head.

"You sure you want me to go?"

She waved me away again.

I took her at her word. She needed to get it all out of her system. She neither needed nor wanted me to sit there with her while she did. We didn't have that kind of relationship. And who was I to tell her she wasn't letting it out correctly? I certainly wouldn't have wanted anyone doing that to me at such a time.

Besides, I could barely keep my own head above water. How could I help my mother when I couldn't even help myself?

———

Grace Beatty took one look at me and I could tell she was shocked.

Maybe I should have glanced at myself in a mirror before driving over. Instead I looked into the mirror of her face and I was shocked, too. It hit me in a new and different way that I was in bad shape.

She rose and walked over to meet me. As she did, her face morphed into a mask of pity. Or it might have been empathy, and I was just primed to see everything the worst possible way.

"Brooke," she said. "You don't look so good. Did you get any sleep at all?"

"Not so you'd notice, no."

"Have you eaten?"

"No."

"That's not the plan, Brooke."

"I'm sorry. I couldn't help it. I couldn't stomach anything."

I was seized with a feeling. Or maybe I should even call it an insight. I was punishing myself. Making myself feel as bad as I possibly could. Not because I really blamed myself, although I could have buckled my damn seat belt. More because it seemed like my job to feel terrible. The idea that I could offer myself any form of comfort seemed downright treasonous. Etta was gone. I belonged at the bottom of the emotional well until I got her back again. Nothing got to be good in the meantime. Not even the tiniest bit good.

She lifted a light jacket off a row of hooks by the door.

"Walker," she said, and a male cop's head shot up. "I'm gone, okay? We're going to go get some breakfast."

I followed her out the door like a faithful dog.

I opened my mouth to speak as we walked down the concrete steps of the station together.

She cut me off.

"No arguments, Brooke. I get it. You don't have to tell me how hard it is to stomach anything. I know. All you have to do is pick the food that sounds least impossible to stomach and put away as much of it as you can bear."

———

"Try to stay away from sugar," she said as we picked up our menus. "I've seen people really go off the rails at a time like this if they eat sweets on an empty stomach. I know it's kind of the opposite of what I said on the walk over here, but protein is your friend right now. Get eggs if you can manage it."

She was raising the bar for me. In increments. I wondered if she was doing it consciously and on purpose.

We were sitting in a booth on benches covered with bright red vinyl. I stared out the window at the neighborhood waking up. People drove by in their cars on their way to work. Bustled by on foot with their shoulders hunched forward as if to keep the world away. Waited at bus stops, seemingly trying to ignore the other riders.

Once again I felt shocked and insulted that life was daring to go on while my Etta was gone.

"That menu's not going to read itself," Grace Beatty said, her voice matter-of-fact and even.

"Right," I said. "Sorry."

I guess I'd fallen into a pattern of seeing her as my authority figure. As if I were a little girl. I felt I needed to answer to her. Maybe I needed her to be the big, strong authority. Because I needed to believe she was big enough and strong enough to find my little girl and bring her home.

I trained my eyes to the menu, absorbing nothing.

"So it'll take a couple of days to get the car back," she said. "There's an evidence procedure we need to go through. Then if you want it as soon as possible, you'll have to go down to San Diego to pick it up. Lots of red tape involved in getting it brought back up here. The good news is, I'm told the chop shop had already replaced the broken window. Thing is, though, you'll need to take it to a paint shop pretty much first thing. They were halfway through repainting it in what I'm told is a pretty ridiculous shade of yellow. You won't want to drive it much until that gets sorted out. You'll probably want to call your mother's insurance company and see if they'll cover that. They'll try not to. They'll say paint jobs aren't covered, but this is a specific damage as a result of it being stolen. If I can help with—"

I shot her a desperate look. She stopped talking immediately.

We held our menus awkwardly for a moment. In silence.

"But why are we talking about the car?" she asked, her voice quiet. Almost reverent. Just at the edge of shame.

"Right," I said, grateful that she had read my look correctly. "Why are we talking about the car?"

The waitress came, and Grace ordered coffee only. The waitress had a pot in her hand and poured us each a cup as I ordered. It dawned on me in that moment that Grace had already had breakfast. She worked the night shift. This coffee shop excursion was only for me.

I ordered two eggs, scrambled, with rye toast. At the edge of my vision I saw Grace nod at me. As if I had just made her very proud.

"When do you get off shift?" I asked when the waitress had left.

I was counting the hours since I'd first walked into that police station. It seemed like a lot of hours in a row for her to have to work.

"About an hour and a half ago."

"Then why were you still there when I got there?"

"I didn't want to stop looking for your little girl."

That just sat on the table for a minute. This amazing, shiny thing that I could only stare at in awe. I opened my mouth to express gratitude, but she beat me to speaking.

"Tell me more about her. About what she means to you."

"Etta."

"Yes."

"Does that help?"

"It doesn't help us find her, no. But sometimes it helps the grieving parent. And I really do want to know."

I took a big, deep breath and started to cry again.

"You have four of your own," I said. "Don't you need to get home to them?"

"Oh, honey. They are so grown and gone it's not even funny."

Part of me had been genuinely concerned for her. And them. I think. Another big part of me was just avoiding steering the conversation to my own truths.

Then I went there anyway.

"She means everything to me. She's all I have."

"You have your mother."

I snorted and rolled my eyes. "That's a net minus."

"Got it."

I pulled another deep breath. It shook going in. Wavered.

I was going to tell her real things. I could feel it. Even though I hardly knew her. Because she had asked for real things. And because this disaster had stripped away everything fake. It was not a time in my life for small talk.

And because this tall, lanky officer was suddenly one of the most important people in my world.

"I always wanted kids," I said. "Always. Ever since I was a little girl myself. But I married a man who didn't want them. It was so stupid, looking back. We were in love, and we thought the problem would take care of itself somehow. He thought I'd change my mind, I thought he'd change his mind. Neither one of us did, of course. I mean, other than us, who didn't see *that* coming? Finally I could feel how much my time was getting short. You know. My biological clock. I was in my late thirties. I didn't want to miss my chance. So I just went ahead and got pregnant. Purposely. Even though I knew it would ruin the marriage."

She waited. Respectfully. In case I was just winding up to say more. But I had never felt so unwound in my life.

Finally she spoke.

"Did you tell him what's happening with his daughter?"

"No. He doesn't want to know. He doesn't want any part of raising her. Or fatherhood. You know. In general. He feels like I tricked him. I guess in some ways I don't blame him. I stopped using birth control and didn't tell him. I guess he *was* tricked. And I don't even have a way to justify myself. Except that desperate people do desperate things. Which isn't a very good justification now that I hear myself say it out loud. We don't speak at all."

"He's still the father. He still might want to know."

"Oh, no. You weren't there. He is *not* the father, according to him. I had to let him off the hook completely on that. I had to assure him that this child was one hundred percent my daughter. My responsibility."

"I'm sorry," she said.

"Yeah. Well. I guess life is just a series of our own choices catching up with us."

We sat silent for a moment. I wondered how what I'd just said applied to this moment. What had I done to deserve what was happening now? I felt as though if I'd ever made a mistake that big, I would remember it.

An uncomfortable thought rose up out of me. I could feel it stick in my throat, wanting to be said. I was too tired to hold it back.

"I heard somewhere . . . some statistic. About how if a child isn't found in the first twenty-four hours . . ."

"I want you to get thoughts like that out of your mind," Grace Beatty said. Her voice was firmer now. "I know it's not easy to avoid going there, but do your best. Statistics are for big groups of people. They don't mean much to the individual. Some people get their kids back after longer searches. Why couldn't you be one of them? Besides, it hasn't been twenty-four hours."

"That's true," I said. "It hasn't been twenty-four hours."

My food came.

I couldn't seem to taste it.

I drowned the eggs in ketchup the way I'd done as a child. I forced down what I could.

———

"I want you to remember one thing," she said a few minutes later.

I was pushing the last of my eggs around on the plate. So I wouldn't have to eat them. She was watching me do it. So I don't know who I thought I was fooling.

Meanwhile I sensed a pep talk coming. And she wasn't going on with it, so I figured she was waiting for me to confirm that one was welcome.

"What do you want me to remember?" I asked, still staring at the uneaten food.

"It's just now getting light. If he put her out of the car in the dark, this is the time somebody might notice. She might have gone unnoticed in the dark. This is when we're most likely to get the break we've been waiting for."

I said nothing.

I guess I was supposed to find it encouraging. In fact, I'm sure I was.

But all I could think of was my precious little girl all alone on a dark street. All night. Would she be wandering around? Or still strapped into her car seat? She would be terrified, wondering where I was. No question about that. Would she ever be the same after a night like that one? Would she ever stop being afraid? Or would she spend the rest of her life with a separation anxiety that no amount of therapy could entirely undo?

But in a way it didn't matter, because it was too late to change that part of the equation. I just wanted her back. I would have to deal with the ugly specifics of the trauma after that.

Grace Beatty's cell phone rang, and it startled me. I had been reaching for my coffee mug, and I nearly upended it. My heart leapt up into my throat the way it had done on the last phone call. It pounded dangerously as she pressed the screen to answer.

"Yes," she said.

A pause. One that nearly killed me.

"Yes, she's still here."

Pause.

"What do they have so far?"

Long pause.

I asked her with my eyes if my daughter had been found. She shook her head just the tiniest bit.

"Okay," she said. "We'll be right back there."

She clicked off the call.

"There's been a break in your case. We still don't know where Etta is. But they arrested your carjacker on a tip from the guys at the chop shop. They're questioning him right now."

She threw a twenty down on the table and grabbed me by the elbow.

"Come on. We have to get back. We'll stay on the phone with San Diego until we hear what he has to say."

We sprinted all the way back to the station. Ran as though our lives depended on it. I could feel my lack of sleep, but it didn't matter. I had sheer adrenaline on my team and nothing was going to hold me back.

———

I sat in a hard wooden chair beside her desk, leaning forward onto my knees. Waiting. Trembling and waiting.

She was on the phone with the police in San Diego.

The suspect, I had been told, was in an interrogation room, being questioned by two detectives. The room had one-way glass, or a one-way mirror. I hadn't quite gotten which. But an officer was outside the room, watching and listening, just like in the cop shows on TV. And that officer was on the other end of the phone with Grace Beatty. So we could hear a secondhand account of what the suspect said the moment he said it.

"He says he put her out of the car," Grace said, covering the mouthpiece of the phone with one palm.

"Where?"

"That's what they're still trying to find out."

"But in West LA, right? I mean, right after he drove away, right?"

I wanted to believe she was in a fairly safe neighborhood. And maybe even a familiar one.

Then I heard my mother in my head. Actually heard these words repeated in her voice.

All of LA is a bad neighborhood. The whole world is dangerous. Not like when I was a girl.

That was the problem with my mother. I could never fully get her voice out of my head.

Meanwhile Grace wasn't answering me. Just listening with her brow furrowed.

I couldn't take the waiting. The words just burst out of me.

"Tell me what he's saying! Please! Tell me *something*! I'm dying here."

She covered the mouthpiece of the phone again.

"He's not being very specific about where he left her. He doesn't remember exactly where he got off the freeway. But he'd been driving south for a good twenty minutes at least before he knew the baby was even there. Apparently she slept through the jacking. Either that or she was too scared to cry."

"So it could be anywhere?"

I was talking around the image of my baby too frozen with fear to cry. Or I was *attempting* to talk around it, anyway.

"They're working to narrow it down with him right now."

My mind filled with geography. At least twenty minutes south of the spot where he took the car and my daughter from me.

Had he taken the 405 Freeway toward San Diego? I had no idea.

But I did know one thing. The neighborhoods got a good bit scarier as he headed south. It was not West LA all the way through.

Chapter Six

Molly: Stress

I slept like a rock after those boys went away, and who would've guessed it, right? I mean, I was so scared about the whole thing, and the weight of being responsible for this baby was sitting on me like an elephant having lunch on my chest, but also I was tired. I mean, really, really tired.

Tired isn't always about how much you moved your body, although that too, because I had been all over that neighborhood all day. But the baby slept like a rock, just like me, and all she'd done was sit strapped into her car seat and then get carried around by yours truly.

I really think it's the stress that takes it out of you.

Anyway, I was sure I'd never even close my eyes for a split second and then the next thing I knew I was having this dream, and a thing that happened in the dream shocked me awake. I was dreaming I was in this dark hole, just like I really was, sleeping hugged tight with this little girl, like I really was, and then all of a sudden somebody picked up the cardboard and found us. In the dream I had this big shot of fear, this jolt, because I figured it was one of those boys. That's what jogged me awake, that jolt of fear. But then I looked up and it was my mother looking down on me, shaking her head. And, now, that part was weird, because I was already sort of awake. But you know how sometimes you're so deep asleep that if something jolts you out of it the dream takes a second or two to fade away?

It was like that.

Then I was more awake and my mother was gone and the cardboard was still over us, and the baby girl was still fast asleep. But it was morning, I could tell, because a little thin line of light was coming in under the edge of our cover.

I lifted up the cardboard just the tiniest bit, an inch maybe, and looked down at the street.

There was a man walking by. A big man with big broad shoulders and a blue work shirt, and I knew then that people would go by on their way to work because it was morning. Actually most people drive in this city, and not too many people walk or take the bus and walk from the bus stop—but here was one guy going by, so probably there would be others.

The reason I figured that mattered was because he was pretty much past us by the time I saw him.

But then I got scared that maybe nobody else would go by, so I wanted to catch him and ask him to make that call for us. But I didn't know whether to wake the little girl up and take her with me or sneak out real quiet and go after the guy. I didn't want to leave her alone, but I also wanted her to sleep as much as possible, because I know about little kids and I knew if she woke up and she still wasn't back with her mommy she was going to get weepy. And how could I even blame her? And even if I did catch the guy and he did make the call for us, we'd still have to hide while we waited for the police to come, and a lot of crying could be a very bad thing for our situation.

So I was trying to decide, but I was getting all frozen up in the deciding, because the whole thing was just too stressful for me.

Finally I figured the guy was getting away, and nothing was more important than that phone call to the police, so I unwrapped myself from her real carefully, hoping she wouldn't wake up.

And I got extra lucky, too, because she didn't.

I ran down the hill to the street, and ran after the guy in the work shirt, and yelled real loud to try to stop him. But the thing is, I didn't start yelling "Hey!" until I got down onto the sidewalk, because I didn't want my yelling to wake the baby. Because if she woke up all alone in that hole and I wasn't even there to comfort her, holy cow would she ever be scared. I figured she would scream bloody murder if that happened.

So I was yelling to this guy but he was already at the end of the block, and I felt this really desperate thing, this desperate feeling pulling me toward him, because he could make a phone call.

But then there was this other desperate thing pulling me back toward the hole, toward our hiding place, because I shouldn't have left the little girl alone, not even for one second. And, let me tell you, it made me feel like I was being ripped apart right down the middle of me.

I got panicky then because he wasn't hearing me, so I put all my panic into one great big shout.

"Hey!"

He stopped and turned around, but right away I wanted to run back up the hill in case I had woke the little girl and she was up there all alone. But I didn't. I stuck it out for a second because we needed that phone call. We just desperately needed that phone call.

It was a lot of stress for me and I don't think I'm built for that much stress. Or maybe nobody is, I don't know.

I waved my arms to him and yelled, "Call the police! Please! I need the police to come here, because I found this baby. Call 9-1-1 and send them here, okay? Will you? Please?"

I know it doesn't make sense after all that trying to be quiet, but it's just what came out of me, because of all that panic.

He was all the way at the end of the block by then and I didn't know if he heard me. I kept expecting him to come closer or give me some kind of sign to let me know if he heard me—if he understood what I needed him to do or not.

He just looked at me, though, like he wasn't sure what to make of me, and like he thought I might be crazy. I know that sounds like a lot to be able to see from the end of the block, but let me tell you, things have a way of coming through. People have a lot of ways to show you what they think of you—if they think you're worth paying attention to at all.

Then he just turned and walked away. And I had no idea if he'd heard me or even believed me, and no idea if he was going to make that call for me or not. But I just ran back up the hill because I had to, because I couldn't leave that little girl alone any more than I already had. I shouldn't even have left her alone that long and I knew it.

And I realized then how much I'd been really stupid to yell so loud about finding that baby, because I didn't know where those boys were, and whether they could hear me.

But what was I supposed to do? There was no phone in that hole with us, and I had no way to make a call, and it didn't look like Bodhi was coming back. If he could've come back, he would have—you know, already. But I couldn't leave her alone to go find a phone, but I also couldn't bring her out into the light with me because those boys could still be out looking.

Every idea I had just ran into a brick wall in my head, and I had no clue what to do, and the stress was too much for me. A sixteen-year-old kid is supposed to be worrying about stuff like tests at the end of the semester and not anything like this. It was hard enough just taking care of myself, and that was when I had Bodhi here to help with that.

The whole thing just kind of came down on my head as I was running up the hill, and I could hear the baby fussing, gearing up for a good cry. Even though there were thousands of cars thumping on the freeway over our heads, with everybody going to work and all, but still I could hear her.

And it was all just too much for me.

I sort of fell apart running up that hill, because of how it was all just too much for me, but in another way I didn't fall apart, because I couldn't, because I had to hold myself together for that baby.

So I sort of broke into a million pieces but didn't let the pieces all tumble apart. Like I tried to just be cracked all over but not shattered.

I dove back under the cardboard and I said, "I'm here, little girl, I'm here, don't cry, I'll take of you."

She kept fussing a little but she didn't actually scream like I knew it would be so easy for a kid her age to do.

I sang to her "Brave girl, quiet girl," over and over and over, and I gave her some more apple juice and some goldfish crackers and that seemed to help.

My mouth was so dry it felt like cotton and my tongue was sticking to my teeth and the roof of my mouth because I'd been giving apple juice to the little girl but not taking any for me. Because I knew we'd run out pretty soon.

And my stomach was so empty it was cramping up, because all I'd had to eat for a whole day was that one banana, and I was saving the crackers for the little girl. I had an apple in my pocket still, but I was saving that for her, too, in case the crackers ran out.

It's more important for a baby her age. They can't be without food and something to drink like we can.

I sang to her and fed her and told myself maybe the guy really did hear me and really did call the police. I listened real close, and peeked out from under the cardboard, hoping to see flashing red lights. But at least an hour or two went by and nobody else walked by on the sidewalk under our hiding place, and the police didn't come.

And it was a lot of stress for me.

Too much stress, let me tell you.

—

I was sitting up under the cardboard, but way hunched over, because that hole we were hiding in was not very deep at all. It was deep enough for the little girl to sit up in, especially since I was holding the cover up a little bit on one side with my back. But for me it put me in a weird and uncomfortable position.

I was facing the top of the hill—in other words I had my back to the street—because I had to leave the cardboard cover down on the street side. But this way some light and air got in, which was a very big deal for the little girl, because she was getting fussy and impatient and pretty scared.

It was hard to blame her, really, because how long can you expect a little kid her age to just lie there holding perfectly still in the dark?

It's not a natural thing to ask a baby to do.

We were playing clapping games. You know, like patty-cake, only for older girls. The kind that have a song or a chant, but I only just hummed it real quiet under my breath, and then you clap each other's hands, or you clap your hands together, or you clap your hands on your knees. There's a pattern to it.

The baby was really sort of more pretending to know how to do it than actually doing it. She couldn't get the pattern of when to clap where, because she was too little to learn a thing like that by heart. So she just sort of mixed it up and clapped wherever she felt like it, whenever she wanted.

Except for one thing—when I held my hands out, she always clapped her hands against mine.

And it just made me love her even more, because her hands were so tiny and perfect and warm, and it sort of broke my heart, especially because her little, helpless, delicate self was in such a bind right now, and she had nobody but me to sort it out for her. And I wasn't enough.

I was mostly frozen up and broken and too scared and confused to be doing her much good, and she deserved way better and I knew it.

But it didn't matter what I knew, because I was all she had and that's just the way it was.

She was too perfect and good to be in so much trouble, but that's the world for you, I guess.

Well. *We* were in so much trouble, I should say.

The fact that she was bad at the game and really didn't know the pattern at all made it easier for me to clap and worry at the same time, because there was nobody there who would notice if I made a mistake.

Then all of a sudden I saw a lady about to go by. An older lady, but not like elderly old—more like maybe fifty. She had hair piled up on her head in this bright shade of red that nobody's hair could actually be without dyeing it.

I had the cardboard angled so I could see left and right a ways up the street, but just the tiniest bit—like I could see somebody's head if they were coming, but the rest of them was blocked by the hill and the edge of our hole.

I stopped clapping.

"I'll be right back," I said. "I have to ask this lady to make a call."

I don't know how many of those words the baby understood, but she got the general meaning of the thing, because she started to cry.

"Oh, no, don't cry, baby girl. I won't go far at all, I just have to ask this nice lady to make a phone call so we can get you back with your mommy."

"Mommy," she cried. "Mommy."

I told her, "Brave girl, quiet girl," but I didn't sing it. I said it kind of firm, like directions. Like, "I'm sorry but this is just what I need you to do."

She didn't stop crying, but she did bring the volume down some.

I slithered out from under the cardboard and ran a couple of steps down the hill.

"Hello!" I yelled, and waved my arms like I was bringing in a plane. "Hello? Lady? I need you to help me. Please! I need you to make a call. Hello?"

The reason I just kept yelling those things is because she heard me but she was pretending like she didn't.

She wrapped her arms tight around her own self and walked a whole bunch faster, and behind me I could hear the little girl crying even though the freeway was loud over our heads.

"Please?" I yelled to the lady again, and I could hear how my voice was getting a lot more desperate. "Please just call 9-1-1 for me and send the police here to where I am?"

I didn't want to say why, because of the way I'd yelled something about finding the kid to that first guy who'd gone by, and then after I did I realized it was a really stupid thing to do because anybody could've heard me, even those horrible boys.

"Please, I need the police!"

I shrieked it that last time, because I was totally losing it by then. Like really falling into panic, and the little girl could hear me and she got louder and more panicky, too.

The lady broke into a trot and ran right by underneath me and just kept running.

For a second I stood there and let it sink in. You know. Like what my situation *really* was right about then.

I looked down at myself and I was filthy from lying in that hole. I had accidentally smooshed the apple in my pocket and now I had a wet spot on my pants that might have made it look like I peed myself, and probably my hair was all matted and disgusting because I hadn't brushed it for more than a day.

People don't help somebody who looks like that, because they just figure you're crazy. They either figure you're not really in any trouble at all, you're just crazy, or they figure whatever trouble you're in is something you brought on yourself and they don't want any part of it because it's a crazy person's trouble.

That was the first time it hit me that maybe a hundred people could go by and nobody would help me or believe me.

That hit me hard, let me tell you.

Then out of the corner of my eye I saw that boy come around the corner. The worst one—the one who was quiet most of the time. I guess they had split up by then but they were still out looking.

I moved faster than I ever have in my life, up the hill and under that cardboard, kind of all in one movement. It scared the heck out of the little girl, and she cried really loud, but I held her tight and sang her "Brave girl, quiet girl" in a whisper under my breath, and she did her best to cry quietly.

We just lay there like that for a long time, my heart pounding, waiting to find out if he'd seen me or not. If he'd heard the baby crying over the noise of the freeway or not.

I know she could feel my heart pounding, and it must've scared her to know I was so scared, but she did her best. She was the bravest, quietest girl she knew how to be at a time like that.

A minute or two later I figured out that he must not have seen me, and so my heart calmed down a little. But I didn't dare look under the cardboard, because he could be right down there on the sidewalk. He could be anywhere on this block still, and how would I know?

So I didn't dare look because I didn't dare do *anything*.

Plus, also, I had no idea what to do.

I have no idea how much time went by like that. I think I already made the point that time is a hard thing to judge. Maybe not for people who live in a house with clocks, or who're out walking around on the street with watches on their wrists. Maybe it's not even that hard when you're watching people walk up and down, and cars go by, and the way the sun moves and changes the spot where it sits in the sky.

But when you're in a dark hole with nothing but a baby you can't properly save and a lot of fear, time is not as easy to judge as you think.

I whispered stories in her ears so she would cry more quietly. Really silly stories that didn't have good plots and didn't go anywhere, but she didn't seem to care.

After a while she tired herself out from the quiet crying and fell asleep again. It might have been hours. Like I say, it was really hard to tell.

I never fell asleep again.

I just lay there in that dark hole with her, knowing I needed to do something, but not having any idea what it was, or how I could do it without losing her to those terrible boys.

The hunger and the tiredness and being so scared for so long was making me feel like I couldn't hold myself together. But I did anyway. Because, really, when you think about it, what choice did I have?

If there was one thing I'd learned since leaving Utah, it was that you can't really just give up. I mean you can give up on some specific thing, but you can't just give up and not live.

You can say whatever you want about being done, but after you say it, you're still a live person. And you still have to do whatever you figure you can.

Chapter Seven

Brooke: Skinless

After that breakfast, I moved into a period of time in which I felt like a person with no skin.

It's a disgusting simile, but it fits the feeling so perfectly that I can't help but use it. Every nerve in my body was exposed, and I was swimming through a sandpaper sea.

That sums it up as well as any words can. It's not really something that can be contained in words anyway.

—

About an hour after I left the police station and Grace Beatty again, I woke up—figuratively speaking—on the front stoop of my ex-husband's house. One hand poised to knock.

I know that sounds unlikely. I know it would be more reasonable to report that some thought or logic had entered into my decision to drive there.

I don't know what to say. I'm reporting this horrible time as accurately as I can.

I went ahead and knocked. Having apparently come all that way.

Then I stood there for a strange length of time, waiting for him to answer the door. I knew he was there. His car was parked in the driveway.

I had one hand on my brand-new cell phone. It was in my pants pocket. I had bought it just after leaving Grace Beatty. I had stopped at one of those stores specific to my cellular provider. I'd had my stolen phone taken off the account and this new one activated.

It was cheaper and flimsier than my old phone. But I had maxed out my last credit card to get it, and I couldn't have afforded even twenty dollars more.

I kept touching it because I didn't trust it to ring. I didn't believe yet that its notification settings could be reliable. I thought Grace Beatty would call and I would miss it.

David opened the door.

At first I saw only the parts of him I had fallen in love with at the start. His long jaw and his lanky body. His hooded, almost aloof-looking blue eyes. I could actually see his legs, his bare legs, because he was wearing only a short robe. Their calf muscles. Their blond hair.

"Brooke?" he asked. Like he might be wrong about that.

"It's eleven o'clock in the morning," I said.

"You came all the way over here to tell me what time it is?"

His voice rumbled through my gut. Smooth and familiar. Remember, I had no skin. Which made it a singularly bad time to see my ex.

"No. No, of course not. I'm just surprised that you were sleeping."

And on that note, a new voice pierced me. It didn't rumble. It was high. It felt discordant. It came from the back of the house.

It said, "Who is it, David?"

"Ah," I said. "It's like that. Got it."

"We've been divorced for two years, Brooke. I have a right to be seeing somebody, you know."

"I never said you didn't."

"Oh," he said. "Right. I guess you didn't."

Then we stood in complete awkwardness. He did not invite me in. I didn't entirely blame him.

I watched his face from the periphery of my vision. His eyes. He has the bluest eyes on the planet. Most people don't have blue eyes. In the movies, in romantic novels, nearly everybody does. In real life, they're rare.

Except at David's house.

"What's wrong?" he asked at last.

It felt as though a day had elapsed. It might have been ten seconds.

"Everything," I said.

"Is Etta okay? Where is she?"

"I have no idea."

"How can you not know where she is?"

"Good question. Seems life is playing a cruel joke on me."

"You literally don't know where she is?"

"I literally don't."

"How is that possible?"

"She was stolen."

"Holy crap," he said.

"Yes. Holy crap." Another awkward moment. "I'm not sure what I'm doing here, David. I guess it doesn't have much to do with you. The cop that's investigating . . . you know, trying to find her . . . she kept asking if I'd told you. And I kept trying to explain that it didn't have much to do with you. But I guess I walked away from that conversation seeing it her way. A little bit, anyway. Feeling like it did concern you. Maybe. Some."

I watched his blue eyes again from the corner of my own. He was staring down at the welcome mat. Except it wasn't a welcome mat. It said **Go Away**. I was beginning to feel as though it were speaking directly to me. Also as though it might be good advice.

When he spoke again, it startled me. Skinless me.

"You know I don't wish any harm on either one of you, right?"

"Of course I do."

"See, this is why."

"This is why *what*?"

"This is why I never wanted kids. Because right off the bat your whole world revolves around them, and you're so attached, and then if something happens, it's like the end of the world. It's too much pressure for me."

A swirl of stunned thoughts ran through my head. This was totally news to me. I had never imagined that David didn't want children because he was afraid he would care too much. I thought he was afraid he wouldn't care enough.

I wanted to tell him that was a ridiculous way to live. Not having something because if you had it you might lose it. But it was a hard point to make in the moment. Because I was in the middle of the horrible loss he had just been describing. Still, I wouldn't have traded having Etta for anything. Even if the unimaginable worst happened. Which I was incapable of even imagining.

I didn't say any of that. It was all too overwhelming in my head.

Another painful pause. But at least it was the last. And I knew it.

I moved into a different emotional moment with him. Suddenly I could see only what had driven us to divorce.

I said, "Well. I'll let you get back to what you were doing."

I stepped down off his stoop. Headed down the stone walkway to my car.

"Keep me posted, okay? Let me know what happens."

I waved my answer without turning around.

As I started my car I wondered, perhaps for the first time, what on earth had possessed me to seek out that exchange.

—

"So, we have it narrowed down," Grace Beatty said. "Or, at least, we hope we do. Of course, we're relying on this guy's memory. But we have patrol cars going up and down the streets in what we think is the most likely radius. And of course they'll gradually spread out if they don't find her there."

I opened my mouth to speak. Then I closed it again.

I was sitting on a hard chair near her desk. It was making my hip bones hurt. I had been sitting there for quite a while. I had my hands in my lap. My skinless lap.

"What?" she asked.

"Nothing."

"You looked like you had a question."

I opened my mouth again. Closed it again.

Then I surprised myself by going for it.

"You think this guy's enough of a monster that he'd purposely give us bad information about where he left her?"

An image flooded into my brain. Behind my eyes. Looking up at the guy's face. In hopes of identifying him later. Seeing only a black ski mask. It *had* made him look like a monster. A faceless monster.

"I don't," she said. "No. But not because I have faith in his good character. Because it's been made painfully clear to him that he's responsible for what happens to Etta. He's already looking at reckless endangerment charges. Possibly even depraved indifference. And that's if he's lucky. That's assuming we find her and she's fine. This guy wants very, very badly for your daughter to be found, and to be okay. But probably only to save his own skin."

I remember thinking he was lucky. To have skin.

I don't believe I said so out loud.

—

After that, and after some time that's too fuzzy to properly relate, I found myself doing something I now see as ridiculous. Even for that horrible day.

I went out and tried to find her.

It was ridiculous because I knew far less than the police knew regarding where to look. I hadn't been there when they questioned The Monster. His every word had not been related back to me.

I knew only that he had been heading south toward San Diego. From West LA. On the 405. And that he had been driving for maybe twenty minutes when he got off the freeway and put her out of the car.

Then again, time could be a very fluid thing. I was proving it that day.

Try to understand. I had to do *something*. If I didn't, I felt as though I might explode.

I found myself cruising down a crowded boulevard north of the airport. Pulled over toward the curb, going slow. Cars honked at my slowness. Pulled around me. A couple of drivers gave me the finger.

I had my windows down, and I was calling my little girl's name.

I guess I figured that was one thing I could do better than the police. If she heard my voice, she would come to me. What if she heard a police officer call to her? What would she do? Hide?

I had no idea. It was a theory we'd never had to test.

So I had my voice, and that was good.

But she'd only hear me if she were maybe twenty yards away. And the range of where she could have been abandoned was maybe twenty square miles or more.

That was bad.

It was an overwhelming, sickening thought. But, oddly, that was not ultimately the realization that turned me for home.

This was the realization:

I was driving slowly because, if she were magically near, she might run into the street. Or she might anyway, just out of fear. I was driving as though my daughter were dodging traffic nearby. Because that was a horrible possibility.

And then it hit me.

The other drivers were not being careful. Nobody was looking out for Etta except me. And there were thousands of them. All *not* driving as though my daughter were dodging traffic nearby.

I pulled over to the curb, where there was no stopping. And I cried. And cried. And cried. And cried. And cried.

———

When I got home—or maybe I should say "back to my mother's house" and leave the concept of home out of this—my mother gave me an odd look.

She was sitting at the kitchen table. Drinking something from a mug. Could have been tea. Could have been booze. I had no time to wonder.

"Where have you been?" she asked me. She sounded distinctly irritated.

"At the police station."

"Well, I called there, and you'd left some time ago."

I was standing in the kitchen, tapping my keys against my thigh. Wanting just to walk away from her. After all, I was an adult. I didn't need to answer to my mother.

Only trouble was, I felt like her minor child in that moment.

"I went to see David. And then I drove around."

"And what if that Officer Beatty had tried to call you?"

"She has my cell number. I told her to call me on my cell."

I watched her face twist into a mass of negative judgment.

"Your cell phone was stolen." She plainly thought it was foolish of me to have forgotten.

"I got a new one. And I called and told her that. Why? Did she call here?"

"No."

"Did somebody else call me here? Anybody? Is that why you're giving me the third degree?"

"David called here," she said, her face untwisting. "Because there was something he wished he'd said when you were there."

I felt a rage boil up in me. Granted, I was angry in general. Skinless. Unable to cope with the slightest irritation. But it was more than that. This was an ancient rage. Festering, and nearly as old as I was.

"Then why did you even ask me where I was?" I shouted.

She looked down into her mug. And did not answer.

I learned a lot from her face in that moment. I always wanted her to tell me why she was the way she was. But it was clear she didn't know. She wasn't concealing an answer from me. She had none. Her life had been set in opposition to the world. To other people. Particularly to me. But she couldn't explain it any better than I could.

I walked away. Or started to, anyway.

"Don't you even want to hear his message?"

I stopped. Wondered if I did want to hear it. It was a bit of a toss-up.

"Fine," I said, because it felt easier. "What did he say?"

"He's afraid he sounded too uncaring when you were at his house. And he didn't mean to. He feels very bad for you and Etta. He hopes you find her soon. And that you'll let him know."

"Thank you," I said.

And I finished walking away.

———

I don't know how much later it was when I climbed out onto the roof again. Just that it was dark.

I had slept some. Out of sheer necessity.

I did it again. Said my prayer again. Though I don't suppose it's right to call it a prayer, since I was talking to a person. To whoever had her.

Then my mind drifted to other possibilities. That no one had her. That she was utterly alone. That she could even be . . .

No. I couldn't go there. I dragged my attention back again.

Somebody had her. I had to believe that.

So why aren't they calling? my brain shrieked to me.

I forced my focus back again. And spoke in my heart to that person. *Please help her not be afraid. Please get her home to me.*

In that moment it was all I had.

Then I realized it. The thing I'd never wanted to come had arrived: it had been about twenty-four hours.

Chapter Eight

Molly: What's Your Name?

"My name is Molly," I said.

We were snuggled up close again, in our hole, and it was getting dark again, and I was getting terrified and she knew it. You can't be that close to someone and not feel their fear, because fear is a real thing that you can feel and kids are actually very good at that—better than grown-ups sometimes, I think.

"Molly," she said.

"What's your name?"

"Molly," she said.

"Your name is Molly, too?"

"Molly," she said again, and this time she pointed at me—pointed one tiny little baby finger right against my heart, so I would know who she meant.

We were out of apple juice and we were getting low on crackers, and I was going to have to come out of hiding with her soon, and I knew it. Even though those boys could be out there, and we might run right smack into them, and they might take her away from me. But still I was going to have to do it because I had nothing to give her to drink, so even if the boys took her away, anything was better than her getting too dehydrated, because she could die, and maybe if they took her away at least they would be smart enough to give her some water.

Still, with them it was hard to know, because smart was not exactly a specialty of theirs.

But I would have to come out with her soon because I was about to have no choice, and I had never been so scared in my life and she knew it. Why she wasn't screaming her head off was beyond me, except she was a very smart little girl, and she knew I desperately needed her to be brave and quiet, and she was trying to do it for me.

Which was pretty amazing for such a little kid. I had so much respect and love for her I almost thought it was going to explode me.

"What's your name?" I asked her again.

"Molly," she said, and pointed to my heart with one tiny finger.

———

"We're going to have to go out there and flag down a car," I said, and she fussed and cried some because she could tell I was getting more and more scared.

But I didn't mean up on the freeway, because I had already decided that was out of the question. The fence was too high to climb with the baby in my arms, and then if we got up there it was too dangerous to be there, and the cars couldn't really stop for us anyway, like I think I said before.

No, we were going to have to go down to the street right below us, and pretty soon, too, because I knew from last night that after a certain hour of the evening the cars just pretty much stop coming there. It's all businesses there, but not like little shops that would stay open. Businesses like industries, like people go to work there in shifts and then they stop going there at all, and then we'd be all alone again for another night. But I didn't know when that would happen, so I figured I'd better hurry.

But here was the thing—the big problem. I didn't hurry—I didn't go at all, because I was so scared I couldn't move, because I kept thinking of running into those boys, and the looks on their faces when they took her away from me. And even worse than that, I thought of the look on her face when she lost me—not that I'm so much or so great, but I knew she trusted me and I was the only thing she had and it had been that way for just about a whole day. I pictured how she would cry and reach her arms out to me and call, "Molly!" I saw that in my head even though I really, really wanted not to.

And then I just got all frozen up like concrete and I couldn't make any muscles in my body move at all.

But something happened that moved me—the baby reached for the apple juice bottle even though she pretty much knew it was empty. And so then I knew she was trying to tell me she was thirsty.

So then I moved, because I just had to. No matter how scared I was, I just had to bring myself to do it.

"Come on," I said to her. "We have to try to get you back to your mommy."

"Mommy!" she said, and then she started to cry a lot.

I had purposely not been reminding her of her mommy—not that I think she forgot—because I figured it might be a little easier for her not to cry if I didn't keep bringing it up.

But now what did it matter anyway, because we were getting ready to walk out in plain sight, so if those boys could see us, they might as well hear us while we were at it.

I started to say a prayer while I was carrying her down the hill, but then I remembered that God and I were not on speaking terms because he hated me—at least according to my mother. I didn't really believe her, but just the fact of someone saying a thing like that to you can leave this bad taste in your mouth that never seems to go away.

No, it was just the two of us—just this baby and me, and that's just the way it was and I had to accept it.

I walked a little bit out into the street because there was a big truck coming. I walked right out where we would be in his headlights but he wouldn't totally run us down if he didn't stop. I was so scared I felt like I was swallowing my heart back down every time I swallowed, which was hard to do anyway because I hadn't had anything to drink for a whole day.

The roar of the truck was getting louder and louder and the baby was screaming and crying because she was so scared, and I was waving my one free arm like crazy trying to get him to stop.

Then at the last minute he just swerved around us and kept going.

I stood there in the street, watching him go, and then I started to cry a little bit myself, because the situation we were in had just gotten so desperate and I was so scared, and I hadn't eaten or even had a drink of water and I was tired and dirty and this terrible thing needed to be over but it just wouldn't end.

It just wouldn't end no matter how bad I needed it to.

I looked all around us in case those boys were coming, but I didn't see them. I didn't see anybody.

Then I saw a car come around the corner and I stood right in front of it. Even though that was a little dangerous for me and the baby, but I had to make them stop this time. It was getting late, and I was afraid it would be night again, and we couldn't make it through another one, and they had to stop.

They just had to stop.

The headlights of the car were making me blind and the baby was still crying in my ear and I was yelling to the driver about how I needed him to stop because I found this baby and somebody needed to call the police and it was a desperate situation. Even though I pretty much knew he probably couldn't hear me.

At the last minute he honked his horn at us, like he was mad that we got in his way, and he swerved around us and kept going.

I just stood there in the middle of the street, waiting for somebody else to come by, but nobody did.

After a time I walked over to the curb with the little girl and sat down and just fell apart. Just freaking fell apart. I started crying even harder than she'd been crying because nobody would stop for us and I had no idea what to do.

And it was a funny thing because when I started crying really hard she started trying to pull herself together.

"Molly," she said, and pointed to my heart.

I was crying too hard to say anything back.

"Brave girl," she said. "Kiet girl."

I couldn't believe she did that. I mean, she was, like, two. It was such an amazing thing for such a tiny kid to do, to pull herself together and start comforting me like that. She was just such an amazing little kid.

Unfortunately, because it was so sweet and amazing it just made me cry even harder.

I sat there on the curb with one arm around her and my face pressed into my knees and cried and cried and cried. And she just mostly watched me, so far as I know.

She was being pretty quiet. Pretty amazingly quiet, considering everything.

Then I looked up and there was a police car turning the corner.

Now, the bad news was that it had gotten to our street and then turned the corner the wrong way without ever shining its headlights on us—and now it was leaving.

I grabbed up the baby in my arms and I ran like I've never run before. I mean, never in my whole life did I ever run like that, even though I was thirsty and hadn't eaten or slept, but I had to put all that out of my head and make it not matter. I had to overcome it all.

The police car was going pretty slow, like they were looking for something, but they also had a big head start on us. But I was actually getting a little closer—gaining a little ground.

My lungs were aching like they were on fire, and I had this stitch in my side that was killing me, and the baby was heavy, but I just kept running and yelling.

I was yelling, "Wait! Police! Wait!"

But it didn't seem like they could hear me.

Then they turned another corner.

Just as they turned, they passed under a streetlight, and I saw that the passenger window was down. The cop who wasn't driving, who was riding on the passenger side, I could see his arm on the top of the door. He was wearing a dark blue uniform with short sleeves and I could see his elbow. It looked really white.

I figured this was it—my last chance.

So I stopped and pulled all the air I could into my lungs and I yelled, "Wait!"

It must have just about blown out that poor little girl's eardrum.

The police car stopped.

The cop attached to the white elbow leaned his head out the window. I looked at him and he looked at me and I breathed again, and I knew it was over.

It was really over. Finally, finally over.

"I found this baby!" I called.

And I ran with her, over to the car.

———

"What about you?" the cop with the very white arms asked me.

We were standing back by the trunk of his squad car, me with the baby still on my hip, and the trunk lid was standing open, and there was water back there. Bottled water, tons of it, on a cardboard tray with plastic over the tops of the bottles.

He pulled one out from under the plastic and handed it to me for the little girl, and I twisted the top off and gave it to her and she took it from me and held it with both tiny hands and drank and drank and drank.

"Yes, sir," I said. "I'm thirsty, too, please. Thank you."

He gave me a little smile that looked like I'd made him feel sad with something I'd said, but I couldn't imagine why, because I didn't think I'd said anything that would make anybody sad. He had a weirdly big forehead and a hairline that was starting to recede, even though he wasn't very old.

He handed me a water and I unscrewed the top and drank it all down in one big series of gulps without ever untipping the bottle again.

I wiped my mouth on my sleeve, but then because we were under the streetlight I could see that my sleeve was really dirty, and that the baby was really dirty, and I wondered if that was what he was so sad about.

I accidentally dropped the cap and he picked it up, which made me like him better, because he was a little bit like me. He didn't just leave litter everywhere like some people do.

He made a three-point shot into the open garbage bin on the corner.

"That wasn't what I meant," he said.

His voice was kind of soft, like he liked me, like exactly the opposite of the lady in the all-night market who right away didn't like me even though she didn't know me well enough to judge.

Problem was, I'd completely lost track of what we were talking about by then.

"What was the question again?"

"When I said, 'What about you?' I didn't mean would you like water, too. I mean, yeah, also that, but I meant it in a bigger sense. Like, you strike me as somebody's little girl who needs to get home to her mom, too."

I think my face got red, but I couldn't say for a fact because I couldn't see it. But it was tingly and hot, which was probably a clue.

I guess I thought they would just take the baby from me and I would walk away and go back to . . . whatever. I didn't know anybody would start looking at my situation.

"I'm older, though," I said.

I couldn't bring myself to look at him, so I was looking down at a wad of gum that somebody threw onto the sidewalk, and wondering how people can do a thing like that when there was a public trash bin on the corner, not even ten feet away.

"Not old *enough*, though," he said. "What are you? Fourteen? Fifteen?"

"Sixteen," I said. I let my eyes flicker up to him and then quick looked away again. "Well, I think. Sixteen around last week, I think, except I don't know exactly what day it is."

"Sixteen-year-old girls need to get back to their moms, too."

"No, sir," I said. "I don't need to get back to my mom."

"Don't you think she wants to know where you are?"

"No, sir. I think if she wanted to know where I was she wouldn't have kicked me out of the house in the first place."

"How long you been on the street?"

"Couple months."

I think I shrugged when I said it.

He opened his mouth to say something, but just then his partner came around to the back of the car where we were standing, and I was relieved because I was totally ready to talk about something else.

He had been doing something up at the driver's seat of the car, the partner, and I wasn't entirely sure what, but I figured he was phoning in that they found the little girl from the Amber Alert.

"It's her," he said.

And even though he was talking to his partner and not to me, I said, "How can you tell who she is?"

"We have pictures of her on the computer, that her mother provided. Her mother is pretty desperate to get this little girl back."

That's when it hit me that I had to give her back, and that it was going to hurt me. I know that sounds incredibly stupid, because, like, how could I not know? But it's just one of those things that hits you in different ways during different parts of the thing.

I tried to hold the little girl out for one of the cops to take her, and right away she got scared and started fussing.

She said, "Molly, Molly, Molly," and held even tighter to me. Like she loved me.

I have to admit it made me feel good.

They didn't take her.

The one who gave us the water, he just looked around and said, "Where's that car seat? You still have it?"

"Oh," I said. "No. I'm sorry. I have no idea where it is. My friend Bodhi had it. Maybe he put it somewhere so those boys couldn't find it, but then he never came back. Bodhi, I mean. I think maybe he got arrested. I think if he hadn't got arrested he would've come back."

"Well, you get in the back seat with her, then," he said. "You can ride with her on your lap and we'll put the seat belt around both of you."

"Wait a minute," I said, and I could feel myself getting scared. "*I'm* going? Why am *I* going? I didn't do anything wrong. I didn't steal her, I just found her. I was trying to get her back to the police, honest I was, but I didn't have a phone."

I could feel them both staring at me while I said all that.

"You're not in any trouble," one of them said. The water guy. He slammed the trunk and it made the baby jump a little. "We just want to get a statement from you. Where you found her and all that. And maybe it would be nice for her if you stayed with her till her mom came to get her, because she's obviously attached to you."

That was pretty literally true in that minute. She was hanging on to my shirt tight with both little hands and doing her best to wrap her legs around my waist but they didn't quite reach.

She was talking quietly in my ear, saying, "Molly, Molly, Molly," over and over again.

She didn't want me to give her to the cops.

"And then I'm free to go?" I said.

"And then I was thinking maybe we talk over some options for getting you off the street and finding you some safer place to live."

I didn't answer for a minute, because I was feeling kind of frozen up with fear. I could feel the fear running up and down the middle of me and it felt like little electrical signals if electrical signals could be icy cold.

Bodhi always said you never go to the police, you never leave anything up to them. You never trust them to solve your problems for you, because they'll only find ways to make them worse. That was one of the first things he taught me, and I believed him. And it had been knocked out of my mind completely by the fact that I had to bring them the baby. But it was back in my mind now.

But right at that minute I was standing under the streetlight with those cops and I was looking at them and they were looking at me, and I decided that Bodhi might have been wrong.

I really wanted him to've been wrong.

I got in the back of their squad car and put the seat belt on both of us, me and the baby—the lap belt and the part that goes across your shoulder, both. I had to hold that part down with my hand so it didn't go right across the baby's face.

She settled right away and stopped saying my name.

I'd never been on the freeway at night, and I thought the palm trees looked spooky but beautiful and I was amazed by the way the gold reflectors on the lane markers glowed like they were on fire. It was weird, but it was almost as though the world looked . . . pretty. Even my world.

"We're going to get you home to your mommy," I said.

"Mommy," she said back to me, but she wasn't crying.

She knew the terrible day was over now, too.

She was an amazing little girl. I was going to miss her when she was gone.

Chapter Nine

Brooke: Why Didn't She Call?

When the phone rang, I very nearly fell off the roof. Twice. Once when I jumped at the sound of the ring. Again as I tried to scramble in through the window. I kicked a shingle off my mother's roof with the sole of one shoe. As it gave way, I lost my footing.

Meanwhile I was literally unable to believe I'd left my new cell phone in the bedroom. Not brought it out onto the roof with me. It seemed so thoughtless in retrospect that I had no way to frame it in my head. I was just baffled.

I also bruised and badly scraped my shinbone on the window sash when my foot slipped. But I wasn't fully aware of it at the time.

I just remember that I picked up the phone and I was wondering why my shin hurt.

It was Grace Beatty.

"We have her," she said. "Ninety-nine percent we have her. She's dirty and she was a bit dehydrated, but she seems okay. You have to come down and identify her, of course. But she's wearing red leggings and a striped tunic, and the boys who are bringing her in say she's the spitting image of your photos."

The world turned weirdly white and silent for a moment. The way the world goes white before you pass out.

Might have been a long moment, because Grace said, "Brooke? Are you there?"

"Yes. But I think I need to sit down."

I plunked onto the carpet because walking over to the bed felt like too much.

I was overwhelmed with the joy of what I'd been told. That was part of it. I was also scared by the one-percent part. Granted, it was nearly impossible to think they had found another girl the same age, lost at the same time, in the same general area, wearing the same kind of clothes. And looking exactly like Etta's photos.

But if it wasn't her, I would die. Actually possibly die.

"Is she right there? Can I talk to her?"

"She's not here yet. They're driving her up. She'll be here soon, though. So don't bother waiting. Jump in the car and get down here."

"I'm on my way," I said, and clicked off the call.

My shin was surprisingly painful but I paid it no mind.

I ran for the bedroom door, screaming for my mother. I knew she had likely gone to bed, even though it was barely eight o'clock. But it didn't matter. Nothing mattered now except this.

"Mom! Mom! They found her! Hurry! We have to get down there!"

She came spilling out into the brightly lit hallway, the soft skin of her face lined from the pillow. She was wearing the most absurd pajamas. Loud and gaudy, with blindingly colorful tropical flowers on a black background.

"Oh dear," she said. "Oh dear. I'll have to get dressed. I'll only slow you down. Just go. Don't wait for me, I'll take a cab and meet you there."

I ran down the stairs two at a time. Then I realized my car keys were still up in my bedroom. In my purse. I flew up the stairs, only one at a time because my shin hurt. Grabbed the purse. Ran down again. Almost tumbled down in my haste.

I sprinted out into the driveway. Opened the door of my old car, whose driver's door always made a discordant metal-on-metal sound when opened. Dropped into the driver's seat. Scrambled for my keys. Found them. Dropped them in the dark at my feet. Found them again.

My hands trembled as I tried to fit the key into the ignition. It took about four tries to get it right.

I turned the key.

Nothing. Not a sound. Not even a grinding of the engine trying to turn over. Damn it, it wasn't even trying! Not a click. Just perfect silence.

I did away with the silence.

I screamed at the car. Cursed it. Called it every name in the book. Pounded its dashboard. Got out and viciously kicked the tires with my good leg.

I felt a hand on my shoulder and nearly jumped out of my body.

"I'll call a cab," my mother said.

She was standing behind me in the driveway in those ridiculous pajamas. In the dark. Looking vulnerable and enormous.

"Too slow," I said.

I ran out into the street and stuck my thumb out to passing cars.

At that moment it was my mother's turn to lose it. We switched roles. I stood, fairly calmly, hitchhiking. She yelled at me the way I'd been yelling at the car.

"Oh, no you do *not*, little girl! You get back here this instant! If you don't know by now what a dangerous world this is, then I don't know what I can say to convince you. Your daughter needs you to get there in one piece, so you get back here and wait for that nice, safe cab!"

She paused her diatribe. Maybe to see if I would obey.

A car pulled over that I recognized as Mrs. Ellis's from three doors down the street. I knew her by her dark-maroon BMW, with its custom plates. I have no idea what they were supposed to have said. It always looked like a random jumble of letters to me. But I guess Mrs. Ellis knew.

She powered down her passenger window.

"Darling, are you all right?" she asked me.

"My car won't start and I have to get to the police station right away. They found Etta!"

"*Found Etta?*" Both words carried a distinct curiosity. "How on earth did you manage to lose her?"

But by then I had opened her passenger door. By then I was already in the car.

"Well, yes," she said, probably accepting the inevitability of her next move. "By all means let's get you there."

As we sped away, her passenger window remained down. I could hear my mother still screaming at me.

Fortunately I could no longer make out the words.

———

"I think I just couldn't bear that," Mrs. Ellis said.

We were stopped at a stoplight. At the intersection of a palm-tree-lined boulevard. But there was nobody coming in either direction. I was wishing she would just run the light. Just brazenly run it. But I guess that wasn't in her nature.

"You would bear it," I said.

It was an answer that left no room for doubt. At least, not my doubt.

"I picture a situation like that with my own children, when they were so little like that. And I think I just couldn't do it."

I stared at the side of her face. Long enough that it made her nervous. I could tell.

"What would you do, then?" I asked.

"Well . . . fall apart, I suppose."

"Okay. Then what?"

"I'm not sure I understand the question."

The light changed. Finally, finally. We drove on.

"I guess what I'm trying to say is something I see very clearly from here. And maybe you don't see it. Because it's not happening to you. You have no choice but to live through whatever's happening. I mean . . . as opposed to what? If you're going to continue to live, then you're going to deal with it. You have no choice. You can say, 'I'm going to fall apart now.' And you can do that. Whatever falling apart looks like to you. But when you're done, it's still right there to deal with. And then you look back and see that what you called falling apart was just another way of dealing with it. We deal with everything, because, short of actually deciding not to live anymore, we don't have any other option. Not one damned option."

I fell silent. The whole world fell silent, from the feel of it. I got the impression I'd said too much.

"I guess that might've sounded like a lot of gibberish," I said.

"Not at all," she said. "I hear what you're saying."

We turned the corner, and I saw the police station two blocks down. I wanted her to go faster. There was one stoplight between us and there. I didn't want her to miss it.

She missed it. Almost purposely, from the feel of the thing. The light went yellow, and she could have sped up. It would've been a legal run. She was apparently just a very cautious driver.

I opened her car door and jumped out.

"Thank you," I yelled, already slamming the door.

I ran the rest of the way. Sprinted. Sailed. My chest hurt from the exertion. My shin hurt every time I jarred it.

I didn't care. I just ran.

———

"Oh my goodness," Grace Beatty said. "What happened to *you*?"

She was looking down at an area below my knees. So I looked down, too. My jeans were soaked through with blood where I'd scraped my shin.

"Oh," I said. "Running for the phone."

"Through barbed wire and land mines?"

"Long story," I said.

I could barely breathe. I could barely talk. Also I didn't want to talk. I wanted her to hurry up and tell me where Etta was.

She pointed to the chair by her desk and I sat in it.

"You've beat her here by a little bit," she said, "but it won't be long. Sit down and I'll tell you a few more of the details."

I didn't answer. Just nodded. At least, I think I nodded. I meant to. I couldn't feel my butt touching the chair. I was nearly outside my body. But I felt my shin ache and throb.

"One of the patrol cars was driving around the area searching for her, and a girl ran up to their car and said she found this baby. Teen girl. Living on the street from the look of it. Said she found Etta strapped into her car seat on the sidewalk."

"Oh my God," I said. I was just barely able to breathe after my sprint. And now the story was taking away my ability to breathe again. "She was strapped into the seat all that time? Oh, my God. That poor girl! And she had nothing to eat and drink and nobody—"

Grace interrupted. "From what I can gather she found her last night. Maybe not all that long after you reported it."

I said nothing. Possibly for a long time. My brain was swirling. My mouth was wide open. I could feel it. I could feel a new emotion gathering up inside me like a storm gaining power. It wasn't fear or grief, which had been such constant companions. It was rage.

"Why. Didn't. She. Call?"

I was trying hard to be calm, because I didn't want to take it out on Grace Beatty.

"We'll know more when they get here. We're going to take a full statement from the girl. Right now what the guys tell me is that she was afraid of some boys. She said they were trying to take Etta away."

"That doesn't make sense," I said. I couldn't get my brain to straighten out. I couldn't process information. I was searching for the end of the rage as though it were light at the end of a long, deep tunnel. I couldn't find it. "Why would they take her?"

"She says they wanted to try to ransom her back to you."

"That . . ." I started to say, again, that it didn't make sense. But I wasn't sure. "Does that make sense? Right now this is sounding like something you hear from an unreliable narrator. Is this a reliable person?"

"No idea," Grace said. "I haven't even met her yet."

Then her eyes left me. Moved to an area above my head and behind me. She tossed her head in the direction she wanted me to look.

I turned around and saw a blue-uniformed officer holding Etta.

She was absolutely filthy. As though someone had purposely rolled her in mud and then let her dry out.

Then I was moving across the room to her. But I couldn't remember standing up. She hadn't seen me yet. She was craning her neck. Looking down the long corridor, with its blinding fluorescent lights.

She was calling, "Molly! Molly! Molly!"

The officer turned his body in such a way that she would be facing me. So she would notice me.

"Look," he said. "There's your mommy."

"Mommy!" Etta cried.

I realize, looking back, that I rewrote history in that moment. I decided she had always been saying "Mommy." That she had never said "Molly" at all.

I took her in my arms and carried her over to Grace Beatty's wooden chair. Sat her down there and fell to my knees in front of her. Threw my arms around her.

Absolutely, utterly lost it.

I mean, I just fell apart in that moment. I sobbed so hard I couldn't breathe.

I kept saying, "I was so scared." Over and over and over, I said it. "I was so scared."

A few minutes later I would remember how to talk to Etta. Comfort her. Ask her how she felt. But in the moment "I was so scared" was the only thing I remembered how to say. And sobbing was the only thing I remembered how to do.

———

"You might want to take her over to the emergency room," Grace Beatty said. "Just to be on the safe side. Just to be sure she's none the worse for wear. While you're gone, I'll see what that girl has to say."

I bristled at the mention of her. That girl who had held my daughter for twenty-four hours without calling. While I lost my mind. While I went through every kind of hell imaginable.

I said nothing about it.

I moved for the door, Etta on my hip. Then I stopped. Turned back.

"Wait," I said. "I don't have a car. My car wouldn't start. A neighbor drove me here."

"I'll take you," the uniformed officer said.

"Oh. Okay. Thanks."

I followed him out to the parking lot, out back, still carrying my child. Probably too tightly.

"I was so scared," I said as he opened the passenger door for me. Inviting us to sit up front.

"I can imagine," he said, and walked around to the driver's side.

We drove away.

The city slid by outside the car windows. I didn't look directly. I was staring at the face of my child in the darkness. Waiting to pass under another streetlight. And then another. So I could see her more clearly.

"What do you think of this girl?" I asked a few blocks later. "The girl who found Etta? Does she seem on the level to you?"

"Not sure what you mean by 'on the level,'" he said. He had a deep voice. Everything he said sounded flat. Matter-of-fact.

"Well. Like . . . this story about why she didn't call the police for twenty-four hours. You believe it?"

"Hard to know what to believe," he said.

I think he was about to say more. I might have cut him off.

"That's what I was thinking. There's a strong correlation between homelessness and mental illness, isn't there?"

I watched his brow furrow. He had a big forehead and a receding hairline. Lots of frown lines.

"I wouldn't really say a strong one," he said, "no. I'm not saying it never happens. But I think it's something that's changed over time. Used to be not so many people lived on the street, and when they did, you could more or less tell why. Addiction or mental illness. But these days you got the majority of your people with, like, one paycheck standing between them and the street. So nowadays, could be anything. Medical bills. Job loss. You know."

"Is she on the street with her family?"

"No. She was alone. She said her mother threw her out."

"Ah," I said. Nodding to myself. "So some kind of behavioral thing."

"If you don't mind my saying so, ma'am . . ."

He paused for a strange length of time. I looked away from Etta for a change. It was hard, but for a second I did it. I watched his brow furrow down even farther.

"What?"

"Seems like you already made up your mind you don't like this girl. And you haven't even met her yet."

"She had my baby for a day without calling. A day! Do you know how much I suffered during that day?"

"Can't really say as I *know*, ma'am, no, but I'm a father, so I can imagine. I'm a father of a girl not much younger than this teenager we're talking about. And maybe that's swaying my opinion here. I look at her and I see my own kid. Only . . . you know. Like they say. 'There but for the grace of God.' I don't know this girl well enough to tell you to like her. I can't even tell you for a fact that you should believe her, because how do I know? But two things I can tell you, because I saw them with my own eyes. One, she ran after our squad car, screaming to get us to stop. She'd been running so long she could hardly breathe. And carrying that heavy toddler. So it looked to me like she wanted your little girl back home."

"Oh," I said.

It's a terrible thing to say, but I was disappointed. I wanted my anger. Maybe I even needed it.

He didn't go on to say more. So I asked, "What's the other thing?"

"She loves your little daughter. That I can tell you. That I know."

I felt my head rock back against the headrest. I was shocked that he would say such a thing.

"She can't love her," I said, my voice hard.

Etta squirmed on my lap because I sounded angry.

"Why can't she?"

"She only knew her for a day."

He chewed on the inside of his lip for a minute. We were stopped at a signal, at a well-lit intersection. And I saw him doing it.

Then he asked, "How long did it take *you* to love her?"

I didn't answer.

We didn't say another word the whole rest of the way there.

Chapter Ten

Molly: Where Did the Dark Go?

I was sitting under those really bright fluorescent lights, talking to that lady cop. Sometimes for a minute I felt like I could just talk to her, pretty much like I'd talk to anybody, because I'd be sort of forgetting for a minute that she was a cop.

But I really hated those terrible lights. We used to have them at my school, and they made my eyes hurt. Actually they sort of made my brain hurt but that's a hard thing to try to explain to somebody who's not sensitive about stuff like that.

But back to that lady cop. She didn't wear a uniform, which is probably why I kept forgetting. She was really tall, and her hair was really short, and I think there might've been a minute in there where I was thinking maybe she was family, as in, like . . . one of us. Bodhi would've known—Bodhi always knew. He was never stupid about anything like that, like I always am. But then she said something about having four kids of her own and then I figured I was guessing wrong. Still, you never know, because lots of different kinds of people have kids, especially these days.

"So how do you know so much about babies?" she asked me.

She sat back in her chair and sort of drilled right into me by looking into my eyes. We'd been sitting quiet for a few seconds, so it surprised me. Also because we hadn't been talking about me right up until just then.

"I had two little sisters," I said.

I was feeling shy for reasons I couldn't quite figure out, and like I wanted to leave that bright room all of a sudden.

"Had?"

"Well. Sort of had. They're not dead, if that's what you mean. I guess they're still my sisters, but I don't see them anymore."

"So what happened that you ended up leaving home?"

I looked down at my hands and I was ashamed of how dirty they were. I wondered if my face and hair were just as bad. I felt ashamed talking to this lady because she was all clean and respectable and I didn't even have a mirror to see what a mess I must've been.

"I don't want to talk about that," I said.

"Okay. No problem. We'll talk about something else. Are you hungry?"

My eyes came right up to hers. I didn't mean for them to, and I didn't ask them to, but the food thing just got a really big reaction out of me when it came up.

"Yes, ma'am. Starving."

"Okay. I'll send somebody out for takeout. You like pizza?"

"Yes, ma'am. I love pizza."

A slice of hot pizza almost sounded too good to be true. I didn't want to look forward to it, because I thought she might be lying about it, because it felt like nothing as good as that could exist in the world anymore, or at least not anywhere near me and my rotten luck.

"What do you like on your pizza?"

"Anything but pineapple," I said. Then I thought it over, about whether I was brave enough to ask. And then suddenly I was just really brave, like all the brave I've ever needed to be, and I said, "Can I please use your bathroom to wash up?"

"Of course," she said.

Probably doesn't sound like much, but it's hard for me to ask people for stuff like that sometimes, because I have to sound like I think I deserve it or something.

And then when she answered me I remember being really surprised that something could be that easy.

We got up and I followed her down the hall and it was still bright with all those fluorescent lights. I felt like I just couldn't get away from that, like I'd come out of the dark in more ways than I could really count up, but not all of them were good.

She stopped at one of those restrooms that are not just for men or just for women. Just one plain single restroom, no stalls or anything, and anybody can use it. She held the door open for me and then reached in and turned on the light, which was on a timer.

"Thank you," I said.

I locked myself in.

It was still really bright, and I was avoiding looking at myself in the mirror, because I was afraid of what I would see.

I looked around to see if there was a window, but there wasn't.

I know that sounds like a weird thing to say, because there was pizza coming, and they wanted to get me off the street. But they also wanted me to have no control over what would happen to me next, and besides, nothing is scarier than the thing you haven't seen yet. It was actually harder to think about moving forward into whatever unknown situation they had planned for me than to ditch out and go back to what I knew.

What I knew was terrible, but at least I knew it, and there's something that's almost a comfort in that.

I used the toilet and then stood at the sink and looked at myself in the mirror. It wasn't really a mirror. It was shiny metal like the kind

Bodhi said they had in jail. It made me wonder if I was under arrest. I mean not literally, but . . . you know. Being underage and everything, I wasn't sure if I was free to go or not.

I washed my hands and face, but there wasn't anything I could do with my hair, because I didn't have a brush or a comb. It was all tangled and matted with dirt, and that made me ashamed, but there wasn't anything I could do about it.

Just as I opened the door again I wondered if that lady cop would be right there waiting for me, and if she wasn't whether I should just walk out the door. If I walked out the door I'd be free, but still on the street, and if she was there I'd have to go to whatever they had planned for me.

I honestly didn't know which I wanted. I couldn't decide.

I opened the door and she was there, so that was that. No decisions to be made.

Then I looked down the hall and saw the baby again. She was being carried in the door by a lady who I figured must be her mother, and that nice cop who gave us water was walking in beside them.

She was older than I thought she'd be, to have a kid so little like that.

When the lady saw me, she held the baby tighter, like maybe I would try to steal her away or something, which I thought was pretty crappy. I mean, if I didn't want her to have her kid back she wouldn't have her. I worked hard to get her back to her mom.

When the baby saw me she started saying my name.

"Molly, Molly, Molly."

Not like she was trying to get to me. She didn't reach out for me or anything. She was with her mom and she wanted to stay with her mom, which any idiot could understand, but she wanted me there, too.

Little kids are like that. They want everybody they love all together in one room with them, and they can never understand why anybody has to leave.

I looked at the mom, right in her eyes, and just for a flash of a second she looked back. Then she looked down at the linoleum, and it hurt me. I felt it like a burn in my stomach, because I expected her to be grateful for what I'd done and she wasn't. She'd already decided she didn't like me, just like everybody else always did.

So that sucked.

"How'd she check out?" the lady cop called down the hall to her.

And the mom gave her a thumbs-up as an answer.

She walked off into a room with the uniformed cop and I followed the lady cop back to her desk so she could ask me more questions and hopefully feed me pizza before too long.

So that was my first experience with the lady, that baby girl's mom, and it wasn't good.

—

"I hope you like anchovies," the lady cop said, "because I got double anchovies."

I guess I had a weird look on my face. I'd never tried anchovies but I figured I wouldn't like them because, so far as I could tell, nobody did. I wasn't even sure why they existed if everybody hated them.

I lifted the lid on the box, sort of slow and careful, like anchovies might bite.

"Well, you said anything but pineapple," she said, and she was smiling too much.

I didn't know what she thought was so funny until I got the lid of the box lifted up and saw it was a regular pepperoni pizza.

"Oh, you were just kidding me," I said.

I was kind of relieved, because I hadn't eaten for a really long time and I hated for anything to ruin it. It had never occurred to me that anything could ruin a pizza until she started joking about those weird little salty fish.

I pulled up a slice and the cheese stretched out like crazy and I tried to get it all onto the napkin but I got cheese and sauce on her desk and had to try to get it up with another napkin, but no matter how much I scrubbed I could see a little grease there.

"Don't worry about it," she said.

I waited for her to take a piece for herself but she never did. She just watched me take a bite, and my eyes sort of rolled back in my head almost, because it was so good. But also I had to remember to go slow with it, because my stomach was all tight and weird from going so long without eating.

"When did you eat last?" she asked me. Like she read minds or something.

"I had a banana right before I found that baby, but also before that I hadn't eaten all day."

"I see. So when you said you were starving, you were speaking literally."

"I guess," I said, because for some reason I was feeling uncomfortable again and like I wanted to run away.

"So the baby had nothing for that whole twenty-four hours?"

"No, she did. She had a bottle of apple juice and a whole box of goldfish crackers. My friend Bodhi got them for us and he found us that hiding place and he went off to call the police and tell them how I found the baby. But then he never came back, so I was thinking he got arrested."

"And you didn't eat a single one of the crackers in all that time?"

"No, ma'am. I was afraid there wouldn't be enough for the baby."

She didn't say anything for a minute. She just had this look on her face that I couldn't quite figure out, but I wasn't afraid of it, so that was a good sign. Mostly I'm afraid of what people are thinking, especially about me. So I just ate my pizza and waited for her to have more questions.

"Why do you think your friend got arrested?" she asked me after a time.

I had finished my piece of pizza, because I wasn't going slow like I was supposed to at all. I was just staring at the box because I wasn't sure if it was okay to take another piece, because maybe the rest was for her.

"He takes things sometimes," I said, and hoped she wouldn't ask me any more about him. I felt bad telling the police things about Bodhi behind his back.

She was staring at her computer and clicking around a little on there, but I could only see the back of the lid of her laptop, not what she was looking at.

"What's your friend's name?" she asked me after a little clicking.

"Well, see, that's the problem right there, ma'am. I don't really know. He calls himself Bodhi but I don't figure that's his real name, more like a street name you give yourself. But as far as, like, his real name that he would have to give to the police, well, I never knew it. When people are on the street like that there are a bunch of things you don't ask them, because not everybody wants to talk about the way it was before."

She frowned, but didn't stop clicking. I was surprised, because I figured she would just close the laptop lid and tell me she couldn't help me if I didn't know the simplest things like my friend's name.

"How old is he?"

"Nineteen, I think."

I sat quiet for a minute and then made myself get brave again and I asked her, "Can I have another piece?"

She seemed surprised that I asked that. She said, "Of course. Have all you want. I got it for you."

I could feel my eyes get big.

"The whole thing?"

"Well, I didn't figure you could eat that much, but I figured you'd eat all you could and then I'd see if one of the guys wanted the leftovers."

I grabbed for the box and pulled it closer and took another piece. But then, before I took a bite, I realized I was not saying what I should be saying—you know, to be a good person and all.

"Thank you," I said. "That was really nice of you."

She just nodded and kept clicking, so I started on the second piece. "Is this your friend?"

She turned the computer around and showed me a mug shot of a boy about Bodhi's age, a stranger, looking really mad and down, like his life was crap in that minute. Which I guess it was, since he was arrested.

"No, ma'am."

She turned the computer back around and looked and clicked some more.

"What was with that lady?" I asked.

I'd been wanting to ask it but also thinking I shouldn't, like it was none of my business or something. Like I really thought she should've been nicer to me, but on the other hand I didn't figure I had a right to feel that way, and any adult would tell me so.

"Which lady is that?" she asked.

It seemed like a weird question, because who else could I be talking about? I guess her mind was just into what she was doing, looking for nineteen-year-old boys who got arrested the night before. In this town there must've been quite a few.

"That lady who's the baby's mother."

"Oh, that," she said. She stopped looking at her computer and looked up at me, which felt uncomfortable and made me wish I'd left well enough alone. "Right. I know you were expecting a little more gratitude than you got."

"How do you know that?"

"Partly I saw it on your face. Partly I just know you felt that way because anybody would've in your situation."

That was an interesting thing for her to say, because it sounded like she meant I was just like everybody else, which I didn't hear a lot or even think was true.

"This has been a very difficult time for her," she said. "Her emotions are all over the map."

"Right, I know, but I was expecting her to be emotional in sort of a different way."

I didn't say I expected her to hug me and kiss me and tell me what a hero I was to her, because it would've sounded stupid. But it was mostly true.

"Here's the thing," she said, still staring right at me, which still made me nervous. "The twenty-four hours she didn't know where her daughter was, they were just torture for her. So I think she's concerned about why you didn't call sooner. So I figure when you're done eating, you can straighten all that out for me. Tell me the story of why connecting her back to the police took you so long."

"Yes, ma'am. I can do that."

She turned the computer around toward me again and showed me another mug shot of another nineteen-year-old stranger. I shook my head again. She turned it back around toward her and kept clicking.

"And then we can tell her your story," she said, "and by then she will have had a little time to process everything she's feeling, and if it makes sense why you didn't call sooner, I think you'll see a different side of her."

"Yes, ma'am," I said, and I tried to take another bite of pizza but my stomach was feeling rocky. Maybe because of what we were talking about. It felt like it went with what we were talking about.

She turned her computer to face me again, and there was a picture of Bodhi. Holding up a number under his chin, and looking sort of like he was embarrassed but also like he thought it was a little bit funny at the same time, which was a very Bodhi thing to do.

"Yes, ma'am, that's him."

She turned it back to her and read me a little of whatever she was seeing there, other than the obvious picture.

"Denver Patterson."

I just stared at her and blinked too much under those terrible lights because I had no idea what those two words meant. It sounded like maybe a place they'd sent him, except I don't think the county jail ships people anywhere, and besides, other than maybe Ann Arbor or something, most places only have one name.

"Denver Patterson," I parroted back to her, because I didn't know what else to say.

"Yes."

"I don't know what that means."

She looked up at me and blinked, like I'd just been doing, and for a second I thought she hated those glary lights, too. But then I decided she was just stunned by how dumb I was being, even though I didn't know why yet.

"That's your friend's name," she said.

Then we both just sat a minute without saying anything. I was thinking how it was weird that I hadn't thought to look at his name or anything else when she had the computer turned my way. I guess I'd just been staring at his picture in shock, because even though I'd been thinking and saying that I knew he got arrested, it was still surprising to see how right I was.

"That's weird," I said. "You feel like you know somebody so well, but then it turns out you sort of don't know them at all."

"Truer words were never spoken." Then, while I was trying to get into what that meant in my head she said, "Petty theft."

"Probably food," I said. "Sometimes he takes food when we really need it."

"Might be. Says grocery items in the amount of seven dollars, fifty-two cents. He was arraigned early this morning. Pled guilty. Sentenced to ninety days."

I felt my eyes go wide again, and I put down my slice of pizza because I would need all of this to settle before I could eat any more.

"Ninety days for seven-fifty worth of food? That seems harsh."

"It wasn't his first offense."

Which I knew.

Then I looked up and that lady was standing in the open doorway, still holding the baby, who said my name when she saw me.

"Molly, Molly, Molly."

And there was another lady with her, a great big heavy lady with a frown that looked like it was carved into her face and could never go away. I figured maybe it was the lady's mother, but that was just a guess.

"We're going to go home now," the baby's mom said, but I couldn't tell if she was talking to the lady cop or me, because she wasn't looking at me. She wasn't looking at either one of us. More like down at the linoleum floor. "But I just want to say . . ." Then she just stood there for a long time, like she had no idea what she wanted to say. "I'm just so happy to have her back, so . . ." Her eyes turned to me for just a flash of a second and then she looked away again. "Thank you."

She turned to go, and I thought, *Well, there goes my second time meeting this lady and it still wasn't good.*

I know it sounded like a step in the right direction, but it was something about the way she said it, like she wished she didn't have to. Like one of the cops told her she had to say it, or maybe her mother, or like she forced herself to do it because she couldn't not do it. But I could tell her heart wasn't in it.

"Wait," I said, and she stopped. All three of them stopped. Well, the baby was in her mom's arms, so what choice did she have? "I still don't know her name. I couldn't get her to tell me."

I watched the lady's face get a little softer.

"Etta," she said.

"Etta?"

But I really messed up in the way I said it, because I said it like that was the weirdest name for a baby in the world. Which I sort of really did think, so the screwup was just in my not keeping that thought to myself.

I should have said something more like "Oh, that's an interesting name for a baby, I never heard it before. Is there a story behind that?"

I tried to do that, but it came out even wronger.

I said, "What kind of a name is Etta?"

I swear I really meant it to be more like that polite way, but it just came out all messed up because when I'm nervous around people I make stupid mistakes.

"It's a perfectly nice name," she said, and she was bristly again by then but I guess I didn't blame her. "You know. Like Etta James."

"I have no idea who that is," I said.

I was actually trying to start a conversation that would get better as it went along, but I'm pretty sure you wouldn't have known it to hear me.

She just shook her head and they all walked away.

It was just me and the lady cop again. I looked at her and she looked at me.

"Boy, I really messed that up," I said, "didn't I?"

"Well," she said, "if it helps any to know, so did she."

And it did help—in fact, it helped a lot. I don't think she ever really knew how much it meant to me when she told me how other people, even fully grown people, mess things up, too.

Chapter Eleven

Brooke: Given Time

I slept a little that night. But only a little. I had Etta in the bed with me. Of course. She was spooned into my chest and belly, and I had an arm over her.

No way was I letting her go again.

Then I woke up and it was dark.

The glowing clock by the bed said it was a little after three. And I just stayed awake, because I wanted to look at her. I had been holding her close in my sleep, but I wanted to *know* I was holding her close.

It struck me that when morning came I would have to call in sick to work at the department store again. Tell them I was not coming in. Because I wasn't letting Etta go to day care so soon. I wasn't letting her go, period. They would ask how long. I had no idea what to tell them. Maybe I would never let her go again.

Maybe I would quit that damn job. Get a better one when Etta and I were over this. If we ever were. My mother would understand that for a time I wouldn't be saving money to move out. She would have to understand.

Etta started talking in her sleep.

She said, "Brave girl, quiet girl."

Which struck me as an odd thing for her to say. She never had before.

She didn't really pronounce the *qu* sound in quiet, because she hadn't gotten that sound down yet. But I knew what she meant. I was her mother and I understood everything she said.

I lay still for a time to see if she would say more.

She didn't.

After a while I reached over her and took my cell phone off the bedside table. Dialed Grace Beatty's direct line by heart. I knew if I waited too long she would go off shift. And then what I needed to say to her would have to go unsaid for another day. I felt like I couldn't carry one more thing inside me. I was so emotionally exhausted. Everything felt impossible.

She picked up on the second ring.

"Beatty," she said.

I said, "It's me." And in the silence that followed, I realized it was a strangely intimate thing to say. Almost embarrassingly so.

"Everything okay over there?"

"Yeah. Fine. I just realized that I left without really saying thank you to you. Without telling you how much I appreciate all you did."

"With all due respect, Brooke . . . ," she began, and her voice sounded firm. Like she was about to school me in something. It chilled me all through my gut. My emotionally exhausted gut. ". . . I'm not the one you need to be thanking, and I think you know it. I do this for a living. I got paid for helping you."

"I did say thank you to her," I said. I sounded like a petulant child. It embarrassed me to hear myself.

"Look," she said. "I'm not the voice of your conscience, Brooke. I can't tell you who to appreciate. But I took a full statement from Molly, and I want you to see it. I want you to read it. But in the morning, after you get some sleep. I can't tell you for a fact that the danger she thought was keeping her from coming out of hiding was everything she thought it was. But I can tell you she thought it was. She had a hellish night protecting your little girl. So take a couple of days to read her story and rest up and get it all sorted out in your head. We're placing her in a foster home today, and we'll give her a little time to settle in, and then if you feel you have more to say to her, you give me a call and I'll work it out so you can see her."

"Okay," I said.

A silence fell. And in the silence, Etta said, "Brave girl, quiet girl." But she was still asleep.

"I'm sorry," Grace said. "I didn't hear that."

"I didn't say anything. That was Etta. Talking in her sleep."

"Oh. What did she say?"

"She said, 'Brave girl, quiet girl.'"

"That's interesting. Any idea why she said that?"

"No idea at all."

But it was not entirely true. Simple common sense dictated that she must have heard the phrase while we were apart. And there was really only one person she could have heard it from.

I made a mental note to find someone who could evaluate her condition in a less physical sense. Someone who could help us sort through the trauma I knew she must be carrying.

The sooner I found such a person, the better.

———

I woke up again because a tone on my new cell phone announced a text. It was light. Etta was still fast asleep.

The clock said it was after nine.

I picked up the phone carefully, without waking her.

It was a number I didn't recognize. No message, just an attachment. When I opened it, I realized it was from Grace Beatty.

It was the police report she had spent most of the night taking from Molly.

It was long. Pages and pages long. That girl could really talk. That girl described just about every minute of the night she spent with my little Etta.

My heart sank lower and lower as I read. It burned over every detail that made it clear how wrong I had been.

When she gave Etta the whole box of goldfish crackers and ate nothing.

When she gave her all the apple juice and went thirsty.

When she tried to stand in front of trucks and cars and flag them down and they wouldn't stop for her.

When she thought one of those boys was coming up the hill to find them but it turned out they were looking on the hill across the street.

When she made it clear how scared she was.

I remembered something Grace had said to me on the phone. *She had a hellish night protecting your little girl.*

It sounded like hell, what she was describing. For her. For Etta, well . . . Molly spoke of singing to her, and chanting with her, and playing clapping games to keep her busy and as happy as possible. Of holding her tightly as she slept.

Something hit me, almost physically from the feel of it. It felt like a fastball connecting hard at the pit of my throat.

The "prayers" I had said out on the roof. Except they were not prayers, because they were not to any deity. They were to whoever had Etta. My silent pleas that the person comfort her. Help her not to be so afraid.

Molly had been the answer to those prayers. Even as I was pushing them out into the night. And I had all but snubbed her. Because I didn't understand why she took so long to call. Because I hadn't waited to hear her side of the story.

I figured Grace would be off shift by now, so I didn't try to call her at the station. I texted her in return.

I wrote:

I've been a fool. Please set up a meeting with the girl when you think she's ready. I need a do-over.

It was more than an hour before she texted me back this:

Thought you might feel that way. We'll give her a couple of days. New foster homes are hard.

I knew it would be a tough couple of days. For both of us.

———

Della was an older woman. Old enough that one would think she'd be retired from her career as a marital, family, and child counselor. Her hair was gray. Not white, but a rich mixture of tones of vibrant gray. It was piled up on her head in a careful style. She had a quick and unselfconscious smile, despite a jumble of teeth that looked both too large and too numerous for her mouth.

"The first thing I want to say," she told me, looking up from the questionnaire I had filled out, "is that it's very soon. You say here this all happened two nights ago. I can't tell you for a fact that any trauma symptoms you're not seeing won't be coming along shortly. But let's be optimistic for now. Why do you think your daughter is doing so well?"

It was a question that caught me off guard.

Etta was sitting quietly in a corner of the office, playing with a teddy bear and a doll. She had been playing for most of the session. I had been doing the work. Except for Etta listening to a series of words and looking at some pictures, I was the one conducting the evaluation with Della. I guess it made sense, given that Etta was so young. For all intents and purposes almost preverbal.

"I'm not sure I understand the question," I said.

"All right. Let me try to make it clearer. You say your daughter is extra clingy and cries when you get out of her sight. That's to be expected, of course. But in a situation as dramatic as hers, frankly, I expected far worse damage. As I say, it's early. But she's doing very well, considering the experience she had to go through. I was just wondering if you had any thoughts on why that might be."

"I was hoping *you* would," I said. "Being the therapist and all."

It was a little bit of a snarky comment. I expected her to react to it that way. She didn't. She smiled. Spoke calmly and evenly.

"But you must appreciate how removed I am from the situation."

"That's true. I'm sorry."

"So . . . any thoughts?"

"Well . . . ," I began. I took a deep breath. Sighed it out. "She did have somebody with her during that time."

"Oh?" Out of the corner of my eye I saw her scribbling on her pad. "You didn't mention that."

Right. I hadn't. And I had been aware that I hadn't. I had felt myself skirting around the issue every time I hadn't brought it up. The only thing I didn't know was why.

I wasn't saying anything. So she added, "Tell me more."

"It was a teenage girl. Living on the street, apparently. She found Etta strapped into her car seat on the sidewalk. And she stayed with her and took care of her until she could get her back to the police."

"I see," she said.

"Molly," Etta said, without looking up from her toys.

Which I found a bit startling. I suppose it's possible that it was coincidental. But I think it makes more sense to believe that she understood a lot of what was being discussed.

"Yes," I said to her. "Molly."

Then Della just wrote and wrote. For a long time. I was quite sure she was writing about me. About how odd it was that I hadn't mentioned Molly sooner. To this day I have no idea what she actually wrote. But it *was* a bit of a psychological mystery that I'd left Molly out of the story for so long. I couldn't imagine Della not wondering. I was wondering myself.

She looked up from her pad. But not at me. She looked over at Etta, who had her back turned to us. Playing with the doll and the bear. Making them look like they were hugging.

"Etta," she said. "Will you please come here and talk with me for just a minute or two?"

Etta looked around at her. But she didn't move. She seemed reluctant to put down the toys.

"Bring them with you if you like," Della said.

Etta dutifully climbed to her feet. She walked to Della and stood a baby step or two away. She looked shy and a little bit cowed. The bear hung from one hand, looking limp and dejected. The doll from the other.

She was so beautiful I thought my chest was going to split open. Maybe to accommodate the swelling of my heart.

"I want to ask you about Molly," Della said.

"Molly," Etta said in return.

"Did you like Molly?"

Etta nodded.

"Did it help that Molly was there with you?"

Etta nodded again.

"Were you still scared, even though she was there?"

Etta stood perfectly quiet and still for a couple of beats. Then she shrugged.

"Okay," I said, aimed at Della. "I feel like I've been holding out on you. Which is pointless if I want to get us both through this."

I took out my phone. Opened the message app. Opened the attachment that Grace Beatty had sent me. Handed the phone over to our new therapist.

For a long time she just stared at the screen, scrolling with her finger. Three or four minutes, maybe. It was a long document. Etta got bored and wandered back into the corner. She dropped the doll and bear and got involved with some interlocking blocks.

"This is quite remarkable," Della said after a time.

"In what way?"

"The various types of support she provided for your daughter. Singing to her and chanting comforting words. Keeping her busy with clapping games. It's very maternal. She seems like a very maternal young woman."

"Okay," I said.

I wasn't sure what this all added up to. And I wasn't sure I wanted to ask.

"I think you can count yourself fortunate," she said. Then, before I could open my mouth to object, she continued. "Oh, I'm sorry, I didn't mean that the way it sounded at all. You both had a terrible experience, and of course there's nothing fortunate about that at all. I just mean . . . given that the experience took place, I think Etta was fortunate to have this kind of support until you could get her back. This girl was clearly trying to mother her, and of course it was no substitute for having her own mother, but it provides a sort of consistency that could prove quite crucial. So I just think it's fortunate that this girl was there to care for Etta."

"Except somebody else might have had a cell phone and gotten her home to me in twenty minutes or less."

"True. Still, I think time is perhaps a less important factor than Etta's fear. Not unimportant, but perhaps less important. If the person who found her had been scary and not very welcoming, well . . . it doesn't take a lot of time to traumatize a child. It can happen in the blink of an eye."

I felt myself getting a little bristly. I wasn't entirely sure why. But I did know that I was tired of feeling it.

"So you're saying that Molly is part of why she's doing fairly well under the circumstances."

"All I can say at this point is that it's too soon to say. I'm hoping you'll come back for at least several more sessions, until we really get a good sense of how she's adjusting after this experience. If you're worried about the cost, I can offer a diagnosis that should satisfy your insurance company."

"Thank you," I said.

"But I'm sorry to say that our time is up for today. Take your daughter home. Hold her close. Talk to her a lot. She seems intelligent and resilient. If I were you, I'd just keep breathing deeply and try to know that you'll both be okay. Given time."

Chapter Twelve

Molly: Denver Patterson

For about a minute and a half the foster home looked good enough, but then my new social worker left, and the whole thing changed out from under me. The cot that had been set up for me in the corner of this lady's real daughter's bedroom got pushed into the closet, so I said, "What, I get it out right before bed?"

She said no, that was my real bedroom—the closet—and my social worker was never supposed to know. She said her real daughter, who was pretty little, needed more privacy and protection, and she wasn't going to force her to share a room with a stranger. Like I was some kind of serial killer or something.

It was a big closet, so that wasn't the deal breaker all by itself, but it was a sign of how things were going to go around that place, if I'd been paying attention.

And it's not that I wasn't bothering to pay attention or anything like that. I mean, this was my life we were talking about. More that the scariness of the whole thing was distracting to me, and I kind of felt like I was floating around that place in a dream.

It was a big apartment in the San Fernando Valley with three bedrooms and walls that were painted this sort of weird lavender color, and it was so close to Ventura Boulevard that you could hear the traffic every minute.

I sat on my cot in that closet for a little bit, but I wasn't sure what to do. I didn't have any books or music like I had at home in Utah, and even when I was out on the street with nothing I could keep busy by walking all over the neighborhood picking up recycling, which stays interesting because recycling is money. I mean, not much of it, but still. It's like a reward built in—find enough of it and you get to eat.

I found the lady in the kitchen, because I didn't know what else to do.

She had on a gray sweat suit with an apron over it, and her hair was up in curlers. There was a man living there, too, lying all sprawled out on the couch in the living room, but I didn't know if he was her boyfriend or her husband. I'd just been introduced to him as Roger, and she'd told me he was on disability for some kind of work accident, which I guess is why he was just lying in front of the TV with no shirt on and with part of one hand shoved down on the diagonal into the waistband of his jeans.

"Can I walk down to Ventura Boulevard?" I asked her, because if I'd had anything at all to do, that would've helped.

"Absolutely not," she said. "I'm responsible for you and I have to know where you are at all times."

She was smoking one of those electronic cigarettes, and it was hanging at the corner of her mouth—no hands—and now and then she puffed out this big cloud of steam that didn't smell like cigarette smoke. It didn't smell like much of anything.

"So what do I do?" I asked.

She said, "Anything you want, as long as I know where you are," which was so not helpful I could hardly stand it.

I walked away to see if I could find the other two girls, because the social worker had told me there were two other foster girls, but I hadn't seen them with my own eyes.

I started to go through the living room but then Roger raised his head and looked at me and I stopped, because I wasn't too sure about him. You know, what kind of a guy he was. So I just looked at him and he looked at me and then I looked over and the lady was standing next to me, staring.

"Come back in the kitchen," she said. "There's something I need to give you."

I followed her back in and I could smell something cooking, which was good, because my social worker had managed to get me over there just late enough that I missed lunch. I probably should've said something, but I'd let the moment go by. So far as I could tell, the only thing about the place that was better than the way I'd been living with Bodhi was the idea that they would feed me a little better here, so I thought it was too bad that I got off to such a lousy start with that.

She handed me a bus pass and a folded piece of paper. I opened the paper, and it was a hand-drawn map with street names and the numbers of the bus routes written along them.

"Tomorrow you go to school," she said. "The day after that you stay home sick. You're going to be sick on Wednesday and Thursday."

"How do you know I'm going to be sick?" I asked, because I totally didn't get what she was all about yet.

"Wow, you're not very bright, are you? I mean we say you're sick, and you stay home and take care of Lisa." Lisa was her five-year-old who couldn't be bothered to share a room with somebody as dangerous as she figured I must be. "The girls take turns. I have to go to work. I have to make a living, you know. And the social worker is not to know about that, either. If she asks, you're having stomach trouble."

"Okay, fine," I said, because what did it really matter? I'd missed months of school, so what would a few more days hurt? But underneath all that I thought it was pretty crappy to take in foster kids and put them in closets just so you get more free babysitters. I mean, who does that?

"One more thing," she said as I was trying to walk away again.

"What?" I said, and I stopped.

But stopping wasn't good enough for her. She wanted me to walk right up to her and she wouldn't say it until our noses were practically touching. She just kept motioning me in until there was no more closer to go.

"A warning about Roger," she said, and it iced my stomach down, because I thought she was telling me he was dangerous. But it turned out that's not where she was going with this warning at all. "Nothing gets by me in this house," she said. "So don't think for a minute I don't see the way you look at him. You just watch your step, little missy."

I took a step back without even meaning to.

"I didn't—"

But she wouldn't let me get a word in.

"Don't you *even* lie to me. If there's one thing I can't stand, it's when a girl looks me right in the eyes and lies to me."

"But I'm not—"

"Don't say another word. Just be careful of what I said and things will go fine around here."

"Yes, ma'am," I said, because I was figuring out that there was no way to really argue with her and besides, I just wanted to get out of the kitchen and get away.

—

I found the other two girls in the backyard. The grass was kind of overgrown, but I could hear them talking so I followed the sound. I found them lying on their backs in the grass with their hands behind their heads, looking up at the sky.

They looked surprised to see me.

"What are you doing?" I asked, because I wasn't sure where to start with them, talking-wise.

They were a lot younger than me, eleven or twelve, maybe, which seemed a little young to babysit a five-year-old. I wondered why the five-year-old wasn't in kindergarten already, and then I wondered why having Roger home wasn't good enough, and then I wondered what these two little girls had done that was so terrible that they had to end up in a foster home. I didn't know at the time that it's usually the parents doing something wrong. I know it now.

"We're looking at the clouds to see what kind of shapes they look like," one of them said.

Nobody said anything for a weird length of time, me included, and then the other girl said, "Who are you?"

"I'm the new foster kid. Didn't anybody tell you I was coming?"

"Nope," they both said, almost exactly at the same time.

I didn't know what to say about that, so I lay down on my back in the long grass—a little ways away because they didn't know me yet—to see what was so great about those clouds. They were kind of puffy, so I guess it didn't seem impossible to make shapes out of them in your mind, but my mind didn't really work that way anymore. Imagining wasn't really something I still did, because nothing I imagined anymore was very good, so why dream it up?

Nobody was talking, and that got weird after a while, so I said, "This place seems kind of bad. Or is that just me?"

"I've had eight foster homes," one of them said, "and this one takes the prize for the very worst."

Then the other girl said, "I had one that was worse. But it's bad enough. Why? Have all your other placements been good?"

"Placements" seemed like a weird word to hear such a young kid using, so I figured it was a language she learned from her social worker or her foster parents.

"This is my first," I said. Then I said, "That one looks a little like an elephant. See? That's his trunk, going off to the right there."

I waited, but nobody said they saw the elephant, so I decided to keep talking. Sometimes when I get nervous I just keep talking.

"So she keeps telling me all these things that I'm not supposed to tell my social worker, but I'm thinking maybe I'll just tell on her anyway. I mean, if she's a bad foster mother, shouldn't somebody know?"

"Don't," one girl said.

And the other one jumped in right away to back her up. "You really are new, aren't you? You *never* do that. You *never* tell on them with your social worker. Especially not with this lady. Because they don't really *do* anything about it. They just go to the foster parent and tell them to fix the problem, and then they walk away and go back to their office. And then you're stuck home with the lady you just told on, and she knows you just told on her. So it gets a lot worse after that."

I didn't say anything for a long time, because I was letting it settle in, about how this lady who more or less owned me, who had total control over my life at that point, would make things worse for me on purpose, as punishment, if I tried to make anything better.

"I wonder why people like that even take in foster kids," I said. More or less talking to myself out loud.

They both laughed.

"Because they get money from the government for every one they take in," one of them said. I never knew which one because they sounded a little bit alike and I never turned my head.

"Well, that solves a lot of mysteries," I said.

It's funny how many times when something seems impossible to explain, it turns out money is the part you weren't getting. You know, once you finally figure it out.

—

Dinner was spaghetti with almost no sauce. She gave us a lot of it but, holy cow, there was almost no sauce. It was like she just waved a jar of sauce over the pasta without really pouring.

Roger didn't even bother to show up, just stayed in the living room watching TV, and the lady didn't even turn off her electronic cigarette or take it out of her mouth.

Then I looked up and saw that the five-year-old, the real daughter, had hot dogs and baked beans for dinner. Two hot dogs on those nice, soft white buns, with ketchup and mustard, and this big sea of baked beans all over her plate. I was amazed that a kid who was only five could eat all that, but Lisa was kind of plump so I guess she was putting away a lot of food on a regular basis.

That's when I started to get mad, and I never stopped being mad after that, because what kind of person takes money from the government to feed a kid and then gives them nothing but cheap white flour for dinner and pockets the difference while they have to watch your real kid get real food to eat?

But I ate all the spaghetti, because I was hungry, and because there was something to be said for having your stomach full of food, almost no matter what kind of food it is.

—

The whole thing really came apart at bedtime when I found out she was going to lock me in, so that's when it hit me that I might be better off the way I'd been living before. I mean, the street was bad in a lot of ways, but at least I was free to try to make things better for myself if I could think of how to do that.

But I still figured I would try to tough it out for the rest of Bodhi's ninety-day jail sentence.

She told me to go to the bathroom before she locked me in, and I did, but just knowing I couldn't go again made me feel like I needed to.

I didn't really sleep much at all, just sat there on the edge of my cot, rocking back and forth. There was a bare light bulb over my head that came on when you pulled a string, and I left it on because when I turned it off for a minute it made me feel like the walls were moving in on me.

I was staring at this little bundle of stuff that was everything I owned, that the social worker had given me. A brush and comb, toothbrush, washcloth, pajamas, bar of soap, all rolled up in a towel. I wasn't wearing the pajamas, because I had never gotten out of my clothes, because I didn't really feel like I was going to bed. Just mostly rocking there on the cot, getting panicky.

At least the lady had washed my clothes, so that was something, but I felt like she did it for herself and not for me. Like I might be bringing some kind of cooties into her house. But maybe I'm reading too much insulting stuff in. It's hard to know.

I felt like in a minute there wouldn't be enough air to breathe, even though there was a pretty big space under the door. Big enough that I knew there actually would be air, and that it was only a false feeling that there wouldn't be, but I still couldn't shake the feeling.

Then all of a sudden somebody banged on the door and I just about jumped out of my skin.

"Turn off the light," Lisa yelled, and I knew it was her, even though she hadn't said a word around me before, because her voice sounded five. And because she would be the only one who could see my light coming out under the door into her bedroom. "It's keeping me awake."

I turned it off and tried to lie down on the cot but I ended up sitting up again and rocking, trying to convince myself that the walls weren't getting closer.

It was a long-ass night.

—

In the morning I didn't go to school.

I pretended to, but then I ditched, and used my bus pass to ride all the way down to the county jail near where Bodhi and I lived. I knew where it was because people we knew from the street got put in there from time to time. Not that we knew them well enough to go see them or anything, but word gets around and we knew where it was.

Now, getting there from Sherman Oaks was a whole other thing. I had to ask a lot of bus drivers a lot of questions. Took me all morning, but I got there.

Then, just as I walked in the door of the jail, I got a bad feeling because it hit me that maybe they would ask my age and why I wasn't in school.

So I walked out again and stood on the street for a minute and tried to work that out in my head. I had ID, sort of, so if they asked for any I could probably squeak by. I still had my wallet, which I'd managed not to lose since I left Utah, and it had a Social Security card and my school ID in it, which had a picture of me and everything.

I walked in, and right up to this round desk with men and women in uniforms sitting behind it. And I just acted like I knew exactly what I was doing. There was a sign that said visiting hours were Monday through Friday from 10:00 a.m. to 3:00 p.m., so I figured so far so good.

A lady with nice, neat braids all over her head asked if she could help me.

I said, "Yes. Thank you. I'm here to visit Denver Patterson."

Everybody behind the desk laughed, except for one guy who I think just wasn't paying attention.

"The Bodhi Tree," one lady said.

"Why is that funny?" I asked them, sort of all of them at once.

"He's just quite a character," the lady who was helping me said.

And, well, hell, I couldn't argue with that.

She gave me a form to fill out, and I had to give my name and address—which was interesting, because I all of a sudden had one—and I had to show ID.

"This is from Utah," she said, looking at my school ID.

"Yes, ma'am. I just moved here."

For a minute she just stared at my ID, and I was waiting for her to ask me why I wasn't in school. But then she just handed it back to me and buzzed me through a door into another room, sort of deeper into the jail.

At first I thought maybe she just didn't care, but then I decided that kids drop out of school at sixteen, which she knew from my ID that I was, and maybe they think that's a terrible idea, but there might not be too much they can do about it, law-wise.

I sat at this table in a big room with a guard in the corner and about ten or twelve tables, but there was nobody else there visiting, which seemed really sad.

Then I looked up and a big, noisy metal door was being opened, and Bodhi walked in. He sat down across the table with me and gave me the biggest grin. His face was shaved clean, and I didn't know if he'd done it as a change of pace or they made you do it in there. And he had this look on his face like it was all a big game—being caught by the police, being stuck in this place. Life in general. That was a very Bodhi way to be. Nothing really seemed to set him back much.

"You okay?" he asked, with that crooked little thing going on with his face.

"I guess so," I said. It was also a very Bodhi thing to worry about how *I* was doing when he was stuck for three months in jail. I think it had only been a couple of days since he got picked up, but that was hard to imagine, because the night I'd found that baby felt like years ago. "What about you?"

"This's as good a place to be as any," he said. "I was just worried about you on the street by yourself. What about the baby? You get her back home okay?"

"Yeah. I did. But then the police stuck me in a foster home."

"Oh crap," he said. "Did not see *that* coming." We sat quiet a minute, and I could almost sort of see him thinking about things, like maybe there were real wheels turning in there, like the old saying goes. "So how is it?" he asked. "Is it okay there? You gonna stay?"

"Not sure," I said. "It's not very okay, no. But I'm going to try to stay till you get out."

"Okay. But here's a tip, in case you change your mind. You know all that money I was stashing for a place to live? Well, it's not *that* much money, but I think I should have a little over two hundred dollars in there. My wallet is in some paper packing stuff at the bottom of that plastic barrel. You know, just to the left of the crate. If things get bad for you, just go get it. Spend it all, I don't care. It'll never be enough for a place, anyway. I was fooling myself. I should've given it to you for food."

It meant a lot to me that he said that, because I always wondered why we couldn't eat better based on how much money he was able to save. But I felt like it was his money and he got to decide, and it wouldn't be right to ask about it. I always figured it was because Bodhi barely ate—he was just one of those people who could live on dirt and air and do fine. One meal a day suited him and didn't slow him down. Nothing did, ever.

"Why did you steal if you had two hundred dollars?" I asked him, and then I wished I hadn't, partly because it wasn't really my business and partly because I already mostly knew. It was part of his nature.

"If I'd had to buy food, you know how much I would've saved up? Zero. That's how much. Don't you ever get mad, Molly? Doesn't it ever make you mad that they have everything and we have nothing and they're just waiting for a chance to lock our asses up because we needed something to eat? Doesn't that piss you off?"

I thought about five-year-old Lisa eating hot dogs and beans in front of us.

"It's starting to," I said.

"Good. Then go take that money and lay low and try to make it last till I get out and I'll come and find you."

"Thanks," I said. "Nice to have a fallback plan, anyway."

I didn't have any specific thoughts on how likely I was to fall back, but my new foster home seemed like a place with a lot of trapdoors and cliffs.

Chapter Thirteen

Brooke: Ready

I stepped into the kitchen with the baby on my hip, and my mother hit me like a falling sandbag.

"I called David," she said.

"Why would you call David?"

"Because *you* obviously didn't plan to."

"Oh," I said. "I just forgot. What with everything that was going on. Why didn't you just remind me?"

She never answered the question. For the second time in only a few days it struck me that maybe she didn't know, either. She had chosen the most confrontational path through the world, and it had become her way. But she truly didn't seem to know why.

"When is the baby going back to day care?" she asked. Hard voiced and loud. Veering the complaints in a different direction. Classic Mom move. Hit a dead end? Crank the wheel, punch the throttle. Keep driving.

"When we've been to the therapist a few more times and I feel like we have a better sense of how she's doing."

"If you don't mind my saying so . . . ," she began.

"I'm sure I will," I said under my breath.

"What?"

"Nothing. I didn't say anything."

"I was just going to say that if you ask me, she's doing fine and you're the one with the problem."

I gave up getting through the kitchen and up to my room. Which had been my original plan. I sat down hard at the kitchen table with my mother. And sighed. And Etta wrapped her arms more tightly around my neck.

"I think it's a combination of the two," I said. "But . . . so what if you're right? I don't get a few days to make an adjustment after a thing like that?"

"You're the grown-up," she said. She was deeply into her harping voice. It felt like a sharp tool, digging into me. Searching for something she could use to dig even deeper. "You're supposed to screw your head back on and keep going. She counts on you for that."

"So . . . in other words . . . just bury it and pretend it never happened? I think it would be better for Etta if I took the time to make my peace with it."

She waved me away with one dismissive swoosh of her hand.

"Oh, that's nothing but a load of New Age claptrap," she said.

"I'm going up to my room." I lifted myself and Etta out of the chair. It wasn't easy without using my hands for leverage. She was getting big. "I'd appreciate being allowed to deal with this in my own way. I'd appreciate not being criticized at a time like this."

I headed for the stairs, but she was not done. Which came as no surprise.

"You quit your darned job," she called after me. "You were living under my roof before, but now you're living under my roof and not even saving up to move out. Just living off me like a minor child. I have a right to say what I think of your actions as long as you're living under my roof."

I stopped. Turned around. I was getting mad, and Etta knew it. I could feel her shifting around. Getting ready to start fussing out loud.

I breathed out my anger. For her sake.

"Thank you," I said to my mother. "Thank you for taking care of us and letting us live here until I can get this sorted through and do better for Etta and myself. I do recognize the generosity of the thing, and I appreciate it."

In addition to the fact that it was true, and I'd meant it, it was an old last-ditch method I used with my mother when all else failed. She seemed to have no mechanism for relating to kindness. She had no comeback for anything suitably divorced from combat.

———

When Etta was asleep for the night, and I thought it was late enough to catch Grace Beatty at work, I called her on my cell phone.

"Beatty," she said when she picked up.

"It's Brooke," I said.

"Oh. Brooke. How are things going over there? How's Etta?"

"Well . . . ," I said. Then I pulled in a deep breath that she could probably hear. "My mother says she's doing fine and I'm the one who can't handle what happened. And, much as I hate to *ever* say this about my mother, she might be right."

"Got a good counselor?"

"I do."

"Ready to have another go at thanking Molly?"

"Yes. I am. That's why I called."

"Good. Good for you. I'm going to hang up and call her social worker, and I'll call you back with a phone number and address."

———

I could have called and said what I needed to say. I didn't.

In the morning I took Etta and drove over there in person.

I had taken out another credit card and put a new battery in my car, and I was driving again. But still, I could have stayed home and called.

The reason I didn't?

I kept thinking about what that police officer had said to me. The uniformed cop who drove Etta and me to the hospital. He said that homeless girl loved Etta. That he could tell me that for a fact.

I thought if that was true, she might like to see her again.

I purposely braved rush hour traffic to get to Sherman Oaks before eight in the morning. Because I knew if I waited longer, she would probably be at school.

I took Etta out of her car seat in the back. The new car seat. One more charge on the new credit card.

As I did, I said, "Let's go see Molly."

"Molly!" she cried out. "Molly, Molly, Molly!"

It hit me that Molly might have already left for school. In which case getting Etta all excited like that would prove to be a serious mistake.

The apartment building had outdoor stairs and hallways, and doors that faced out onto the street. I knocked on the door of apartment B. At first, no answer. Though I could hear a flurry of activity on the other side of the door. It sounded like a herd of baby elephants running for cover.

Then, just as I thought no one ever would, someone answered the door. It was a woman of about forty with curlers in her hair. She looked tired and worn down. Also upset about being tired. She had an e-cigarette dangling from her lips. To say she did not look happy to see me would be a laughable understatement.

"What?" she said. "I'm trying to get the girls ready for school."

"I'm here to see Molly."

She snorted a laugh that sounded derogatory. As though it had been truly stupid of me even to consider such a plan.

"Molly, Molly, Molly," Etta said from her perch on my hip.

"Yeah, I'd like to see Molly, too," the woman said. "Nothing pisses me off more than having to call a girl's social worker and tell them she's gone. But that's what I had to do last night, when Molly didn't come home. I'm surprised nobody bothered to tell you."

"She ran away?"

"Looks like it. Now if you'll excuse me . . ."

"Do you have any idea why?"

She stopped with her hand on the door. Clearly disappointed that she didn't get to slam it yet. She sighed deeply.

"I could make you a wild guess, yeah. I *disciplined* her. Kids don't like that if they're not used to it. These kids, they been running wild forever and they're not used to having to answer to anyone. Me, I reintroduce them to discipline. Some take it, some don't."

"What did she do wrong?"

"Skipped school. I called the school to see if she was there for her first day, and it turned out she never showed. So when she got home, I waited to see if she would fess up. She didn't, so I let her have it."

She started to swing the door again. I stopped it with my left hand. My right hand was holding Etta onto my hip.

"Let her have it? As in, struck her?"

Her eyes narrowed.

"I got kids to look after," she said.

Then she put her hip to the door and closed it against my will.

"Molly, Molly, Molly," Etta chanted as I carried her back to the car. She no longer sounded excited. She was brokenhearted now. It made my chest hurt to hear her tone.

She chanted it again as I strapped her into her car seat. And again as I started up the car. "Molly, Molly, Molly."

"I'm sorry, honey," I said. "Molly wasn't there."

"Where Molly?"

"I'm sorry, honey. I don't know."

I texted Grace Beatty on her cell phone before driving away. Because I knew she would be off shift by then.

She's gone, I typed. She ran away.

No answer.

I drove most of the way back to West LA before I heard the tone of her text coming through. Fortunately I was off the freeway and waiting at a stoplight when I heard it.

It said: Damn. I hate it when that happens.

I drove the rest of the way home without answering her text. I mean, what do you say in response to a statement like that?

I heard another text come through a few minutes later, but I was driving, so I didn't dare look.

As I pulled into my mother's driveway I stopped and read. There was more than one. They were fairly long.

I'll never understand this fascination with the street. Had one guy tell me it was addictive. Can you believe that? Homelessness. Addictive. He said it was because you had zero responsibilities. Nothing to do all day. He couldn't hack having any structure in his life. Makes no sense to me at all.

Then the second one:

If you still want to try to find her, I'll give you an address. I'll find it and send it in the next text. Ask for a young man named Denver Patterson. He might know something regarding her whereabouts. Bring ID.

She hadn't yet sent the text with the address.

I didn't get out of the car. I sat there typing an answer. Even though I could hear Etta getting squirmy in the back.

I typed: This young guy needs me to bring ID before he'll talk to me?

Her answer was nearly immediate:

No, but his jailers will expect it.

I sighed and took Etta out of her car seat. Carried her into the house.

"Where Molly?" she asked me.

"I don't know, honey," I said.

But I couldn't hide my irritation from her. I wondered how long it would be before she forgot to ask. Or at least stopped asking. Whether she forgot or not.

I stuck my head into the kitchen. My mother was not around.

I breathed a huge sigh of relief and carried Etta upstairs.

I heard another tone from my cell phone and looked down at it. Grace Beatty had texted me the address.

I set Etta in front of her toy basket and sat on the edge of the bed. I don't know about this, I typed in reply.

What don't you know?

I don't know about going to a jail. See, this was my problem with the whole situation to begin with. These were not the people I meant to bring into my life. If you know what I mean.

Then, while I was waiting for her answer, I worried that she *would* know what I meant. Or that *I* would. Because, if you really dissected that statement, I did not come off well for making it. I also wondered how true my statement had been. The homeless youth aspect might have been *a* problem with the whole thing. But I'm not sure it was *the* problem.

A tone made me jump.

If it helps or changes anything, this kid is in jail for stealing about seven dollars' worth of food. Everybody has to eat.

I sat for a strange length of time, waiting for the whole situation to settle inside my gut. It never did.

I'll sleep on it, I typed back to her.

But it turned out to be a mostly figurative statement. Because bedtime came and went that night, and I didn't get much sleep at all.

When I told the lady at the jail I was there to see Denver Patterson, her eyebrows arched up high. Then she laughed a short little burst of a laugh.

"What's funny?" I asked.

I had the baby on my hip, even though I didn't want to bring her into a jail. Because I hadn't wanted to leave her at home with my mother. I figured she'd dump her at preschool.

Hell, I might as well be honest: I didn't want to leave her. Period.

"Just surprised he's such a popular guy," she said.

I filled out a form and showed her my driver's license.

She buzzed me through a door into a stark-looking hallway. There was only one open door, and I walked through it. It led me into a room full of tables, most empty. A guard was watching over a woman and child sitting with a man who was clearly an inmate.

I sat for a time, feeling more nervous than the situation likely required.

Then I heard a voice, and it made me jump.

"Hey there, girl! Good to see you again!"

I half stood, Etta and all, and looked around. A young man was standing behind me. Hair buzzed short. Clean shaven. He was wearing a jumpsuit, but it was not the inmate orange the movies had conditioned me to expect. More of a pea soup green. His face looked bizarrely cheery. You know—under the circumstances.

"We've never met before," I said.

"I was talking to the little one."

He reached out to pat her on the head, but I flinched us both away. He got the message and took his hand back.

I found myself surprisingly furious that someone I'd never met or even seen before could claim to know my baby daughter. It made me feel as though life had spun hopelessly out of my control.

"Sit down," he said. Expansively, with a sweeping gesture to go along. As though he were a host making me welcome in his home.

Reluctantly, I sat.

"How do you know my daughter?" I asked him.

If that girl had brought Etta down to the jail during the time she claimed to be hiding, I would be furious. I would abandon trying to find her. Or maybe I would try to find her just to tell her I was furious.

"I was there," he said. "Right after Molly found her. I swiped her a bottle of apple juice and a box of goldfish crackers. That's why I'm in here."

Then I felt stupid. Because it was quite obvious who he was. He was the friend of Molly's who I read about in her statement to Grace Beatty. The one who went off to call the police and never came back. I guess I hadn't connected the two because this boy was in jail. It hadn't occurred to me that his incarceration had begun so recently. And then, of course, there was the name difference to throw me off.

"Wait a minute," I said.

"Okay."

He had a quirky grin on his face. As though everything was funny to him. Even in a place like that.

"If you got arrested for stealing apple juice and crackers . . ."

I paused, and he jumped in.

"And two candy bars for me."

"Then how did Molly have the apple juice and crackers to give to my daughter?"

"Well," he said. "It's like this. I got away with it. Or at least, I thought I did. The lady saw me take 'em, but I was a much faster runner. But then I was out looking for a phone and I ran into two cops who were out looking for *me*."

I sat still and quiet for a minute. I was wondering what I owed him. For going to jail so Etta could have apple juice and crackers. And how I could possibly repay such a debt.

"I was hoping you knew where I could find Molly."

"Molly, Molly, Molly," Etta said.

"Oh. She's not in that foster place anymore?"

"No. She ran away. You didn't know that?"

"I did *not* know that, no. I *did* know that the place they put her bites."

"Any idea where she might have gone?"

"Possibly."

"Any chance you'll tell me?"

"Not much of one, no."

"Why not?"

"Because you'll tell on her. And get her put back there. I know you will."

"You can't possibly know anything about me."

"I know you're one of *them*," he said. He waved his hand in a stylized arc on the word "them." Like a magician pointing out a magic trick. Or distracting me from one. "You're *establishment*. You believe in the *power structures*. You think they know best."

"Actually," I said, "I met that woman who was supposed to be her foster mom. And I didn't like her at all."

"But you'll still try to turn her in."

"No. Not necessarily. Not if she doesn't want to go back."

For a moment I scanned back over my words and wondered. Could I really find her on the street, thank her . . . then leave her on the street? Then again, who was I to force her to be someplace she didn't want to be? Especially when she would just take off again.

"Then why do you even want to find her?"

"I just need to . . . I never really thanked her properly. When I saw her at the police station that night, I made a mess of things. I just need to tell her how much I appreciate what she did."

He was staring into my eyes like a laser as I spoke. I got the eerie feeling that he was something of a human lie detector. That he could see right through me with his X-ray vision.

Fortunately I was telling the truth.

"Well, then," he said. "If that's really how it is, I might have a thought or two on where Molly could be hanging out."

"Molly, Molly, Molly," Etta said.

Chapter Fourteen

Molly: Special Delivery

I thought about going back, but I didn't go back.

I don't mean to that awful foster family, because I never thought about going back there, not even one time and not even for a second. But I thought about going back to that lady cop and asking her to call my social worker and see if she could put me someplace better.

I never did, because I was afraid I was in trouble for running away, plus I was afraid nobody would believe me and everybody would believe that terrible lady, and they'd send me back to her, and then I hate to even think how much trouble I'd be in.

It was cold without Bodhi, and I'd been sleeping by myself in the cold for maybe a week. I know people think it never gets cold in LA, but they don't know. If they don't live there, they don't know, and if they do live there they still don't know, because at night in the winter they're inside their house.

As soon as it got the tiniest bit light, I'd go out on the street and start picking up bottles and cans, because I wanted to use as little of Bodhi's money as I possibly could—partly because it needed to last for nearly three months, and partly because it was his. It was one thing to eat off it if I needed it, but that didn't mean I was supposed to sit around on my butt all day like a slug and just waste it. He spent months saving up that money so maybe we could get some kind of place. Just a cheap room at a weekly motel, maybe, where we'd have a shower and a heater and a bed.

But he was right, what he said to me at the jail. He was kidding himself, and I knew that was true because even at the really cheap weekly motels you wouldn't be able to stay much more than a week for around two hundred dollars.

I hated to even think about what he might've done to get that kind of money, so that was another good reason to spend it as slow as possible.

Besides, if you're not going to walk around looking for stuff to recycle, then what the hell *would* you do all day? It's not like I had a TV set or a bunch of fun hobbies.

———

It took about a week for other homeless people to start asking about Bodhi when I saw them on the street, because I guess before that they just figured he didn't happen to be with me that one time, or the time after it.

I felt like I didn't really know any of the people who lived in the neighborhood with us, but somehow they all knew Bodhi. Everybody knew Bodhi.

There was something about that seventh day—that was when everybody seemed to notice how long it had been since they'd seen Bodhi with me.

I'd spent all day walking around, and then cashed in what I found at the big, nice market that closes at night. I'd had a really good day, so I bought a hard roll and a little bit of salami at their deli, and then put it together on my way out of the store and ate it on the walk back.

An old man with a long beard was living on the hill inside the freeway fence, which was sliced open, and he called to me, "Hey, what happened to your boyfriend?" when I went by.

"He's not my boyfriend," I called back.

Then I kept walking, because I had a bad idea that maybe this was the kind of guy that, if you're going to tell him you're single, you better keep walking.

A minute later I turned a corner and ran into those three guys. The Three Musketeers.

"Well, well," the supposedly smart one said.

I had about three bites of sandwich left, and I wolfed it down without hardly chewing, because I was worried they would take it away from me or knock it out of my hand onto the dirty sidewalk. If they were going to kill me, at least I was going to eat my sandwich first.

"What?" I said. I was scared, but I was doing my best to make them think I wasn't. I have no idea if it was working or not, but I tried.

"What happened to that baby?" the dumb guy said.

He had hair that was really red—or actually orange like a carrot, but people still call that red—and I'd never noticed that before. He always had it stuffed under a knit cap, but it was getting longer and shaggier, and it was sticking out and curling all around his face.

"I gave her back to the police," I said. "What do you think?"

"Did you know we were looking for her?"

I don't know which one said that, because I was purposely looking down at the sidewalk. I didn't want to look at them because I didn't want them to see that I was scared, but maybe looking down wasn't good, either.

"No," I said, real nice and casual. "How would I know that?"

I looked up, because I sort of had to, because if something was coming at me I needed to see it. I could see the freeway out of the corner of my eye, off to our left and up over our heads, and I could see the cars really well, which was good. If we could see them then all those drivers could see us, and it was still daylight—kind of late toward dusk, but light enough for the drivers to see us. That didn't absolutely guarantee they wouldn't do something terrible to me, but it was a step in the right direction. It helped me like my chances a little better.

The smart one was looking into my face, and his eyebrows were all pressed down, and he walked a few steps closer to me, which I didn't like. But what was I supposed to do?

"How long did you have her?" he asked me, and I could smell his breath. It didn't smell good.

"Like, maybe ten minutes," I said. "The cops were out driving around looking for her and one of them saw us right away. It was like no time at all."

"Are you stupid?" he asked me. Still too close.

"No, we're the stupid ones," his stupid friend said. "I told you it was a waste of time. Pounding up and down the streets and the police already had her back for hours. What a waste of good energy."

"Speaking of waste," the smart guy said right into my face, "why did you give her back? That was a gold mine right there. Why did you give her back if she was worth her weight in gold?"

"What choice did I have? The cops saw me with her."

"You could've run away. You know how to run away from the cops, right? Your boyfriend sure knows how."

"She was heavy," I said. "You're not the one who was lugging her around. You can't run fast when you're carrying a little kid like that. Besides. How was she a gold mine? The only ones who knew who her parents are were the police. And what was I supposed to do? Go up to them and say, 'I'd like to ransom this little girl back to her mom, so please hook me up?'"

Then I decided I should've kept my mouth shut, because I wasn't supposed to know it was a ransom thing with them, and I wasn't supposed to know that it was just a mom, not a set of two parents.

I waited, but fortunately none of that seemed to stick with them, or to ring any alarm bells in their heads.

"You're supposed to play it cool," the smart guy said. "You bide your time. Two or three days later the parents go on the TV news with this impassioned plea to anyone who's seen their kid. We would've been smart enough to bide our time. But you blew it for us."

I remember thinking his idea was still pretty stupid, because none of us owned a TV, or probably knew where to go to watch one. But I didn't say so, because he was still right in my face and I didn't want to piss him off.

Then all of a sudden the quiet one opened his mouth. And I think I was right about him being a little dangerous, because I noticed that when he finally did say something, everybody listened.

"Look," he said, "just leave her alone, okay? She didn't know we were looking for the kid. How could she've known that? Our timing was just wrong."

I waited to see how that would settle in with his two friends, and a minute later the guy with his face right up to mine moved it away, and they all cut around me and kept walking.

I started shaking, which I guess I'd been smart enough not to do when they were watching, and I ran all the way home.

Well, to that crate. Home was a really stupid thing to call it.

I was still shaking when I got there, and when I opened up the crate and climbed in I saw there was something in there that hadn't been there before. It scared me, even though it was only some folded-up sheets of paper, because nobody should have been in there to leave anything, and besides, I was scared to begin with.

I opened up the papers.

There was just a little last bit of sun coming in at a slant between the boards of the crate, and I sat where it would fall on the paper. There were two sheets, with writing on the front and back—loopy handwriting like the kind they teach you in school.

It said on the first line, "Dear Molly," so I knew it was for me, and then I got a little panicky again, because nobody was supposed to know I was here. Only Bodhi was supposed to know our spot.

I started reading to see who knew, and what they wanted to say to me.

Dear Molly,

Your friend Denver told me where you might be staying. I went and saw him in jail. At first he didn't want to tell me, but I think I convinced him that I only wanted to say a better thank you for everything you did for Etta.

I've been by every day this week but you're never here. So maybe he lied about where you are. Or maybe he was mistaken. Or maybe you're just away during the day like anybody else.

In case it's that last thing, I've decided to leave you this letter. I'm going to write my address and phone number at the end of it. If you ever want to call or come by, you can. And I'll tell you in person what I really need to say.

In the meantime, the short version is this:

I acted badly on the night I met you. I really didn't understand the situation yet. I thought you were too slow to get her back to me because I didn't know what you went through that night. Now I do, and I'd like to try again to say thank you.

The reason I thought you might want to come to my house instead of calling on the phone is this: Remember that policeman? One of the uniformed ones who drove you and Etta back to West LA? He drove us to the hospital that night to get Etta checked out. (She's fine, by the way.) He said something that seemed strange to me at the time. He said you love Etta. He seemed very sure of that.

I don't know if you think he's right about that or not. But if so, I thought you might want to see her again.

But I also know you might not. Might not call or come by, either one. After the way I treated you that night, I wouldn't blame you.

If that's the way this works out, then at least I can say this in writing and hope you find this letter and read what I'm about to say.

When Etta was gone and I was waiting to see if I would ever get her back, I said a couple of prayers out into the night. It was a kind of pleading. That whoever had her please be comforting to her, and help her not be too scared.

Now I see that you were the answer to those prayers.

Etta is doing well, by the way. We have a therapist now, and she's very impressed with the way Etta handled that terrible night. She thinks it's because you helped her. She thinks you were very mothering with her, and that even though she didn't have her mother, she had a mother figure to see her through.

So I really owe you one for that.

I hope I get to tell you any and all of this in person. But if not, it's nobody's fault but my own.

Etta says your name all the time. And sometimes in her sleep she says, "Brave girl, quiet girl," and I wonder if she heard that from you.

Thank you,

Etta's mom, Brooke Hollister

And then underneath she had written her address and her phone number, just like she said she would.

The light was starting to fade and I knew it would get dark soon, so I folded up the letter and stuck it in my pocket and tried not to be scared. But the combination of running into those boys and then somebody finding me here, somebody who knew who I was, well . . . it just kind of had me rattled.

I lay awake for a long time and decided it was nice of her to write me that letter, but I was pretty sure I wasn't going to go over there or even call her on the phone. They were lots of pretty words, but I saw what she thought of me that night when I looked into her eyes, and I knew she probably had pretty much the same opinion of me now, even though I think she didn't know it herself. But I still knew.

I think we all more or less know where we stand with people, whether we like to admit it to ourselves or not.

———

I guess it was around two nights later, but also maybe it could have been three. Sometimes all the days seem to melt into all the other days, you know? And then who remembers?

Anyway, I'd gotten back with almost nothing to eat, because I hadn't found enough recycling to buy anything more than a candy bar. I should never eat a candy bar on an empty stomach, because it makes me jumpy and makes it harder to sleep, but then I went and did it anyway.

The plan was to get back, get a little money out of Bodhi's wallet, and then go out and get some real food. But then when I got there I just crawled into the crate and flopped.

I guess I told myself I was just too tired to go out again, and I'm not saying that's entirely not true. But also it was dark—not really late, just winter-dark—and after running into those boys, and everything that happened when I had the baby, I might've been a little bit afraid but just not talking to myself about it.

And then, speaking of afraid, I started hearing the noises of somebody coming through the vacant lot, and I just knew I was about to be robbed, or worse. I figured all the people on the street knew Bodhi wasn't here with me, and so it was just a matter of time until they found out where I slept.

I could see a little bit of light, but not a big light like a flashlight would throw off. Maybe just somebody's cell phone or those little lights you put on your keychain so you can see to stick the key in your front door at night. If you're lucky enough to have a front door at night.

Bodhi's wallet wasn't in the crate with me—it was still in the packing paper at the bottom of that plastic barrel. Because I'm not stupid, and I know that when somebody finds the place where they can see you've been sleeping, that's the place they toss for anything you might actually own.

The only thing that was in the crate with me, except for a couple of raggedy blankets, was the black plastic squirt gun Bodhi used to keep around. He told me never to point it at anybody in the daylight, because they'd right away see what it was and what it wasn't. It wasn't going to fool anybody in the middle of the day, but he said hardly anybody's going to rob you in the middle of the day anyway, so maybe it might come in handy.

The noises were getting closer, so I took hold of the squirt gun and jumped out. I didn't want to do it, but I knew I had to, because once somebody actually got to the front end of the crate, which was the only end that opened up, they'd have me pretty well trapped.

I could make out a person, but it was just a shape in the dark, and the only thing I could really see was a glowing phone making just a little bit of light to walk by. It was down near the person's hip. My heart was banging and I could feel the blood in my ears doing this pounding thing, and when I called out, my voice sounded squeaky and high and not scary like I wanted it to be.

"Don't come any closer! I've got a gun!"

"It's only me," a voice said, and it was a lady voice. Which I guess was a little bit better, but who knows?

"Who?"

"Brooke. It's only Brooke."

Then I laughed, but I think it was mostly all that fear rushing out of me. I don't think I really thought it was very funny how she scared me like that.

"What're you doing here?" I asked her.

She said, "Could you please put the gun down and then I'll tell you?"

"Oh, this?" I said. "This's not even a gun, it's a squirt gun. I was just trying to fool you." I showed her by squirting it against my hand, even though she couldn't see it in the dark, most likely, but I figured she could hear it. "Now what are you doing here? I thought you said you were going to sort of leave it up to me whether I wanted to see you or not."

Then I tossed the squirt gun back into the open crate, and it made a noise when it landed, and she jumped.

For a minute nobody said anything. We just stood there in the dark, not even really seeing each other, and it felt stupid. I just felt like we were both being stupid somehow, but I can't really explain how.

Then she said, "So you did get my note."

"Yeah," I said.

"I wasn't sure if you did. If you would. That's why I came by. Because I knew I would always wonder if you saw the note but didn't want to talk to me, or if you just hadn't seen it. And then I'd never know if I said sorry properly."

We stood quiet for another stupid minute.

I was thinking about how sometimes when people want to tell you how sorry they are, it feels a little bit like they want to make *themselves* feel better. You know. More than *you*. But I don't even know for a fact if they can tell that's what they're doing or not.

I didn't say any of that.

After a while I just said, "Where's the baby?"

"Home sleeping."

"You left her alone?"

I was shocked. Seriously shocked that she would do a thing like that.

"My mother is home with her," she said.

"Oh."

Then we had no idea what to say.

I shouldn't speak for her, because I can't really say for a fact what was going on in her head, but there was this big awkward thing hanging between us and you could just feel it. It felt like you could take a fork and poke holes in it, it was that real. You know, if you had a fork.

"Maybe I could just say a little more before I go," she said.

And I said, "No."

I think it surprised us both.

"Any special reason?"

"Because I can't see you. I can't see your face or your eyes, so I can't tell what you're thinking about me. So I won't know what to think about anything you say to me, because I won't know if you're still looking down on me or not."

"Oh," she said.

She sounded . . . I can't quite get the right word for it. Like life was more complicated than she expected. Maybe even like *I* was more complicated than she expected. Like she was discouraged or depressed by that, or something, and didn't feel up to handling whatever came next.

The phone had gone dark, but she held it up near her head and touched the screen, and it put a glow on her face. But it wasn't enough. I couldn't see much of anything.

"That won't do it," I said.

She let the hand with the phone drop down, and we stood there not talking, and after a while the screen went dark again.

"Have you eaten?" she asked me after a while.

"Not so much," I said.

"You want to go out and get something?"

"What do you mean?"

"I didn't know there was more than one meaning to a thing like that."

But there was. She could've meant walk to a store or a restaurant and we each buy something, but maybe she'd choose a place where everything cost more than I wanted to spend.

"Are you . . . ," I started out, and then I wasn't sure if I should ask, ". . . offering to, like . . . buy me something to eat or something like that?"

"I am," she said.

"Like where?"

"Anywhere you want."

"You're telling me you'll take me to any kind of restaurant I want and I can order whatever sounds good to me and you'll pay for it, and all I have to do is listen to you talk about whatever you're still wanting to say about that night?"

"Exactly."

I thought about pizza places, and restaurants that sell burgers and fries. Maybe we could even go to the kind of place that has food like your mother makes at home. You know, like meat loaf and mashed potatoes, or fried chicken with okra. I couldn't decide what I wanted, but I definitely wanted something, and I couldn't really see what I had to lose.

"I guess . . . ," I said, ". . . why not?"

Chapter Fifteen

Brooke: Maybe

"Ooh," Molly said. But she drew it out a lot longer than that. It was a syllable that just kept going. "I know what I want."

"What looks good?"

"This open-face hot turkey sandwich with gravy. And mashed potatoes and gravy on the side. I haven't had that for so long. I bet you can guess how long it's been since I had it."

"Last Thanksgiving?"

"Right. But it wasn't a sandwich, just turkey with gravy and mashed potatoes. But I had rolls with it, so that's pretty close, right?"

I opened my mouth to ask her a question I probably had no right to ask. Or maybe that's redundant. Maybe every question was a question I had no right to ask.

Before I could, the waitress showed up.

She took one look at Molly and then backed up a step. Which I thought was rude.

Molly had used the restroom to wash her hands and face, which is at least decent before you eat. But her hair was filthy, and her clothes were filthy. And she smelled as though she hadn't had a bath or shower for a while. Which I suppose she hadn't.

I watched the waitress's face and wished she would look at me. So I could ask her with my eyes to downplay her reaction. But she was staring at Molly. When she finally caught my eye, she was giving me this "You're a saint" look.

I didn't like that, either.

It wasn't that I didn't have some of those same feelings about Molly. I'd noticed the odor. I'd felt a little embarrassed bringing her into a restaurant in that condition. But at least I'd had the good grace to keep those reactions a secret. At least, I hoped I had.

"What'll it be, ladies?" she asked.

While Molly ordered the open-faced turkey sandwich, I changed my mind about my own food. I'd planned to have either a chef salad with no cheese or an egg-white omelet. Then I thought, *Why am I obsessing about weight? For whom?*

"I'll have the same," I said.

And the waitress, fortunately, left.

I sipped at my coffee for a minute, and Molly stared out the window and said nothing.

"Sounds like you're nostalgic for home," I said after a time.

"Sometimes."

"If you miss it, you could always go back."

"Nope," she said, still staring out the window. "Not an option."

"Did your parents abuse you?"

"No."

"Then you could go back."

"Not really."

"I know you think they're terrible. A lot of kids go through a stage where they think their parents are terrible. But you could try to work it out with them. I mean, my mother is the worst. Has been as long as I've known her. I didn't just decide that because I was going through a stage. She's a very unpleasant person. So if I can work out my stuff with her . . ."

"She's not the worst," Molly said.

She had ordered a glass of milk but she wasn't drinking it yet. Wasn't even looking at it. She was still just staring out the window.

"Well, you don't really know that," I said. Trying to sound patient. But instead of sounding patient I just ended up sounding like I was *trying* to be. "You haven't met her."

"Did you live with her till you were eighteen?"

"I did, yes. Nineteen, actually."

"So she never told you to go away and never darken her doorstep again. And she never said you couldn't ever see your little sisters again as long as you all lived. So she's not the worst."

I realized then that I had been told this already. I had known she'd been thrown out of the house, rather than running away. And then I'd forgotten it. That time had been such an emotional whirlwind for me. Nothing got in. Or maybe everything fell right back out again. I felt deeply ashamed for bringing it up.

"I'm sorry," I said. "I guess I see your point. I'll have to think about that."

We said nothing more until the food came. It was awkward. I'd been the one who felt I had so much to say to her. And suddenly I wasn't sure what it was. All those thoughts had flown away, but to where?

I wondered again what she'd done to get herself thrown out of the house. Must've been something big. Mothers don't put their kids out on the street for nothing.

She looked at her food, and then at mine. It seemed to please her that I had chosen the same meal.

"Do you really love my daughter?" I asked.

She had just taken her first big bite. She took a moment to savor the food. Then she answered with her mouth full.

"I really do." She finished chewing. Swallowed. Fixed me with an almost curious look. "Not as much as you do, of course, because I just knew her that one night, and she didn't come out of my own body or anything like that. But she's just an amazing little kid."

I still wasn't eating. For some reason just listening to her was occupying all my faculties.

"What do you think is amazing about her?"

"You don't think she's amazing?"

"Of course I do. I just wondered what you noticed most."

"She's only two," Molly said. And took another enormous bite. Talked with her mouth full again. "But she was quiet when I told her we needed to be. I mean, sometimes she couldn't stop crying completely. She's a baby. But she understood, and she really tried to do what I asked, and she barely knew me. At first, I mean. And she's so little."

"She cares for you, too," I said.

She stopped chewing and just stared at me. "How do you know that?"

"She says your name over and over."

I watched her eyes go soft. I realized something about Molly in that moment. She had been searching for somebody who would love her as she currently stood. Who wouldn't judge her. And she had found that person. But it wasn't me.

"Didn't I say that in my note?" I asked her. "I thought I did."

"Yeah, I guess you did, but I didn't know you meant she said it like she loved me. Or . . . cared for me, or whatever you just said."

"Sometimes in her sleep," I added, "she'll say something that I'm guessing she heard from you. She'll whisper, 'Brave girl, quiet girl.' Did I say that in the note, too?"

"I think you did, yeah. Yeah, I said that to her. Kind of sang it to her. I think it helped."

"Obviously."

"Oh!" she said. So loudly I jumped. "I just remembered! The most amazing thing she did! Right before the police drove by, when I was trying to flag down a car and nobody would stop for me and I sort of gave up and walked back over to the curb with her and sat down. I guess I was having this meltdown, because it was too much responsibility for me, and so *she* said it to *me*. She said 'Brave girl, quiet girl' back to me, because she knew it's what you say when somebody needs comforting, and she knew I needed it right about then. And she remembered. I mean, isn't that amazing? And she's only two!"

I opened my mouth to speak. To say that it *was* amazing. Even to me, and I adored her. But surprise tears spilled over, and my voice quavered too much. Enough that I didn't try to follow through.

"I'm sorry," she said. "I didn't mean to make you cry."

"It's okay. It's not your fault. I've just been unusually emotional since the incident."

"Yeah," she said. "I can relate."

Then she put her head down and pitched back into her food. And I put my own head down and ate, too.

It helped.

—

"I know you're going to try to get me to go back to that foster home," she said.

It was several minutes later. She had just downed the last bite of her dinner. Set down her fork. She wiped her mouth with her napkin and stared straight into my eyes. Possibly for the first time ever. No, not literally the first time. There had been that one time at the police station. But it had been short.

"I met her," I said.

"'Her' who?"

"That foster mother."

"Oh. Her."

"I don't like her," I said.

"I don't either."

"I think she hit you."

She quickly looked away again. She didn't answer.

"*Did* she hit you?" I asked. I felt it was an issue I needed to press.

At first, nothing. Then she muttered something so quiet as to be inaudible.

"I'm sorry. What?"

"With a broom handle," she said. A little louder this time. "Ten times."

"That's abuse."

"You're telling *me*."

"Just tell your social worker. Maybe she can put you someplace better."

"Exactly," she said. "*Maybe*. It's the *maybe* part that I'm worried about."

———

"How about dessert?" I asked her.

We had been quiet for a while. Nursing a pall that had fallen over the table. Over our attempts at conversation.

She let out a long, loud syllable. Something between a groan and a growl.

"I'd really, really like that," she said. "But I couldn't fit one more bite of food down there. I'm not used to eating such big meals."

"Take it to go, then."

No answer. I looked up to see her staring at my face. As if she were doing math in her head. As if the answer were hiding in my eyes.

"I can really *do* that?" she asked. Her voice sounded awed. "It's not cheating?"

I laughed. I couldn't help it.

"There's no cheating, Molly. I'm offering to buy you dessert. Get something that doesn't melt, like a piece of pie. Take it home for later."

But my voice stuck on the word "home." I looked away again, embarrassed.

"This is weird," I said after a time.

"What part of it is weird?"

"Taking you out for a meal and getting to know you a little, and then I'm supposed to take you back to that . . . crate. And just leave you there in that awful industrial neighborhood in the dark by yourself. Like somehow I'm supposed to pretend it's a suitable place for you to live."

She didn't answer for a long time. I was looking down at the table. I wasn't sure I wanted to brave a look at her face.

When I finally did, it seemed to unstick her ability to speak.

"*You* could talk to my social worker," she said. "That lady cop knows who she is. You could ask her if she'd put me someplace better, but if she isn't sure she can, or you don't think she will, you can't tell her where I am. You have to promise not to tell her where I am unless she can put me someplace better."

"Okay," I said. "I think I can do that."

Actually, it worried me. It might be against the law to know where a runaway foster teen is living and refuse to say. And what if something terrible happened to Molly in the meantime? But I agreed to try because I had to do something. After everything she had done for Etta and me. Even if I did think she'd done it too slowly.

I caught the waitress's eye, and she came to our table, pulling two dessert menus out of her apron pocket.

She held a menu out in my direction. I waved it away.

"Nothing for me," I said.

Molly grabbed hers and ran her finger down the items. If she was really absorbing all those dessert choices, she was a lightning-fast reader.

"I'll have a piece of the chocolate peanut butter pie to go," she said. And she handed back the miniature menu.

"Coming right up, hon."

The waitress retreated, and I sat frozen in my own thoughts. Or lack of thoughts. And my own sense of inadequacy.

"I'm back living at my mother's house for a time," I said.

"Okay."

It was clear from her tone that she had no idea why I was telling her this.

"If I had my own place, you'd be welcome on my couch for a couple of days."

But my face burned with shame when I said it. Because it might have been a lie. I didn't mean for it to be. I *wanted* it to be true. But I'm not sure it *was* true.

"Right," she said. "Got it."

"It's just . . . if you knew my mother. She's so negative. She's just against everything. I couldn't even ask an old college friend to stay for a few days without her pitching a fit."

"Right," she said again. "I get it."

I got a sickeningly uncomfortable sense that she did get it. All of it. All the subtext. All the parts I was trying to keep under wraps.

She was not a stupid young woman. Not by any means. She got me. And that was an unfortunate turn of events.

———

We sat in my car. In the dark. Near the trash-filled vacant lot where she had been living.

She was holding the little Styrofoam to-go container on her lap. Running her finger back and forth along the edge of it. It made a strange squeaking sound.

I knew she didn't really want to get out of the car and go back to that awful place. Who would? I felt like a beast for even bringing her back there.

"Maybe I could take you to an inexpensive motel," I said. "Pay for a night."

"I'm fine," she said. "You've done enough. Just talk to my social worker for me." But still she didn't get out of the car. "There's just one thing, though. You said you wanted to take me out to eat so you could talk to me. You know, tell me all kinds of things about that night when I had your little girl, and how you felt about all that. But then you sort of . . . didn't."

"True," I said.

We sat in silence for an awkward length of time.

"I guess the truth is . . . ," I began. Then I paused. And wondered if I even knew. "I guess I really said what I needed to say in the note. How thrilled I am to have Etta safely back and how much I appreciate the fact that you kept her so comforted. And how that was the answer to something almost like a prayer for me. And that I'm sorry I got it so wrong that first night at the police station. That was what I wanted to say, but I said it all in the note. But it didn't feel like enough somehow. I needed more. I guess I wanted to talk to you in person to see how you felt about all of it."

"Oh, I get it," she said. Her voice sounded more sure of itself. Suddenly. "You want me to forgive you."

"Maybe," I said.

"That's just so typical. People always say they're sorry for what they did to you, and maybe they are, but they just want to tell you so *they'll* feel better, not so *you* will. Fine. I forgive you. There, are you happy now?"

She opened my passenger door and stepped out into the night.

I jumped out, too. Called after her.

"Molly!"

I didn't think she would stop. She was stomping away fast. Very determined to get me out of her life again. But I was wrong. She paused. To see what else I had to say, I suppose. I walked closer.

She was standing in the vacant lot, in the dirt. Next to a discarded sofa. A massive thing with no cushions. I got as close as I thought she'd let me. In other words, I stayed a few steps back.

"I guess I've got no right to ask you this," I said.

She was still facing away. As if just about to resume stomping off.

"Probably not," she said.

But if I could just break through that one brick wall. If I could just understand *why* she was out there. What she had done to bring it on. Then maybe the idea of inviting her closer into my life to help her wouldn't feel so terrifying.

"What?" she asked. When she got tired of waiting.

"Why did your mother make you leave? What happened?"

"What difference does it make? I didn't do anything wrong."

"Something must've happened."

"You think it's my fault, don't you? You just don't get it at all."

"No. I don't get it. So tell me. Help me get it."

She breathed out a sigh that was almost more of a snort. I could tell she was angry. "My mother just has these things she's prejudiced about," she said.

"I don't understand that. That doesn't make any sense. What kind of mother throws her kid out on the street because of prejudice?"

"*You're* going to have to tell *me*," she said. "Because I have no idea."

Then she walked away into the night.

When I got home, my mother was in the living room. Watching TV. Blaring the volume, as always.

When she saw me, she hit the mute button. The silence felt stunning.

"Where have *you* been?" she asked. Her voice was loud and hard. As it usually was, but even more so.

"I just had dinner with a friend."

She narrowed her eyes suspiciously.

My gut instinct was to run. Trot up to my room and leave her behind. I didn't. I sat on the couch with her. She was clearly taken aback.

"I just wanted to tell you something," I said. And paused. My voice was soft, and I watched her face change as a result of it. Become even less comfortable. My mother liked the familiar. Conflict was familiar. This moment was not. "I wanted to tell you . . . thank you. For being a better mother than some. Making sure I had a roof over my head all those years."

"And now," she said.

"Yes. And now."

She continued to study my face for clues. Clues to what, I had no idea.

"You've been drinking," she said.

I burst out laughing. I couldn't help it. It was a bitter sort of laughter. I couldn't believe communication with her was so impossible. Even when I was sincere, and really trying.

"I have not been drinking."

"Let me smell your breath."

I leaned over and breathed into her face. She sniffed audibly.

"You're on drugs," she said.

I laughed again. I couldn't help it. It was all so absurd.

"How can you even say that?" I asked. "Are things really so horrible between us that you can't believe I would say thank you for putting a roof over my head?"

"Well, you never did before. And you're laughing like a fool when nothing is funny. What's so darned funny? Nothing that I can see."

"Us," I said.

We sat in silence for a moment.

Then I went upstairs, checked in on my sleeping baby, and put myself to bed.

While I was waiting for sleep, I tried not to imagine how it would feel to sleep in a crate with openings between the slats. In a bad neighborhood. In the dark and cold. Alone. At age sixteen.

Chapter Sixteen

Molly: Different Kind of Home

It was a day or two later, and I was just minding my own business, going out in the morning looking for stuff to recycle. The sun wasn't really on me yet, because it was early, and it was cold, and I didn't have anything like a jacket.

I was thinking I'd have to take money out of Bodhi's wallet and buy something when we got into the really deep, cold part of winter. Better LA than Utah, but it was still cold enough that you needed some kind of jacket.

For the first block everything was okay, but then I noticed how a car was following me.

I turned a corner, kind of fast, and did a quick look over my shoulder. I sort of looked and tried to pretend I wasn't looking at the same time. Then I looked where I was going again, but I heard the car turn the corner behind me, so I walked faster. And while I did that, I was sort of reacting to what I'd seen in my brain, almost like I looked so fast that I didn't really see what I saw until a second later.

It was a real nice car, as in a luxury car like rich people have, but it had the craziest paint job I'd ever seen. This midnight-blue base, but then half the hood was yellow. And not an exact half, either. Not with a ruler right down the middle. I mean like somebody was spraying yellow paint over the hood of this really nice car and then just changed their mind for some reason.

Right around the time I was thinking that made the person following me some kind of insane freak, I heard somebody call my name. I jumped a mile.

"Molly!"

It was a lady's voice, so just for a second I didn't run.

I stopped and turned around, and it was that Brooke lady, the one whose baby I found. I couldn't believe she was driving that crazy car. The last time I'd seen her, when she took me out and bought me turkey and mashed potatoes and pie, she'd been driving a different car. The other one was old and not a luxury car and not what a rich person would drive at all, but at least it had a normal paint job.

She had her window down, so I walked right up to her driver's side door, which meant I had to walk out into the street, but there was nobody coming because there was nobody else out at that hour.

The whole driver's side of the car was yellow, and a nice, neat yellow, too, like a real paint job. Like if you only saw the car from where I was standing you'd almost think it was a perfectly normal bright-yellow car. If you didn't look at the hood. And if there even *is* such a thing.

"Did you talk to my social worker?" I asked her right off the bat, before she even had time to say anything, because if she hadn't done that one simple little thing for me then I didn't want to hear whatever she'd come to say.

"Yes."

"Is it good news? Will I like it?"

"No."

I turned and walked away again. Up onto the sidewalk and back to my normal route past all the trash bins that might've had bottles or cans. I didn't know why she came and I didn't really want to hear why, because I was mad.

I could hear her driving along behind me.

"Molly!" she called again.

And this time, because now both her windows were down, I heard the baby girl in the back seat, and she was calling my name, too. It was a little bit quiet, but I could hear her saying "Molly, Molly, Molly," and it melted all my mad away. I could just feel it turn to water and pour out of me, like I was all leaky and full of holes.

I turned around, and the lady pulled over to the curb and stopped, and I could see the baby in the back seat, in a car seat sort of like the one I'd found her in, but newer. Then I wondered why I hadn't seen her the first time I walked up to the car, but I hadn't walked very close, and the light had been in my eyes from that direction.

I tried to open the door to jump into the back with her, but it was locked. I should've known. The lady was all paranoid about driving in a bad neighborhood with her kid, not that I blame her. When she saw I was trying to get in, I heard her unlock all the doors. It made this clunking sound, and I saw the lock button pop up.

I got in and started talking to the little girl, and I heard the clunk of the doors locking again. The baby had this big smile and her eyes were all wide to see me, and it was the best thing that'd happened to me in as long as I could remember, just that look on her face.

I played clapping games with her for a minute, and she was just as bad at them as she'd been that night when I taught her, but she always knew to clap against my hands when I held them out to her. It was hard, though, because her seat was strapped in backward, the way the safety people say your baby is supposed to ride. We had to sort of clap sideways. Out of the corner of my eye I saw her mom watching us in the rearview mirror.

"What did my social worker say?" I asked her, because I was still a little bit mad about that. "Does she just not care at all that somebody was beating me with a broom handle?"

"She wasn't that bad," Brooke said.

"How bad was she?"

"She just has a different perspective on the things that can go wrong in foster homes. She says she takes allegations of abuse very seriously. But she feels they have to be proven. She says it's common to find there's been corporal punishment in a placement. But it's also common, if a teen doesn't like a foster home, to make up something they think will be a deal breaker."

"Got it," I said, even madder now. "So she thinks I'm lying."

"She just wants to investigate the situation. Try to prove who's telling the truth."

"How do you prove a thing like that? Nobody was there watching it happen."

"I guess she wants to talk to the other foster kids in the home. About their experience."

"They won't tell her the truth."

"How do you know that?"

"Because they know all about the system and how things go. They know if they tell on her they still might not get taken out of the home, and then that terrible lady knows they ratted her out, and things get even worse for them."

I didn't say anything for a minute and neither did she. And I wasn't clapping with the baby and she wasn't smiling anymore, because she knew we were talking about something dead serious, and she knew I was mad.

"You think I'm lying, too," I said. "Don't you?"

"Me? *Me?* I'm the one who told you right off the bat I thought she hit you. Before you ever said a word about it. *I* brought it up."

"Oh," I said. "That's right. I forgot about that. How did you know, anyway?"

"It was something she said to me. But now I don't remember her words exactly."

I waited around without talking for a minute in case she wanted to say more, but she didn't.

"So you know that's not good enough," I said to her. "The way my social worker wants to take care of it. Right?"

"Yeah," she said. "I do know that's not enough for you."

"Then what are you even doing here? Aren't you afraid to be driving around this neighborhood with your baby after what happened?"

My grandpa always taught me that it's stupid to be that way, like leaving your front door unlocked because you think you'll never get robbed, but then after you get robbed putting ten locks on the door. By then it's too late, because you were robbed already, and you're no more likely to get robbed again just because you were that one time. He said it was stupid but it was just part of how people's brains were made. Like, if it never happened before, you think it never will, and that's wrong, but if it just happened, you think it always will, and that's wrong, too. He called it locking the barn door after the horse was stolen.

I looked up at her eyes in the rearview mirror.

"Why do you think I'm driving around with a can of pepper spray between my knees?" she asked me.

"Didn't know you were," I said.

So she held it up and showed me, and it was big. Not like those little cans you keep on your key chain or stick in your pocket. It was probably seven or eight inches long.

"Looks like something you'd use to scare off a grizzly bear," I said.

In the mirror I saw her eyes get softer, and saw her do something like a smile, even though I couldn't see her mouth. But it turns out you can see a smile on other parts of a person's face and I just hadn't known it.

"Let me drive you where you're going," she said.

"You can't really."

"Why can't I?"

"It's not just one single spot that you drive somebody to. It's like a route I walk for most of the day, where I stop at all the trash bins and pick out bottles and cans to take to the recycling place."

"I can drive from one trash container to the next," she said.

And, like she needed to show me how that was possible, she stepped on the gas and drove to the next corner and stopped right next to the trash bin. But I knew there wouldn't be anything in it, because I'd been by it late in the afternoon the day before, and besides, this was one of the streets where hardly anybody ever walked around on their feet. If you wanted bottles and cans you at least had to go six or seven blocks to one of the busy avenues where people walk around and wait for their buses and stuff like that.

I didn't want to explain all that to her, so I just got out and looked around in there and found nothing. I heard her lock the doors after I got out and then unlock them when I was ready to get back in again.

"This is weird," I said, and got into the back seat with the baby again.

"What's weird about it?"

"Driving around in a Mercedes to pick up recycling," I said, because I knew by then that it was a Mercedes, because I had eyes in my head. "I mean, who does that? And also, what's wrong with the paint on this car? Why would you have it like this? Don't people stare at you wherever you go?"

She wasn't driving to the next corner—she was just sitting there behind the wheel, listening to me complain about her car.

"This is the one that got carjacked," she said. "It's my mother's car. The guy who stole it took it to a chop shop and they started to repaint it. And then I guess they got interrupted by the police. My mother just got it back. She's in this fight with her insurance company to try to get them to cover repainting it."

"Oh," I said. I didn't know what more to say about a thing like that.

I was staring through the windshield at the hood of the car, and the way the solid-yellow paint faded into this sort of mist of tiny drops, the way paint does when you're spraying and haven't had a chance to go back over it with the sprayer again. And at the same time I was wondering why she wasn't talking and also wasn't driving.

"You need to put on your seat belt," she said after a while.

"That'll take all day! Every time I get out I have to take it off, and then every time I get in again I have to put it on, and we're stopping at just about every corner. It'll take forever!"

"It's still faster than walking," she said.

I couldn't argue with that, even though I wished I could have because it all sounded like a lot of trouble. Also I guess I wasn't used to having somebody looking over my shoulder while I picked through the trash, especially not some regular clean person with a nice house. I guess I was wishing I could just do this on my own like every other day.

While I was thinking all this, she still wasn't driving.

"I had a thought," she said.

I could just tell by the way she said it that this was going to be the heart of the thing—like all my wondering about why she was here again was about to be answered by this thought.

"Okay . . . ," I said. But I said it like it wasn't really very okay, because I had no idea if it was okay until I heard it.

"I was thinking maybe I could drive you home. But I don't mean to where you've been staying. And I don't mean the foster place. I mean actually home."

I burst out laughing, and it made the baby laugh, too, and bounce her hands up and down against the padded bar that held her into her car seat.

"What's so funny?" the Brooke lady asked, and she sounded a little hurt or offended that I was laughing at her idea—or maybe both.

"You think the only thing keeping me from going home is that I don't have a ride?"

"No. I don't think that. I know there was trouble between you and your mother. I don't know what kind of trouble, because you won't tell me. And I guess that's okay. Because what business is it of mine, really? But I just know she's your mother. And I know how much I love my daughter. And I just think there's a chance it's something that can be worked out."

I didn't answer, because I was thinking about what she'd just said, and for a minute I was wondering if she was right. It was a dangerous thought and I knew it, because I knew my mother and she didn't. But you know how sometimes a person will tell you how they look at something, and it's totally different from how you see it, but their view of things starts to seem just as right as yours, and then you don't know which to believe? It was like that.

"Where's home?" she asked me, because I still wasn't saying anything.

"Utah."

"Oh," she said, and I could tell she was disappointed. "I was hoping you'd say something closer, like Orange County or Sacramento."

"Well, it doesn't matter," I said, "because you don't have to do it."

"No, I'll still do it," she said.

Then she started driving again, driving me to all my regular trash bins in that wild blue-and-yellow half-repainted Mercedes-Benz.

It was just such a weird thing and I didn't know what to say about it. So we drove around and stopped at every trash bin, and I put on and took off my seat belt every time, and I just kept avoiding saying yes or no to her idea, because I had no idea what to say.

———

"I came out to her," I said.

It was maybe half an hour later when I told her the thing I didn't want to tell her. I'd found a big paper grocery sack in one of the garbage bins and I had it in the back with me, half full of bottles and cans.

The reason I said the thing I didn't want to say is because I was tired of wondering if I could believe in her version of things—that my problems with my mother could be worked out. If she thought this was a deal breaker and she decided never mind about trying, then I could stop going back and forth about it in my head. And then I would know not to get my hopes up any higher for any longer.

"Wait," she said. "*What* now?"

"My mother. I came out to her. That's what happened."

The baby was falling asleep. The driving was putting her into a nap mode, and her eyes kept flickering from most of the way closed to all the way closed. It was the sweetest thing I'd seen in a very long time. Then again, that wasn't a hard contest to win.

"There must have been more to it than that," she said.

Then I got mad again, because she didn't know anything—she hadn't even been there, and I had, so who was she to tell me I was wrong?

"There wasn't," I said. "I told you exactly what happened, and I wish you would give me credit for having eyes and ears and having *been* there."

I wasn't being loud, but the baby's eyes shot open again because, even though I was saying words quietly, she knew they were mad words.

"How can a mother put her daughter out on the street just for that?"

"Wow, you don't know much," I said, and the baby started to fuss and cry because I was even madder, and keeping even less of a secret about it. "Because kids are getting turned out on the street every day for being gay. It happens all the time, and just because you live in a comfy little world where you don't have to know about it doesn't mean it isn't happening. My parents are very religious. You know, like fundamentalist religious. To them everything is black and white and exactly what the Bible says it is."

"But the Bible can say pretty much anything you want it to say."

"Don't tell me, tell my parents. I'm not the one who needs convincing."

I had settled a little by then, so the baby settled, too, and we drove along and she didn't cry anymore.

Also we weren't stopping at any trash bins, so I figured Brooke had gotten all wrapped up in what we were talking about and forgotten about what we were doing out there. I didn't remind her, because it was a stupid thing to be doing. I mean, all she had to do was give me a dollar and I'd be better off for that whole day than if we finished checking all my usual trash bins. It probably cost more in gas than I could earn.

"Mormon?" she asked after a time.

"No, not Mormon. Everybody says that. Everybody figures if you're from Utah your family has to be Mormon, but they have other religions there, too, you know. They're Baptist, actually, and they go to this church where the preacher is pretty hard-nosed about stuff like that. Whatever he tells them, they just automatically believe him, which I think is sad. It's like they don't even think for themselves anymore. So now you know my story and now you know why it would be a stupid idea to try to go back there."

"Actually . . . ," she said. And then she didn't go on for a minute. Like what she was saying had gotten ahead of her thinking about it, and she needed time to catch up. "If what you say is the whole truth, and there really isn't anything else that happened . . ."

Then I got a little mad again, because she wouldn't believe me.

"You still think it's my fault," I said. "With everything you know about me you still won't believe me."

The baby started to fuss and cry again.

And then I realized I'd said a really stupid thing, because she didn't know me at all. I was just some kid on the street, and even if I hadn't been on the street, some kids just lie, especially when you ask them if something was their fault or not. All of a sudden I could see it from her eyes, how she'd just met me and I could be anything. But I didn't say any of that, because it was all a jumble in my head, and besides, it seemed more important to comfort the baby.

"Okay," she said, and I caught her eyes again in the rearview mirror. "Okay. Let's just take you at your word on that. Nothing else happened. Then I think it's more important than ever that we try to get you home. Sometimes a thing like that . . . and by 'that' I mean something where you turn out to be different than what they thought you were . . . different from them and different from what they were expecting . . . there might be some time required. Like it might be an idea they could adjust to over time. And we should at least try. Oh," she added suddenly. "I'm sorry. I'm forgetting to stop."

"It doesn't matter," I said. "If you buy me a hot dog I'm in better shape than I would be with every bit of recycling from every one of those trash cans."

I didn't answer that other thing, because I didn't dare. Because I would get my hopes up, and then she might turn out to be wrong, and then it would be a long fall down to that crate on the street again.

"Where can you get a hot dog around here? At this hour?"

"Straight down three blocks," I said. "On the right."

—

Just as we were getting out of the car and walking up to the hot dog place, I asked her my really important question. I was scared to ask, because I was about to find out what she really thought of me. The real me, on the inside. Not just the stupid unimportant stuff like whether I had a house to go home to, or if my hair was clean, because that's all stuff that can be temporary. I was about to hear her thoughts about the real parts of me that I could never change even if I wanted to.

"What would *you* do?" I asked her.

"What would I do about what?"

She was bouncing the baby on her hip, and acting like her mind was a million miles away.

There was no line, so we stepped right up to the window. The place was open twenty-four hours a day, so even though it was pretty weird to want a hot dog for breakfast, you could get one if that's what you wanted.

I ordered one with chili and cheese and tomatoes and onions, and she paid for it, and then we sat at one of the outside tables to wait. She was nervous, and looking around, and she still had the pepper spray tight in one hand. The benches were stone and really cold right through my pants.

"What would I do about what?" she asked again.

"What if Etta grew up and came out to you? What would you do?"

She answered without taking any time to think, and her face didn't change at all. The question was nothing to her. Nowhere near the everything it was to me.

"Oh, hell, I don't care," she said. "So long as she's happy. I don't care *how* she's happy."

I knew then. I knew I was okay being with her, but . . . more than okay. Almost like I was home with her, in a weird way. I mean, it wasn't as good as having a real home, because I couldn't actually live in a thing like I'd found with her, but it still felt something like home, because it was a place where I could bring my whole self.

"Okay," I said, "let's try it. Let's go back to Utah and see if she got used to the idea at all by now."

I didn't really think it would work, because I knew my mother better than that. I didn't say yes because I thought I'd get to stay in our house in Utah with my little sisters. I said yes because it was a few more days I'd get to stay with Brooke, who would buy me meals, and let me be around her little daughter, and who wouldn't care at all if Etta came out to her later when she was older.

Maybe she'd even get to know me too well to throw me back out on the street again.

"What changed your mind?" she asked me.

"Just sounds like a better few days than what I had planned."

"What did you have planned?"

"Pretty much this," I said.

And I put my arms out wide, like I was a tour guide showing her my world.

"Got it," she said. "We'll leave tomorrow. Hell, what am I waiting for? We'll leave today."

Chapter Seventeen

Brooke: Fool

I guess we'd been driving for about an hour when it hit me. I was a complete idiot. A total, unmitigated fool.

It was as though the truth had been there all along. Hanging over my head like a bunch of sandbags. Totally real. Totally present. But not touching me in any way. And then it all just let go and landed on me.

There was no way the truth could have been as simple as her story had made it out to be.

I mean, you ask a teenager, "What did you do?" And they say, "Nothing. Honest. I was perfect. I was just being myself, which is a perfectly reasonable thing to be. And then this totally unfair adult just punished me for something that nobody in their right mind would punish a kid for, and I was completely right and they were completely wrong, and it wasn't my fault in any way."

Now I ask you: What kind of fool believes a story like that?

I glanced at her in the rearview mirror and accepted the truth: that I would likely show up at her mother's door and be faced with a reality quite different from the one I'd been sold.

But I wasn't turning back. Mostly because I needed to feel I'd done my part for the girl. After everything she'd done for Etta and me, it wasn't too much to ask. Especially when I had no job from which I was missing time. And I had the car for as long as I needed it because my mother refused to drive it until the paint situation was sorted out.

And maybe, just maybe . . . because there was a one percent of one percent chance she might be telling the truth. But that was a damn slim chance. Based on my experience with the world, the truth is never as simple as the answer you get when you ask one of the two parties to tell you their side of a thing.

Molly was riding in the back seat with Etta. As though I were their chauffeur. But I knew she didn't mean it that way. She just wanted time with the baby and vice versa.

When I'd told my mom about the trip, she not only hadn't argued with me over the use of her car, she'd seemed more than a little bit relieved. I guess we all needed time alone.

While I'd packed the trunk full of necessary items, nine-tenths of them for the baby, Molly had walked to a gas station restroom and cleaned herself, and washed her clothes out in the sink. She had showed up back at the car wearing sopping-wet clothes, but smelling decent. Her hair was still filthy.

I'd made a mental note to stop and buy her at least one change of clothes.

She caught my eye in the rearview mirror. Caught me staring at her. I could tell it made her feel a little defensive.

I looked away.

I watched the road over the ridiculous half-yellow hood of the Mercedes. I still hadn't gotten used to that. In fact, by then I might even have accepted the simple truth: there *was* no getting used to it.

I watched other drivers pull level with our car, slow down, and stare. And point. And laugh.

I listened to Molly playing road games with Etta.

"Blue car!" Molly shouted.

I glanced in the mirror and watched her pretend to punch Etta on the upper arm. But very, very gently.

Etta laughed. It was such a magical sound. Not that I hadn't heard it before. Not that I didn't hear it nearly every day. It was just magical. Every time.

"Boo car," Etta said.

"Blue," I said. I used my talking-to-Etta voice. So she would know.

"Boo," Etta said.

"Blue. Ba. Loo."

"Ba. Loo."

"Blue."

"Boo."

Molly laughed. "She'll get it," she said. "She's only two."

"I'm not worried about it," I said.

I was worried about quite a few things in that moment. But I was not worried about the word "blue."

———

When I'd driven as far as I felt I could for the day, I had to stop. I had to find us a motel. And that's one of the things I was worried about.

I didn't know this girl. I only knew that her mother never wanted Molly around her little sisters ever again. Still, she'd clearly been good to Etta over an extended time alone.

But to fall asleep in the presence of this unknown homeless teen?

I could have gotten her a separate room. But that would have been twice as expensive. And that went straight to my other worry: Would all these trip expenses fit onto my new credit card? And, if not, how would we get home?

I pushed it all out of my head and stopped at the first place that presented itself.

It was a cheap motel on a vast dirt lot, with a broken neon sign that read **Stagecoach Motel**, and a flashing **Vacancy** sign underneath. A massive wooden wagon wheel was secured beside the sign. It looked like a throwback to the old west. A century before I was born. And yet just beyond it, an easy walk away, sat a thoroughly modern strip mall with outlet stores and a big-box department store, and chain fast-food restaurants.

I pulled into the parking lot and found a spot near the office. It wasn't hard. The place was nearly deserted.

"Oh," Molly said. "This is as far as we drive today?"

"I think so," I said. "I'm tired."

Etta was fast asleep. Car rides had that effect on her. I unbuckled her and pulled her into my arms. Molly held her while I emptied the trunk.

"Whoa," she said as I pulled out bag after bag. She peered inside. "We're only going to be gone a few days, you know."

For some reason I felt defensive about how much stuff I'd packed. I snapped at her. A little bit, anyway.

I said, "Not everybody travels as light as you do, Molly. In fact, hardly anybody does. You must know it's something of an aberration."

She looked away. Looked around. As if suddenly fascinated by our surroundings. She didn't answer.

"I'm sorry. I shouldn't have said that. It's mostly stuff I needed to bring for the baby. You need a lot of supplies for a baby."

Then again, I was talking to the girl who had kept Etta reasonably happy for twenty-four hours on apple juice and goldfish crackers. And imagination.

I handed her the diaper bag, and she slung its strap over her shoulder.

"But seriously," I said, "did you really walk out of your parents' house with nothing but the clothes you have on your back now?"

"No," she said. Still looking around. Still not looking at me. "I packed a few things to take with me. But then they got stolen."

"Do you have a hairbrush?"

"I used to, but I lost it somehow. A while ago I lost it. I used to take it with me when I went to gas stations to use their bathroom and clean up so I guess I must've left it at one, but I swear I looked at every place I ever took it. It's a little bit of a mystery."

"Toothbrush?"

"Yeah, but not *with* me. We didn't stop back at the crate to get my things. Well. That's pretty much all my things at this point—the toothbrush."

I hefted two of the big bags and she took the smaller one with her free hand. And we walked to the office together.

"Where are we?" she asked, still looking around.

"Not sure. But somewhere in Nevada. Past Las Vegas."

"How did we get past Las Vegas? Where was I?"

"Maybe you fell asleep."

Actually, I knew she had. I'd seen it.

"Oh. Yeah. Maybe."

We walked inside.

The rates were clearly posted on the office wall. I was a bit shocked to see that they wanted ninety-five dollars plus tax for a room. It didn't seem like much of a place to charge ninety-five dollars for. Then again, I hadn't stayed in a hotel or motel for years. And everything goes up in price.

The desk clerk was a tired-looking man in his forties with thin hair and narrow features. "One room?" he asked, looking at the three of us. As though we were a hard group to figure out.

"Yes," I said. "One room."

He slid a form across the counter.

I began filling it out with a pen that dispensed ink in fits and starts as I scribbled. About one letter out of two came out looking legible.

I handed him my credit card.

When I had done my best with the form—I didn't know the license plate number of my mother's car by heart—I slid it back.

"I need your car license number," he said.

"I don't have it memorized. I could go back out if I absolutely have to. But there are only about three cars out there."

"We need to know who's authorized to park in the lot and who isn't."

"Oh. I see. You figure my car will be hard to identify. Well, try this on for size. It's half painted yellow. It's a midnight-blue Mercedes with yellow paint on one side, and on half the hood. That should pretty much clear up who owns it, right? I mean, what are the chances of two cars matching that description showing up in your lot tonight?"

He furrowed his brow and scribbled a few notes on the form. Handed me back my credit card and a room key. An actual metal key, like in the old days.

"You and your daughters enjoy your stay," he said.

And we lugged everything outside again.

As we tromped through the dirt to our room, Molly said, "He thought we were a family!" Her voice sounded breathy and excited. As though something miraculous had happened.

"It's a logical assumption. I'm old enough to have a daughter your age."

"Yeah. You are. I actually think my mother is a couple of years younger than you. She had me when she was nineteen."

I winced at the thought. It might be hard to explain why. Or maybe it didn't need explaining. I don't know.

"If I'd had my way," I said, "I'd have had kids when I was in my early twenties."

"Kids? As in more than one?"

"Yeah. I wanted two."

"So if you'd had your way you'd have a kid just about my age now."

"Pretty much," I said. "Yeah."

"Why didn't you?"

Then we had to lug all those bags up a flight of outdoor stairs. It ticked me off. Because the place was nearly empty. So why couldn't he have given us a room on the ground floor? At least, I think that's what was ticking me off. Could have been more than one thorn sticking into my side right about then.

"Kind of a long story," I said as we climbed.

But it wasn't, really. It was a short one. David didn't want them. Somehow it was easier to call it a long story rather than admit the truth: it was a story I didn't particularly want to tell again.

We arrived at the landing, puffing. Or I was puffing, anyway. Etta began to wake up on Molly's shoulder. I knew it would be hard to get her to sleep that night because she'd napped so much in the car.

I stuck the key in the door. Swung it open into a plain but acceptable room. It had two beds, at least.

"I have a question for you," I said. "Why did you even *tell* your mother? I mean, if you knew how she felt about things like that."

"Long story," she said.

While we dumped the bags onto one of the beds, I wondered: Was it really long? Or, like my story, simply one she preferred not to tell?

———

Molly took a thirty-five-minute shower. I know. I timed it.

I'm not sure why I cared. It wasn't my water, and it wasn't my gas heating it. For the money I'd paid for the room, she might as well get some value back for the dollars.

Etta was sitting on the bedspread near my hip. Playing with one of the toys I'd brought from home. The one that let her point a big red arrow at different barnyard animals. And then, when she pulled the string, the toy would play a recording of a quack or a moo or a neigh.

I took my phone off the bedside table and checked the bars of reception. I was getting plenty. So I opened the browser. Started typing into the search bar.

"LGBT homeless . . ." Before I could type the word "youth," the browser suggested it for me.

I clicked. Read the first couple of sentences of a Wikipedia article, which was displayed in the phone equivalent of a sidebar.

"Research shows that a disproportionate number of homeless youth in the United States identify as lesbian, gay, bisexual, or transgender, or LGBT. Researchers suggest that this is primarily a result of hostility or abuse from the young people's families leading to eviction or running away."

I didn't click through. Instead I read a few more of the search results.

The title of the fourth article down was "LGBT Youth Are 120% More Likely To Be Homeless Than Straight . . ." It cut off there. And yes, the capitalization was wrong. So I thought maybe it was a fringe publication. I looked under the link of the title to see who had published it.

It was *Newsweek*.

"What're you doing?" Molly's voice asked. From very close by.

Her tone was casual, but it still startled me.

She was standing at the end of the bed wrapped in a bright-white motel towel. Her hair was clean and wet, and looked curly and a little bit red. It had red highlights. Somehow that red had been hidden under the filth.

"Oh, nothing," I said. "Just killing time. Put your clothes on and we'll walk over to that little mall and get you something else to wear. That way you can wash one set and wear the other while you're doing it. And we'll get you a toothbrush and a hairbrush. And then we need something to eat."

"Thank you," she said. "That's very nice of you." But her mind seemed miles away. "I'm scared about seeing my mother tomorrow. Is it okay to say that to you? Because it really feels like a problem and I don't know how to make it not a problem but I thought talking about it might help. Because we'll get there tomorrow if we're already past Las Vegas, and so now it all seems really real and really close, and so now I'm getting scared about it, because what if she slams the door in my face?"

"I wasn't thinking of sending you to the door. Actually. I've been thinking about it. And I thought *I'd* go. Talk to her in advance. If she's not open to the idea of seeing you, then you never have to face her. We won't even give her a chance to say something terrible."

"Thank you," she said again. "That's a really good idea. You know how I know it's a really good idea? Because a second ago I wasn't even hungry, but then you said that and now all of a sudden I'm starved. Let's go. I can carry the baby. Let's eat first and shop later."

———

"I can't eat another bite," Molly said, "and it's so good it's killing me, that's the tough part, but even so, my stomach won't let me eat even one bite more. Can I ask the waiter to wrap up this last enchilada and I'll take it up to our room?"

I'd been staring out the window. Into the pitch dark. Just the lights of a few businesses and a stream of cars along the interstate. I'd been thinking about more or less nothing. Mostly feeling instead.

I was feeling that I needed to go to the restroom. But I was resisting.

"We don't have a fridge up there," I said, dragging my mind back to the moment.

Etta was sitting up in a booster chair. Disturbingly wide awake. Her eyes lit up when I looked at her face and she looked back at mine. She was eating refried beans with a spoon, or anyway, she had been. Now she was drumming the spoon on the table, sending bits of beans flying.

"Doesn't matter," Molly said, "because it won't be sitting out long. I only need, like, forty-five minutes or an hour and by then I'll digest what I just ate and then it'll be gone."

"I have to go to the restroom," I said.

My eyes were still locked with those of my beautiful daughter. We seemed to be enjoying staring at each other. I wondered briefly if we had stared at each other like this before we almost lost each other. Maybe. But I couldn't remember.

I didn't want to go to the restroom, because I didn't want to leave her. I decided I'd pick her up and take her there with me.

I'd been allowing myself to get dehydrated through that long day of driving. And then, once we sat down at the restaurant, I put away about five glasses of iced tea, nursing that bottomless drink like a person dying of thirst in the desert. And it had caught up to me.

But I didn't want to leave my daughter alone with this girl.

In a way it was silly. Because Etta had already been alone with this girl. Who then gave her back to me.

In another way it wasn't silly. I barely knew her. Her mental and emotional stability level was a great unknown. She could have been anything. I had no idea why her own mother had thrown her out of the house.

More importantly, I was paranoid now. I had a sort of PTSD over losing her.

"So go," Molly said, knocking me out of my thoughts.

I rose. Leaned over the table and lifted Etta out of her booster seat.

"She can stay here," Molly said. "I'll look after her."

"She might need to go, too."

"You just took her before we started eating."

I paused. Stammered over some lame explanation that never quite came out into the light.

"I just don't like being apart from her," I said at last.

And we hurried away. Before I could hear any more of Molly's thoughts on the matter.

———

When we arrived back at the table, Molly had her last enchilada wrapped to go. Her face seemed sullen. She avoided looking me in the eye.

The baby still on my hip, I grabbed up the check from the edge of the table.

"I'll go pay this at the cashier," I said. "And then we'll walk back."

"Fine. Whatever." But before I could walk away, more words spilled out of her. "You know," she said, her voice harder now, "if I couldn't be trusted to take good care of her, you wouldn't *have* her right now."

I sighed. Tried to form my words carefully.

"That's very true," I said.

"So then what was that all about?"

"I've just been really paranoid since . . . you know."

"But I would still think you would trust *me*. I mean, I'm the reason you got her back."

"It's not just you," I said. "Anybody could come along and grab her. And why put it on you to be the one who has to be fast enough or strong enough to keep it from happening?"

"Right," she said. "Fine. Whatever."

And I walked off to pay the check. With Etta.

———

It was after midnight when I had to get up and use the bathroom again. Etta and I were in one bed. I'd finally gotten her to sleep just moments earlier. Molly was in the other bed, over by the window. I thought she was asleep, too, but I wasn't sure.

I didn't want to risk waking Etta. And if I dragged her into the bathroom with me, she would definitely wake up.

I watched Molly's back in a thin stream of desert moonlight. It poured into our room through a gap in the curtains. I watched for several minutes, looking for any irregularity. Any movement that would suggest she was awake.

I decided to chance it. Or, rather, I simply needed to.

I literally ran to the bathroom. Used the toilet as fast as I possibly could. Ran back out without stopping to wash my hands. I couldn't see Etta, who was all lost in the bedsheets. Not in that absence of light. So I rushed over and felt around.

She was there.

I sat on the edge of the bed and let out a panicky sigh. Or, more accurately, the sigh of panic leaving my body. The borderline of crossing back into no panic.

I lay down carefully, so as not to wake her.

"So what was your excuse *that* time?" Molly asked. Her voice was quiet, probably out of respect for the baby. But also even and sure of itself.

"I don't know what you're talking about," I said.

But I knew.

"I just think it sucks that you don't trust me. Especially with the baby. When was I ever anything but good to that baby?"

"I know," I said. "I'm sorry. I've just been finding it hard to trust lately."

She didn't say another word that night and neither did I. I'm not sure if she slept or not. I wrapped one arm tightly around my sleeping child. And somewhere in the very early morning I might have gotten three or four much-needed hours.

Chapter Eighteen

Molly: Queasy

I had to go into the bathroom while Brooke was in the shower, because I thought I was maybe going to throw up.

I'd been lying on that motel bed with the baby, just sort of nursing this really ugly feeling that was sitting sort of in my stomach, but sort of lower, like I'd eaten a big piece of evil and it had gone all the way down into my intestines but now it wanted to come back up again. Or kill me, I wasn't sure which.

"I'm sorry," I said when I got to the bathroom door. "I'm not trying to look or get all up in your privacy or anything and I wouldn't do this if I didn't have to, but I think maybe I'm about to be sick."

Then I fell down onto my knees in front of the toilet and just waited, feeling my face get hot. But then, after all that, nothing seemed to happen. It was like the evil I'd swallowed decided to stay inside and kill me.

She turned off the water and looked around from behind the shower curtain, so I could see just her head. She was holding the curtain to cover the rest of her, and it was a nice solid curtain that you couldn't see through, so there was nothing weird or indecent about the situation.

"Something you ate?" she asked me.

"I don't know. I'm sorry. It just sort of came over me. I'll get back out with the baby in a minute."

I couldn't believe I'd left Etta alone, even for a second, even just in the next room, after everything I went through trying to get Brooke to go take a shower and let me look after her. I mean, it was like pulling teeth trying to get her to just go into the bathroom and shut herself in and trust me for a split second.

She tossed her head in the direction of the open bathroom door, so I looked there. The baby was standing in the doorway, holding the edge of the door to steady herself, and giving me this look like she was worried about me.

"I'm okay, Etta," I said. "I just got to feeling a little sick."

"Sick?" she asked.

And her face was so sad with hurting for me, and her voice was so sweet and soft, I just fell in love with her all over again. I remember thinking how lucky I was that I ever got to see her again after that terrible night. I really hadn't seen any of this coming. I mean, who would?

I just froze there on my knees for a while with everybody staring at me. Well, both of them, which is only two—I'm not sure if that qualifies as an everybody or not. I was really aware of how I felt, not even in terms of my belly, but more that I was clean, and my hair was brushed, and I was wearing the brand-new jeans and sweatshirt Brooke had bought me the night before, and I felt like a real person. But I don't mean that like I thought I hadn't been a real person before. I'm not quite sure how to explain what I mean. I guess I mean I felt like I could go anywhere and meet anybody and they wouldn't look at me funny, and they would treat me like a real person just like everybody else.

And while I was noticing all that I also started noticing that I probably wasn't going to throw up. I wasn't exactly feeling great down there, but it seemed like the moment had passed.

"Sorry," I said, and got up off my knees. "False alarm, I guess."

The baby looked super relieved and Brooke turned the water on and went back to taking her shower, and I left the bathroom and closed the door to give her some privacy.

Like I would have all along if I'd figured I had any choice about the thing.

—

When you're going from LA to Utah, where I used to live, it's mostly California and Nevada all the way through. But then there's this one little tiny piece of Arizona. It's just a little corner, and when you get to Mesquite you know you're about to hit it, and then you better not blink, because it's going to be over fast. I mean, not literally, because really it might be thirty or forty miles, but I'm just saying it's not much when you think about how you're driving through a whole state. And then you're about to cross the state line into Utah, right at that south-west corner, and the very first city that comes up is St. George, and that's where I grew up, and that's where my parents still lived.

And that's where we were going.

So we passed through Mesquite and I started to feel sick to my stomach again, because I knew we were really close to there, and that's when I think it dawned on me that it wasn't about something I ate.

"Could you pull over?" I asked. "I think I might need to throw up again."

Except it wasn't a very good way to describe the thing, because I hadn't thrown up before, but I guess I was trying to say I felt like I *needed to* again.

We were on the I-15, which is a pretty big highway, and people go really fast on it. The speed limit is 70, but then people go even faster than that. There was a pretty good, pretty wide shoulder, but I guess it was only for emergencies, so I was waiting to see if she would think this was emergency enough.

"Sick?" Etta asked from the back seat.

I was riding up front with Brooke because I was all nervous and frazzled and I didn't want the baby to pick it up from me.

"A little," I said to her.

And while Etta and I were talking about that, Brooke pulled over onto the shoulder.

I opened the door of that crazy half-yellow car and just sat there, sideways, my feet out and resting on the dirt, leaning forward. But nothing happened. But I still sat there for a long time, hearing and feeling the cars and trucks race past us. They made this sort of sucking wind that pulled our parked car over and kind of rocked it as it settled back again.

Finally I gave up and put my legs back in and closed the door. I shook my head at Brooke and she drove on. I liked her in that moment, because I thought she was going to dredge it all up in words and go into how I was probably just sick from stress, but she didn't. She kept her mouth shut and left me alone, and, let me tell you, that's a good quality in a person.

We crossed the state line into Arizona, and then I opened my mouth and said something that I'd had no idea I was about to say. I think it was because I was starting to trust her more, but I can't say so for a fact. I just know I surprised myself with this next thing that came out of me.

"There was a girl," I said.

I sat for what felt like a long time, feeling my face burn hot and watching Arizona rush by the window, and she didn't say anything. I thought it was weird that she didn't say anything, like she was pretending she never heard me, but looking back I think she was just waiting to see if I wanted to say any more on my own.

Just when I thought the whole thing would drop forever and she would never admit she'd heard me, she all of a sudden said, "Okay. And . . ."

"I'm telling you my long story," I said.

"Ah," she said. "Got it."

"She was just sort of . . . she was different about it. About . . . you know . . . things. I just wanted to be who we were and I didn't figure it was anybody's business but ours, but she wasn't like that. She was into this whole 'living out loud' thing. She wanted to be out and proud and right in everybody's face and I was too ashamed to tell her that my parents were the way they were. I knew it would be bad when I told them. I actually didn't know it would be *that* bad. I mean, it's weird looking back, but the whole getting thrown out onto the street thing really never occurred to me, and now I don't know why not. It actually occurred to me that they might have somebody kidnap me and take me to one of those conversion camps, but I never thought of this. But I knew it was a terrible, terrible idea to tell them. But . . . you know how it is when you love somebody. Right? I mean, I don't know you very well, but I'm guessing you do because I figure just about everybody does. But then, I don't really know all that much, or all that many people, so I don't know why I'm talking about it like I'm some big expert or something."

We drove in silence for another few seconds, and again I think maybe she was just giving me the space to say more if I wanted to. I stole a look over at her face and it looked kind of soft, and also like I'd made her really sad with what I said.

"Yeah," she said. "I know how it is when you love somebody."

We drove without talking for another minute. I felt pretty done, talking-wise. Hell, I was mostly surprised I'd even said *that* much.

"Why did you leave Utah?" she asked me after a bit.

"Well, Bodhi wanted to go to LA, and there was winter coming on, and it gets pretty cold where we were. I mean, not like *winter* winter like where it snows, but it gets down around freezing at night."

"I guess I meant . . ." But then she trailed off and I thought she'd never tell me what she meant. "I'm just surprised you left if you had someone there."

"Oh, no," I said. "I didn't have her. She dropped me right away after that whole mess came down the way it did."

"Oh," she said. "That's . . ."

I could tell she had an opinion on the situation but she wasn't quite sure how to say it in a nice way, so I did it for her.

"I know," I said. "It sucks. It was really bad. She didn't turn out to be anything like who I thought she was. I thought she loved me, but I was just being really stupid. I look back and I can't believe how stupid I was being."

Some of the feelings around that whole thing tried to come up, but I was careful not to let them. You can't just let them have their way, those kinds of feelings, because they knock you down and then they're in control, and it's all over and you might never get up again. You have to be strong and keep them back behind the wall where they belong.

"What was her name?" she asked me.

I was really surprised that she would ask me that, because I had no idea why she would want to know. I guess she was trying to understand the whole thing, or she wanted it to feel more real to her, but I figured she would've wanted exactly the opposite.

"Gail," I said.

It burned coming out. It made my face burn and my arms and legs tingle and my throat get tight, like I was trying to keep it from getting out into the world. I wished I hadn't said it at all. You can't just let those feelings have their way.

"First love tends to be a disaster," she said.

"Really? I thought it was just me."

"Definitely not just you."

We didn't talk for a few miles, and I knew the Utah state line was coming up pretty soon, and it made me feel all queasy again. I made up my mind that I wouldn't ask her to stop this time. I just kept my finger on the power button for the window, so I could get it down really fast if I all of a sudden needed to.

"Okay," she said, and it made me jump. I wasn't expecting anything in the way of words. "You told me your long story. So I guess I might as well tell you mine. My husband was dead set against having kids."

"Oh," I said. I thought about it for a minute, and then I added, "That's really not a very long story."

"Right," she said. "It's not. I know."

"Well, long or short, you told it, anyway."

I thought she was done, but then she started up again.

"I should have looked it right in the eye. Asked for a divorce so I could move on to a marriage with someone who wanted what I wanted. Or even so I could have children on my own, like I more or less ended up doing anyway. I shouldn't have stayed and stayed and stayed and somehow convinced myself that something would change. Looking back, any fool could see that nothing would ever change. But you know how it is when you love somebody."

I could feel myself smile a little when she said that, and wow, I really hadn't seen any smiles coming.

"I really do know how that is," I said.

"I just thought you might want to know that you're not the only person who looks back and thinks they were very stupid about love. I just thought it might do you some good to know that."

"Thanks," I said. "It totally does."

It totally did—I wasn't just saying that. And it was the second time it had happened to me. That lady cop had been nice enough to tell me that grown-ups mess up and make mistakes just like me, and now Brooke was nice enough to say it, too. When you hear something a couple of different times in a couple of different places, you start thinking there must be something to it.

"What was his name?" I asked her.

"Why?"

"I don't know. Why did you ask me my person's name?"

She never exactly answered that one. She just said, "David. His name was David."

"That's a nice name."

"I used to think so, too. Now I just get a little sick to my stomach every time I hear it."

"Oh," I said. "So you know exactly how I feel."

But the funny thing was, after that I took my finger off the power button for the window, because I wasn't feeling so queasy anymore.

I felt like it was nice that she was talking to me and I really didn't want her to stop, so I started asking questions that I thought maybe I shouldn't ask. But I did anyway, maybe because I was a little nervous. I tend to talk when I get nervous.

"So why did you move in with your mother? Since your mother is so . . . you know . . ."

She sighed, but I didn't really get a feeling like she minded my asking. More like thinking about the whole thing just made her sigh.

"I guess I figured I didn't have any other choice."

"You didn't have friends?"

"Well . . . once upon a time I did, of course. But I just sort of . . . After I got married I stopped paying attention to those friendships. I guess part of me didn't realize how much you can't just stop taking care of them and expect them to keep being there. I guess I made the mistake of letting David fill all those roles after we got married. And then, after I had Etta, I let Etta be my whole world. And when I left David, I started paying the price for it. I thought about asking my friend Caroline if I could stay with her. She was somebody I'd known since high school. But I felt guilty about ignoring her. And . . . I don't know. In the end I just couldn't bring myself to ask."

I watched the scenery go by for a minute, even though it wasn't much to look at.

Then I asked her, "Why is she so terrible?"

"Caroline's not terrible."

"No. Your mother."

"Oh. A lot of ways, I guess. She's loud and controlling, and she just criticizes everything I—"

"No, that's *how*. That's *how* she's terrible. I wanted to know *why*."

That just sat there in the car for a minute, and it was weird, because I could sort of almost literally feel it sitting there. I guess it was a thing she didn't know quite what to do with.

"How would I know?" she said at last. "Why is anybody the way they are?"

"You've known her all your life."

"And she's been this way as long as I've known her."

"You don't know anything about how her life was when she was growing up?"

I could see her hands flexing and relaxing on the steering wheel. Flexing and letting go. So I guess the conversation was making her a little uneasy.

"I do and I don't," she said. Her voice sounded kind of tight and squashed, like somebody was sitting on it. "To hear her tell it, her childhood was all just fine. But I knew my grandparents, and it couldn't possibly have been. They were terrible, terrible people. Angry and critical and abusive. Really bad."

"So being a terrible person sort of . . . runs in the family."

That was the first time I thought I saw her get mad at anything I was saying.

"And what is that supposed to mean?"

"I didn't mean it like . . . I didn't mean you were terrible. Not at all. I guess I just meant, like . . . now you know what your big job is in life. It's like life has given you this huge challenge to make sure that what was running in your family stops with you and doesn't go on any more than it has. You know. Like, to Etta."

She never said anything back to that. After that we were just quiet for a really long time. But I felt like I could see her thinking about it.

—

"I'm starting to think this was a really bad idea," I said.

We were pulling into St. George, and the red rock hills all around the town looked so weirdly familiar to me. Part of me had missed them like crazy, just for their actual beauty, but another part of me had them all mixed up with every bad thing that had ever happened to me here, which was pretty much my whole entire life. The good news was, I wasn't feeling queasy anymore, but the bad news was how I was halfway into a full-on panic attack.

"We drove all this way," she said. "You're honestly not suggesting we go back without my even talking to her. Are you?"

"I don't know," I said, and I closed my eyes so I wouldn't see those red rock hills. "I don't know what I'm suggesting."

"You don't have to go to the door. Like I said."

"But I'll be right outside in the car, and what if she sees me there? She told me never to come back, ever, and what if she calls the police on me or something?"

"She can't call the police on you for sitting in a car at the curb."

"Why can't she?"

"Because it's not her property."

"Oh. Okay. Get off at this exit."

It wasn't okay, nothing was okay, but I had to take a break from talking about how okay everything wasn't, so I could tell her where to get off the interstate.

"You want to be somewhere else while I talk to her?"

"Yes, please," I said, and actually started to breathe again. Not that I hadn't been breathing—I mean, enough to keep me alive and all—but when she said that, I started breathing in enough air to break up the panic a little.

"The library?"

"Maybe the coffee place," I said.

"But first we have to go by the house so you can show me where it is."

"Couldn't I just draw you a little map or something?"

"I'd really appreciate it if you would go by with me and point out the house. It's going to be hard enough to go up and knock on a stranger's door without worrying that it'll be the wrong house and the wrong stranger."

"Okay," I said. "Fine. But you can see it from the end of the block, so just promise you won't take me very close."

———

She pulled up into a loading zone in front of the coffee place and I got scared again. Because it was really near my house and my school, and everybody I knew showed up here pretty much every day, and I wasn't sure why I picked the place or how I thought I could get in or get out without running into everybody I knew.

But I didn't figure I had a right to say all that, because I *had* picked the place, and after I'd pointed out the house she'd been nice enough to drive me somewhere that wasn't right where my mom could see me from the front door.

I just got out and stood there on the street, with the door of her car open, kind of bent forward and looking back in at her like I wished I didn't have to go. Because I wished I didn't have to go. Out of the corners of my eyes I saw people stop to stare at her mother's crazy half-yellow Mercedes, but they weren't anybody I knew.

"Molly, Molly, Molly," Etta sang from her car seat in the back. She was nervous because I was going, and I knew her well enough to be able to tell.

"I'll come around and get you after I've talked to her," Brooke said to me. It sounded like a nice, polite way to say "Go ahead and close the door and go now, so we can get on with this." And then, to the baby, she said, "We'll see Molly soon, honey. We'll come back for her. She's just going to get a coffee and then we'll see her again."

"Okay," I said, but I didn't close the door and we didn't get on with anything.

"Oh," she said. "You need a couple dollars for a coffee?"

"That would be very nice," I said. "Thank you."

But that wasn't why I didn't close the door. I actually hadn't even thought of that yet. She handed me a five-dollar bill, and I said thank you again, but I still didn't close her car door.

"Seriously," she said. "I'd like to get this over with."

That made a lot of sense to me, because it made me think of how much better I'd feel when we were driving out of town again and it was all over. I didn't say anything, because my mouth wasn't working very well right about then, but I did close her door and then I walked into the coffee place.

There was a clock hanging behind the counter, which I already knew because I knew the place, and it was around 11:30. I breathed a little more and a little deeper, because I figured everybody I knew would be at school. But the minute the door swung closed behind me I saw my science teacher sitting at a little round table right in front of me with his wife.

"Molly," he said.

"Hey," I said.

I put my head down and looked at the linoleum and tried to get around his table, but he just kept talking.

"Where've you been?" he asked me. He said, "We haven't seen you for ages."

I wondered if he knew and, if he knew, how much he knew. I wondered what kind of story had gone around about me since I'd left home. People must've noticed that my whole family still lived there in town. Well, not my whole family, but everybody except me. Did they think I ran away or something, or did they know the whole truth? Or did my family have some kind of story to make them look better than the actual truth would make them seem? I had no idea, so I didn't know what to say and I didn't want to say much anyway.

"LA." That was all I said to him. And I tried to walk away again.

"Well, you look great," he said. "You've lost a lot of weight, haven't you?"

But he said that like it was a good thing, which felt weird to me, because it showed me how much he didn't know. He was about forty or fifty pounds overweight, so I guess he just figured everybody has all the food they want anytime they want it, so if they get thinner it's because they wanted to. Because they tried.

I didn't answer, so he asked, "How did you get so slim?"

"Starving," I said.

And this next part was weird, but they both smiled at me, like they still thought this was a really great thing to be able to say.

"*Tell* me about it," his wife said, even though we had only ever seen each other from a distance and she'd never talked to me before. "It's so hard to stay on a diet. I don't know how you managed."

I had no idea how to hack through all that distance between where their heads were and the way I'd been living, so I just smiled and walked away from them.

I walked up to the counter and ordered a latte, because that had a lot of milk in it, and I hadn't eaten anything. Brooke would've bought me breakfast, but I'd been too queasy to eat any.

"Can I get the key to your bathroom?" I asked the girl behind the counter. Weirdly, I didn't know her, so she must've been a new hire or something.

She gave me the key and I told her my name so she could write it on the cup. I had to walk right by my science teacher's table to get to the bathroom.

"It was good to see you again, Molly," he said.

And I completely decided right then that he didn't know the real truth, because he wasn't acting like any of this was a tragic thing. I stopped because I was confused about something, and all of a sudden I couldn't walk and be confused at the same time.

"How come you're not in school?" I asked him.

"It's Sunday," he said.

"Oh. Is it?"

Then I got a little embarrassed because most people know those simple things like what day it is.

I let myself into the bathroom with the key and looked at myself in the mirror, and what I saw was just a regular girl. Clean clothes, clean hair, clean face. Thin enough to look like I was trying to be a fashion model. But the look felt like a fake, because I knew that's not who I really was at all. I felt like I was wearing a normal-girl costume. Like I was trying to fool everybody about my life.

I looked away from the mirror and used the bathroom and washed my hands.

And then I stepped out of the bathroom and ran right into Gail. I mean banged right into her hard enough to almost knock her off-balance.

"Molly," she said. "What are you doing here?"

"Nothing," I said, which was a stupid answer.

My heart was hammering around in there, and I could feel my face getting hot and tingly, which meant it was turning red because I was embarrassed. And the redder it got, the more she would see how embarrassed I was, and I knew it, so that made me even more embarrassed. And I couldn't bring myself to look at her. I mean, I was literally looking away, kind of desperate, like I had to do that to save my life. I could see her hair out of the corner of my eye so I knew she still wore it slicked back with product and, like, purposeful comb marks, but other than that I can't even tell you if she looked good to me anymore, because I literally didn't even look.

She had just been walking up to the counter, to order I guess, and she was with Jason Miller, which was just too weird for my brain to process.

"You look great," she said. "You lost a lot of weight."

That I decided I couldn't forgive. I forgave my science teacher for saying it—in fact, there was nothing to forgive with him, because I never really blamed him for saying it, because he didn't know. But Gail knew what I'd been through. Then again, I guess there were a lot of things I couldn't forgive Gail for.

"I was just leaving," I said.

And I walked out the door without my latte, which I had already paid for. I had no idea where I was going, but I had to get away.

Then, as I was walking along really fast with my head down, I realized that in a minute the new girl barista was going to call my name and say my drink was ready, and then Gail would know I'd walked out without it. And then she would know I hadn't just been leaving at all.

My face burned hotter and hotter the more I thought about it, but, like everything else in my life, it was a done-deal disaster and there was nothing I could do to make it right.

Chapter Nineteen

Brooke: The Devil

I was taking Etta out of her car seat. To take her up to the house with me.

That's when I noticed my hands were shaking.

It came as a surprise to me. Because, as my mother tended to say, I didn't have a dog in this fight.

At first I wrote it off to the general stress of anticipating having words with a stranger. But, you know what? I'm pretty damned good at that. I'm no coward about such things. I'll talk to anybody about anything, provided there's no actual threat of physical violence.

I lifted Etta into my arms. She caught on to my worry. I could feel her take it into herself. Like a contagion. Like a virus that needed no time at all to incubate.

"Where Molly?" she asked in a whiny voice.

"We'll see her soon, honey."

I started up the walkway.

The house was gray. Almost a dark gray, which seemed fitting somehow. Like some kind of statement from its occupants. Or from the house, regarding its occupants.

The window trim was white, but also filthy from years of weather. It was not a shabby or poor house. It was large and fairly new. But little

if any pride showed through in the care that had been taken of it. The
yard was overgrown, the windows streaked with months of old rain.

"Where Molly?" Etta asked again.

I almost snapped at her.

I didn't. I stopped myself in time.

We were both nervous. And we had melded our nervousness into
being nervous together. But we were nervous over two entirely different
issues. And she could only tell me what was on her mind.

I stopped walking for a second or two. And it came over me. What
was really at stake here. I had a lot of my worldview riding on this
moment. I was about to find out if the world was really a place where a
mother would put her child out on the street for no good reason.

The idea that I had almost snapped at my daughter when she was
to blame for nothing . . . the pain at the thought of my almost hurting
her in that small way . . . I guess it just brought it all together for me.

Being forcibly separated from my daughter had been the worst
thing that had ever happened to me. Hands down. If Molly had done
something horrible, that would be a bad thing to find out. Because I was
traveling with her. But what if she hadn't? That would be even worse.
How would I fit that into my view of what was possible in the world?
Where could I file it in my brain?

"We're going to go talk to Molly's mother," I said to Etta.

Gently. Because she was my daughter. And that, after all, is a sacred
trust.

I walked up onto the porch and knocked.

At first, no reply.

As I waited I was looking through the front window. Not peering
in like a Peeping Tom. Just seeing what I could see from the doormat.
The place was packed to overflowing with knickknacks and little bits
of statuary. Vases and ornately framed photos. If the whole house held
true to what I saw of the living room, I couldn't imagine how a family
of people would even fit in there.

I got a deep, sinking feeling at the idea that no one would answer the door. Then what would we do? It was an outcome I hadn't thought to anticipate.

I knocked again, and at almost that exact same moment the door swung inward.

The woman who stood in the doorway looked nothing like Molly. She was small and slight, with perfectly straight blonde hair. Pinned up in the back, with every hair just so. She wore an apron over a polka-dot housedress. There was something pixie-like about her. She looked like an old photograph of a model housewife from a black-and-white 1950s laundry detergent ad, except in color. Well. Marginally in color. Her dress was gray, like the house.

She smiled at Etta, and then at me. It looked to be a genuine enough smile.

"Yes? Something I can do for you?"

It struck me suddenly that I had no idea what to call her. I didn't know her name. I wanted to call her Mrs. Blank. Mrs. Molly's Last Name. But I didn't know Molly's last name. It made me marvel at what I was doing here. Trying to help or defend this girl I didn't even know.

"I'm a friend of your daughter Molly's," I said.

Her face changed.

I won't say it went dark, or cold. That would be a bit of a stereo-typical way for things to go. But it wasn't like that. It's hard to explain the change I witnessed. I think the best description would be to say she seemed to vacate herself in that moment. To leave the area, leaving her body in place. I looked into those same light-brown eyes and it seemed as though no one was at home inside.

She wasn't answering. While I waited, my heart began to pound harder. I guess because I had a sense that this was not about to go well.

"You *are* Molly's mother?" I asked. Just in case I had the wrong house or something.

She nodded. It was only the tiniest gesture. Nearly imperceptible. She offered no words to go with it.

"Molly's been in a bad way since she left Utah. She's been living on the street in LA. Sleeping in an old packing crate. In a very sketchy neighborhood. She's lost too much weight. I don't know if you know any of this."

I waited. Again. At first, nothing happened at all.

Then she seemed to rouse herself to speak.

"And you know my daughter how?"

"We were thrown together in a strange way. I lost my little baby girl, Etta." I indicated the girl in question with a flip of my chin. "We'd gotten separated. Molly found her and got her back to the police so she could be returned to me."

She narrowed her eyes at me. In that moment, she seemed marginally at home behind those eyes.

"How do you go about losing a little girl?"

You're a fine one to talk, I thought.

I didn't say it. Blasting her with my anger would get me nowhere. Though I had plenty of ammunition.

"She was taken from me in a violent carjacking."

"Oh," she said. Her tone seemed to change. The look in her eyes softened. "I'm sorry to hear that."

She looked past me and out to the street. I turned to see what she found so interesting. All I saw was my mother's car parked at the curb. I wondered if she was looking to see if I had Molly with me.

"That your car?" she asked.

"Yes."

It wasn't worth explaining that I'd borrowed it from my mother.

"Why d'you drive around with it in that ridiculous shape? Why don't you pick a color and get it painted that color all over?"

"Can we please get back to the subject at hand?" I tried to keep my voice even. But I was growing peeved. And I'm sure she knew it.

"You want me to feel guilty," she said. "But I don't."

"You don't."

"No. Not at all. I told her she could come back anytime."

I stood a moment. Silent. Reeling. My mind was going a dozen directions at once. I gave up trying to follow any of them. An overriding voice reminded me that I'd known to expect the unexpected. I'd seen something like this coming. Some big piece of information that Molly had neglected to tell me.

Still, I had no special confidence that this woman would prove to be a reliable narrator. No more than I had in Molly. I knew her even less. And something about her statement wasn't adding up.

"Wait," I said. "Let me get this straight. You put her out of your home. But then you told her she could come back anytime? That doesn't make sense. If she can come back anytime, why put her out in the first place?"

"There's no welcome in my home for the devil," she said. Flatly. The words sounded almost rehearsed. I heard no emotion behind them whatsoever.

It was a stunning statement. To me, anyway. A bit of cool sureness had come into her presence. She had found some kind of firm foothold in this conversation.

"You think Molly is the devil?"

"I didn't say that. But she brought the devil into my home." Her voice sounded even more solid now. Like a wall, holding me back from wherever she thought I meant to go.

"So she could come back home anytime . . . how?"

"Just so long as she doesn't bring the devil with her. I don't see how that's asking too much."

I held Etta more closely against my chest. I'm not sure why. I guess I wanted to protect her. I wondered what she was making of all this. I knew she didn't understand the words. But she must have felt the energy of the conflict on some level.

"Let me just get this straight," I said. "Let me just make sure I understand you correctly. What you're saying is that she could come home . . . I mean, what does that even mean? She can come home if she doesn't bring the devil? I don't understand that." Actually, I thought I might know what she meant. But it was such a wild theory. Still, I had to know. I had to get this clarified. "Do you mean you told her she could live with you again if she just stopped being gay?"

"Prayer can heal all things," she said. Quiet and calm. Like it was a perfectly reasonable statement to end any discussion.

"That's it?" I was raising my voice now. Trying not to, but failing. "And there was nothing else? That's really the whole story? She wasn't violent, or on drugs? She didn't break the law? That was her only transgression against your values?"

"You get off my property now," she said.

Her face didn't change in the slightest as she said it. Neither did her voice. Which I found a little bit scary.

"You're not even willing to discuss this?"

"I will not have a conversation with somebody who thinks that's not plenty reason enough. Now you take your permissive ways and go back to California with them. They're not needed here."

And, with that, she slammed the door in my face.

———

Something strange happened as I was putting Etta back into her car seat. Her mood suddenly and utterly fell apart.

She waged a full-on tantrum.

I won't say it had never happened before. She was a small child, after all. But it was rare for her. And when it did happen, it was usually for a very obvious reason. She was overtired, for example, and something stressed her to the breaking point. But she had slept almost all the way into Utah. And I was only asking her to sit still so I could buckle her in.

She resisted mightily. She stretched her legs out and locked her knees and used those straight limbs to push against the seat. To keep her upright. She would not relax into a sitting position so I could place the straps.

And she shrieked her displeasure.

At first I fought with her. I used my physical strength to try to overpower her. I was furious, but not with her. But I had no room for her tantrum in my current mood.

But she was so resistant. I couldn't overpower her without hurting her.

My right ear was aching from her screaming into it. It felt as though she were jamming knives through my eardrum.

I almost lost it. I was right on the edge of losing it. I almost blew like an old steam boiler. But, at the last minute, I realized what was happening. I understood how much my fury was driving hers.

I stopped fighting her. I stopped struggling.

I sat down on the seat in the back, next to her car seat. I let her remain suspended above it. I stopped trying to buckle her in.

I sighed deeply. Tried to let some of my rage flow away.

"I'm sorry," I said. "I'm not mad at you, baby. I'm mad at that lady."

"Lady?" she asked.

Her demeanor transformed immediately. Every muscle in her body seemed to go slack. She sank down into her car seat.

"Yes, the lady we were just talking to. She wasn't very nice and I guess I'm still upset about it."

She reached out and took hold of a strand of my hair. She didn't pull it angrily. Neither did she stroke it tenderly. I was left unclear as to whether it was a loving gesture or not. I suppose she just wanted to connect with me.

"You're always welcome with me, Etta," I told her. "I promise you that. You're my daughter, no matter what."

We sat for a moment in silence. The mood in the back of that car felt strangely peaceful. The silence echoed in my right ear, which was still stinging from its recent abuse.

I looked back at the house. But there was no outward sign of life. It was just a gray house. It no longer showed its true nature in any way.

I sighed again.

"We should go find Molly," I said after a time.

"Molly, Molly, Molly."

"But before we go get her, you have to be strapped in. Is it okay if I strap you in now?"

"Okay," she said.

And I did, without issue.

We drove away from that house, and from that experience.

———

I got lost on the way back to the coffee place, which didn't help my mood in the slightest. It took maybe twenty minutes to get back there. To finish what should have been a three-minute drive.

I had navigation, but I didn't remember the name of the coffeehouse, and all the streets seemed to dump me where I didn't want to be.

And then, when I finally found the place, Molly wasn't there. It piled onto all the other elements of my morning and left me feeling as though I was living a nightmare. There seemed to be no way to break its grasp.

I sat in the car outside the coffee place for a minute or two, staring through the window. I could see every table in there. I don't know why I thought staring longer would somehow make her appear.

It occurred to me that she might be in the restroom, so I waited. I was trying to avoid taking Etta out of her car seat again. But the waiting did not pay off.

I couldn't just drive off without her. What could I do? I had no plan for this, and my brain was tired, and I was too upset to think clearly. It was all too much.

Finally I got out, and took Etta out of her seat, and we went inside. No Molly. We checked the restroom, but it was locked. We waited there to see who would come out.

"You need a key for it," the young girl behind the counter called to us.

"Maybe there's somebody in there," I called back.

"Nope. I've got the key." And she held it up for me to see, on its long strip of polished wood.

"Thanks anyway," I said, and we walked outside.

I stood blinking in the sun. I was so utterly without a plan.

"Molly?" I called as loudly as I could. It was a long shot. But I didn't know what else to try.

"Molly?" Etta called. With less volume, but all the volume her little lungs could muster.

It broke my heart in ways I could never describe or explain.

We stood in the sun for a few minutes more. Helpless. That was the feeling. Helpless against my life in that moment.

Then I buckled Etta back into her car seat and we started driving around. Aimless. And yet panicky at the same time. I couldn't leave this little city without Molly. But I had no idea where to begin looking.

We started by just driving around the block.

"You tell me if you see Molly," I said to Etta.

"Molly," she said back to me. But not as though she saw her.

Then we drove around two blocks at once.

Why hadn't I given her my cell phone? Of course, then *I* wouldn't have had one, but I could have stopped at a pay phone, or borrowed a phone. I shook the thoughts away because they were of no use to me now.

Then for a while I just drove. Just aimlessly drove.

My gut was still buzzing with anxiety from my talk with that woman. The dark cloud that had settled over me at her doorstep had only gotten darker. And now I had lost Molly. And the panic of that fact, mixed with everything else . . . well, it was a very bad combination. I'll leave it at that.

Finally, for lack of any better options, I drove by her mother's house again.

"Molly!" Etta cried as soon as we turned that last corner.

But I had eyes. And I had already seen her, too.

She was sitting on the curb in front of her family's home. Leaning on her bent knees. Elbows pressed to the new jeans I had bought her. Her head was so low as to be nearly between her knees, like a person who's trying not to be sick. She seemed to be gazing blankly down at the pavement.

I pulled up. Reached over and swung open the passenger door. Nearly hit her with it, though I hadn't meant to.

She looked up, and I unloaded on her.

"What the hell are you doing, Molly? Why didn't you just stay at the coffee place? The plan was I'd come pick you up at the coffee place! You said you didn't want to be here. So I looked every other place in town before I looked here. I've been driving around forever!"

Or anyway, it felt like forever.

She only blinked at me. Clearly hurt.

"Get in the car," I barked at her.

She did.

We drove away. Back toward the interstate. I couldn't get out of that town fast enough. When I saw the cars zipping along the highway in the distance, I felt myself breathe for what felt like the first time in a long time.

"I thought I'd never see you again," she said.

"Then why didn't you just stay put where I was supposed to meet you?"

"I kept running into people I knew."

"And for that it was worth our getting separated indefinitely?"

My voice had come up to a near screech. Etta started to cry. I realized I was losing it in a big way.

I stepped on the brake and the car behind us blared its horn. I pulled over to the curb and shifted into park. In a red zone. I rested my forehead on the steering wheel and closed my eyes.

Silence reigned. Even Etta was silent. Everybody was waiting to see what I would do next. Even me.

"I'm sorry," I said to Molly. "I'm not mad at you. Well, I'm a little mad at you. But not mostly."

I heard her let out a long, slow breath. Relief.

"Oh, good," she said. "I thought you were pulling over to tell me to get out of the car. Who are you mad at mostly?"

"Your mother."

"Oh. So you did talk to her."

"Yes."

"So we're both going back to LA."

"Yes."

"That's what I figured."

I looked up again. Through the windshield. Watched the cars stream along the I-15.

"I can't say you didn't warn me," I said.

"What did she say?"

"Something about the devil. Quite a bit about the devil, actually."

"Yup. That's my mom. Did she tell you I could come home if I didn't bring the devil with me? I meant to warn you about that, but then I got all scared and all the thoughts dropped out of my head. But she said it, right?"

"She absolutely did say that."

"You know what that means?"

"I didn't at first. But as we were talking I figured it out."

"And you know I can't do that, right? I mean, literally can't?"

"Of course you can't. Nobody can. You can't change who you are. It was wrong of her to ask you to try. Now come on. Let's go home."

I shifted into drive again and pulled carefully into the traffic lane. Headed for the on-ramp.

"Easy for you to say," Molly said.

"Meaning what?"

"Meaning you have a home to go to. I have to go back to that crate on the street."

"No, you don't. No way. I'm not dumping you back there."

"So where do I go?"

"I have no idea. But I'll figure it out. I'll come up with something. I don't know. I'll talk to your social worker. Or find some kind of program or some kind of group home or . . . I don't know, Molly. I can't think right now. I'm too upset. I need more time to think. All I know right now is that I'm not throwing you back out on the street. Bad enough that happened to you once in your life. It's not going to happen with me."

Another long breath out of her.

"Thanks," she said. And left it at that.

Then we were all quiet for a time. I accelerated to seventy on the interstate, and we drove southwest, toward home, for many miles without talking.

"I ran into Gail," she said. Just out of nowhere. Her voice sounded grave and dispirited.

"At the coffee place?"

"Yeah."

"So that's why you didn't stay there for me to pick you up."

"Right."

"So we both had a really terrible day."

"You can say that again," she said.

Chapter Twenty

Molly: Ouch

We were on our way back through that little corner of Arizona, the one you might miss if you blinked, and I was feeling like I shouldn't talk to her because it seemed like she was falling apart at the seams. Kind of driving and falling apart at the same time, but she was still doing a pretty good job of driving anyway. I mean, she wasn't scaring me. The bad stuff was mostly a thing that looked like it was happening on the inside of her.

I wasn't exactly what you might call on top of the world myself, but I swear she looked worse than I felt, and I wasn't even sure I knew why.

While I wasn't talking to her, I was thinking about what she'd said about getting me someplace to live, but I didn't figure it would work out that way.

Nothing against her personally, but it reminded me of Bodhi when we started getting to be friends. The way he said to me, "Come on, Molly, we'll go someplace better, and don't worry about anything because you'll always have me looking after you."

It's not that he turned out to be a liar, because he wasn't, and it's not like he ever really betrayed me on purpose. More like he just couldn't do everything he said he could—like he just sort of overestimated his own power to work things out and made a bunch of promises too big to fill. I figured it would be like that with Brooke, too.

I looked over at her, and I was surprised to see her looking back—like we each snuck a look to size the other up, and at exactly the same time, and then we both got caught.

Then she had to look back at the road again, because . . . well, you know. She was driving.

"I feel like I shouldn't talk to you," I said to her a little later.

"Why not?"

"You seem so upset."

"I don't know that talking to me would make it any worse."

I squirmed around a little in my seat and then I said, "I guess what I mean is, I feel like I shouldn't ask you about it. About why you're so upset. Or maybe I'm just afraid to ask about it, because I have this crazy idea that it's sort of a nice thing for me, like a compliment to me. You know, like you actually care that my mom was bad to me or something, but now that I've gone and said all that out loud I'm worried you'll tell me I'm wrong."

"You're not entirely wrong," she said, and then she brushed her hair back off her forehead with this big sweep of her hand, like her fingers were a comb. "But you have to understand that there's some of my own situation mixed into it."

I didn't know which part of her own situation, and I didn't want to ask, but I knew she was telling the truth, because anytime a person gets that upset about somebody else's situation, it's a little bit their own situation, too. That's one of those things that other people don't always seem to notice, but I think you can pick up on stuff like that if you're even halfway paying attention. Or anyway, that's what I always figured and it seemed to work for me.

I watched some more of Arizona slide by the window, and then she started talking about it again on her own.

"I don't have to tell you how much I love my daughter. At least, I don't think I do."

"No, you don't. I know it."

"I suppose it shook my faith. You know. To see how something can come between a mother and a daughter like that. And it might be a little bit about how I almost lost Etta. I think at this point in my life there's a piece of that in everything. Every feeling, everything I go through."

"I can understand that," I said.

And I really could, because, you know, we've all almost lost something. If we're lucky. If we're not so lucky then there's no "almost" about it.

"Was she with another girl?" she asked, and for a minute I had no idea what she was talking about.

"Was who with another girl?"

But before she even answered, I figured out who she must mean.

"Gail," she said. Kind of quiet, like Gail's name was a bomb she had to be careful to set down real gently.

"Oh. That. Right. No. She was with Jason Miller, which is, like, so weird I can hardly process it in my brain."

"Is he just a friend? I hope?"

"I have no idea."

"Does she like boys, too?"

"I didn't think so. But you never really know about somebody. People can always surprise you. But I'm kind of sitting here trying to decide that no, she doesn't. You know, like trying really hard to believe she doesn't, because I really don't want what happened to be anything I can't handle. Because I really don't feel like I could handle that. It's hard even just talking about it like we're doing."

I watched her wrinkle up her forehead before she answered.

"I'm sorry," she said after some wrinkling. "I guess I shouldn't have brought it up."

"No, it's okay. I'm glad you brought it up. At least, I think I am. If you brought it up for the reason I think you brought it up, then I'm glad, even though I hate talking about it. But I think the reason you want to know is because you feel bad for me if it happened like that, because you know how hard it is to see your ex with somebody new. At least, I think you know."

"Oh, I do."

"I figured you must, because I figured everybody must. Except maybe the luckiest person in the whole world who I guess fell in love with their high school sweetheart or something and then they never broke up again and were still together when they died. I wonder how often that happens."

"Not often," she said.

I could hear the baby snoring in her car seat in the back, which meant it would be another long night of not being able to get her to sleep. I wondered if we would stop at a motel again or just keep driving.

"When Etta was gone," she said, "I drove over to see my ex-husband. Because I felt like I had to tell him. And he was in bed in the middle of the day with some new woman he's been seeing."

"Ouch," I said.

"Yeah. Ouch. So I know."

"Well, anyway, it was nice of you to care how bad my day was. And that's one more thing we have in common—we both hate bumping into our exes. Except maybe the whole world has that in common, I don't know."

"It'll do for something in common," she said.

I thought that was a nice thing to say—a small nice thing, but still nice. Almost like she was trying or something.

———

We stopped at a motel, so that was the answer to that question. It wasn't anything like the last motel. It was in a newer section of Barstow, and all on concrete, and it was a big box of a place that looked just like the big box of a place on either side of it. I wondered how she even chose it, since there were a bunch and they all looked alike and their signs all said they had vacancies, but I did see her staring at her phone while we were waiting at a stoplight, so maybe she figured out that this was the cheapest one.

We hauled all that stuff for the baby out of the trunk again and she hung all these different straps on my shoulders and took a few herself, and then she hauled the baby out of the car seat.

Etta was still pretty deep asleep from all the driving.

"I'll take her if you want," I said, because I could see Brooke was tired. Not even just tired in her body, although probably that, too, but more like all the way down to her spirit she just seemed exhausted.

"Maybe she'll sleep straight through," she said.

But I don't even know why she said that, because we both knew it would never happen that way. Anybody who knows anything about babies would know it would never happen that way, because they don't sleep all day and then all night. One or the other—and even that's only if you're really lucky—but definitely not both.

She handed the baby over, and I let her sleep on my shoulder, but then, as we were walking to the office, she started waking up.

I could see Brooke's face in the light that was shining outside the office door, and I swear she looked like she was about to cry. Like it was all just too much for her. It kind of scared me, what with her being the grown-up and all.

"Don't worry about it," I said. "You just get a good night's sleep. I'll stay up and take care of her."

She stopped walking and looked at me for a long time. Like she'd never met me or something. Like she was trying to figure out who I was and how I could be the way I was being.

"Why would you do that? It's not really fair to make her your responsibility."

"But you have to drive in the morning. And besides, you came all the way out here just to see if my mom would take me back and that's more than anybody has tried to do for me for a really long time."

Also because I wanted to be really helpful and agreeable, and good to have around, so she'd want to keep me and help me even more, but I didn't say that. I also didn't say the last reason—or at least the last reason I knew about—which was that now I actually knew her well enough and liked her well enough that I cared about how she felt.

"I shouldn't put it on you," she said. "But I'm going to take you up on it. Because I really need the help tonight."

"I know you do," I said.

And then, after that, other than the stuff she had to say to the motel desk clerk, we didn't talk for a really long time.

———

She took an extra-long shower, which I can relate to. I didn't take one that night, because I didn't want her to have to look after the baby, but I know how good that can feel.

When she came out, in pajamas, and with a hotel towel wrapped around her wet hair, Etta and I were out on the little balcony playing with her toys.

Etta was a little amped up from sleeping all day, so she was running around in sort of a squished circle in that little space. There was a railing and all, though, so it was safe enough. I had almost everything Brooke had brought for her to wear on her at once. Two pairs of leggings, one on top of the other, and a shirt with a sweater and her jacket, because it gets cold at night in the desert. Then I had a blanket from one of the two beds wrapped around her shoulders, but when she started running it flapped out like a cape, which made her look like some kind of tiny superhero.

Brooke came to the sliding glass door and looked out at us, and she had this look on her face like we were the cutest things she'd ever seen in her life. But then, after I got all happy about that for a minute, I decided she was only thinking that about her daughter.

She slid the door open.

"What are you doing out there?" she asked me.

"So you can sleep," I said. "She's not in much of a mood to be quiet."

She got this really nice look on her face, like she was touched by what I said, and Etta stopped running for, like, a split second, and Brooke came out and kissed her on the top of her hair. And then, before she went back inside, she took my head in both her hands and kissed *me* on the top of *my* hair, too. Like we were both her daughters.

Then she went back inside.

I watched through the glass while she got ready for bed, and I could still feel where her hands had been on my head and where her lips kissed me. I started thinking what it would be like if Brooke were my mother instead. I'd have another, even littler, sister to look after, and I wouldn't have to be homeless, and if I came out to her, which I already had, she would just say she couldn't care less. So long as I was happy she wouldn't care *how* I was happy.

But then I made myself stop thinking about it, because those kinds of ideas can set you up for a long fall. You have to be careful what you want and how much you want it, because I knew there were people who usually got what they wanted, and I didn't seem to be one of them.

———

So then it was the next morning and we were driving, and we hadn't said much over breakfast, and we still weren't saying much. We were going to get home that day, whatever a home was in my case, and she knew it and I knew it, and I didn't know what that meant for me. I think she didn't either, and I think maybe that's what was making it so quiet in that car.

Even Etta was quiet, and I knew she was awake so far.

I'd been looking out the window for a long time, even though there wasn't much out there—just flat California desert and clouds that looked kind of puffy and nice.

Then I looked over at Brooke and she was crying.

There wasn't any sound to it—she wasn't sobbing or anything. It was just these quiet tears running down her face and dripping off her chin. I could see where they'd been landing on her shirt, leaving all these little dark spots.

"What?" I said. "What happened?"

For a long time she didn't say anything at all, like she wasn't even home in there, like she hadn't even heard me, and that scared me a little.

Then she opened her mouth, and still nothing.

And then after a while of that she said, "I'm so sorry, Molly."

"About what?"

"I didn't believe you. I thought you did something terrible that made your mother decide to throw you out of the house."

"I know you did," I said.

If it had been any earlier I would've been mad when I said it, because I already knew she believed that, and as long as I'd known it I'd always minded it a lot. But now she was crying about it, so once you've made a mistake like that you really can't do much better than to be sorry about it.

"I needed to," she said. "I needed to believe that it could only happen if you'd done something truly horrible. Violence against a family member or something unacceptable like that. Why did I do that, though? Why did I need to make it your fault?"

"Because then it could never happen to you," I said.

I'm not stupid. I'm young but I have eyes, and I'm not an idiot, and I know that people like to pretend you got yourself into the trouble you're in by doing something that they would know better than to do. That way they can pretend that bad stuff like that happens for a reason and they can just stay out of the way of that reason.

It's not really a very good way to live, in my opinion, but I guess it helps people get to sleep at night.

"Because then it could never happen to Etta," she said.

"It could never happen to Etta. You're not like that."

"Thank you. Even thinking about it scares me, though."

Then we didn't talk, either one of us, for miles and miles.

And then, just out of nowhere, she said, "Think you can forgive me for that?"

I said, "I think I already did."

And then we rode most of the rest of the way back to LA without talking.

Chapter Twenty-One

Brooke: Wrong

We were about thirty miles outside of LA when the silence broke. Molly broke it. She had a question.

"So, do we have a plan?" she asked.

I immediately felt the sense of pressure it placed on me. I'd told her I was going to find her some kind of solution. But I couldn't do my promised research and drive home from Utah at the same time. Still, I felt the weight of the big promise I'd made.

"I need time to put a plan together, Molly."

"I meant tonight."

"Oh. Tonight."

That was a reasonable thing to ask. We were almost home. My home, that is. She wanted to know her immediate fate.

I could hear the edge of tension in her voice. It wasn't overt. In fact, she might have been doing her best to keep it to herself. The fact that I recognized it probably meant I was getting to know her a little.

It struck me that the trip had changed something about her situation. It had removed her from the jaws of the unpredictable streets, if for only a few days. I had been in similar situations, only with much smaller fears. When you're immersed in them, and treading water every day, it feels just barely doable. But step away for a time, and it's hard to imagine you ever successfully navigated those waters.

I had given Molly a few days of feeling found, and now she was dreading getting lost again. Hard to blame her for that. I had told her I wasn't throwing her back to that terrible crate on that vacant lot full of trash. Now she was ready to find out if that was just talk. Or if she could really depend on me.

I'd been thinking about a plan for our first night back. Of course I'd given it thought. And I did have one idea. But it felt wrong.

"I had a thought," I said. Trying to ignore how wrong it was.

"Okay. I'd like to hear it."

"It doesn't feel right to me, though."

"Still want to hear it."

I looked in the rearview mirror to see if there was any movement from Etta. I was pretty sure she was asleep. But I wanted to know for a fact. I'm not sure why it felt important in that moment.

"I can't bring you into my mother's house," I said. "She'd have a fit."

"Right. You said that."

She was staring out the window. Her face was turned fully away. Maybe so I couldn't see what was happening in her eyes.

"I could put you up in a motel for the night. Problem is, it would have to be a really long way away. I'd have to drive a long way to find the right one. Because the ones within a few miles of my mother's house would be a lot more expensive than I could afford."

"Was that the idea you said was wrong?"

"No."

"I didn't think so. What was the idea?"

"I'm not comfortable with it," I said.

"Can I please just hear it anyway?"

"I was thinking . . . my mother has a rollaway bed. And I was thinking maybe I could move it into the garage for tonight. There's no real need to put the car inside. It's just about to be repainted anyway.

Although my mother will want it in the garage all the same, because she thinks it's an eyesore for the neighbors. But anyway. It's a terrible idea. I don't know what I was thinking."

"Why is it a terrible idea? Because then the neighbors will have to look at the weird car?"

"No. Because it's a *garage*. You deserve better than a garage. People make their dogs sleep in the garage. It's not for human children. I think you'd be better off if I drove you to a motel."

She turned her head to look at me. But I had to keep my eyes on the road in that moment.

At least, I think I did.

"I'd rather be closer to you and Etta," she said.

There was a lot to unpack in that simple sentence. A bunch of hopes. A boatload of emotion. I think that was the moment it struck me that Molly had latched on to us as her family. Or was trying to, anyway. She wanted to be part of what Etta and I had together. She wanted in. I couldn't see what I had to give her except disappointment.

I talked over all that.

"A garage, though. It doesn't seem good enough."

"Seems good enough to me. It has four walls. And a bed. Whatever kind of bed you said your mother had. I don't know what that kind of bed means, but it's a bed, so it's better than what I'm used to."

"A foster home would have to give you more than a garage."

"When I was in that foster home I had to sleep in a closet. Locked in."

I said nothing for a minute. I was digesting that. Trying to make my peace with what that terrible foster home had offered Molly. And what another placement might offer her again when I entrusted her to someone else. But there was no peace to be found there.

"It's just for one night," she said while I was thinking.

"Okay. I guess it's good enough for one night."

But there was a hefty dose of denial in those pronouncements. And I think we both knew it. Somehow we were both willing to pretend that I could solve her homelessness problem tomorrow. In a single day.

—

"You sure you don't need to use the bathroom one last time?"

"Positive," she said.

She was sitting on the edge of the rollaway bed. We had made it up for her with sheets and a blanket. I had brought out two bottles of water and a plastic cup. A towel and washcloth, because I had learned that you bring your guest a towel and a washcloth. It had been ingrained in me as part of some kind of social contract. But it was absurd in this case, because she wasn't allowed near any of my mother's four bathrooms, despite the fact that I had snuck her into the downstairs one once.

Etta was running around the garage like a maniac. The soles of her light-up sneakers were flashing blue and red sparkly lights. She was nearly bouncing off the walls. She looked like she was imitating a pinball in a machine.

Again she had slept far too much on the drive. I would probably never get her to sleep.

Molly was watching her bounce around.

"You can come get me," she said. "You know. If you need to sleep and you want somebody to look after her."

"That's not fair to you," I said.

"I don't mind. But . . . Oh. Never mind. That won't work because I can't come into the house to watch her. But if you didn't mind her being out here . . ."

I could feel us skirting around an uncomfortable truth. The garage was not good enough for Etta, and we both knew it. I had put Molly in accommodations that were not up to par for my own daughter. And I knew that was wrong.

"What else can I get you before bed?" I asked her. Ignoring the rest of the problems.

"Nothing. I'm fine. This is fine."

"Okay. We'll leave you, then. The light switch is here."

I pointed to it on my way to the door that led into my mother's kitchen.

Suddenly Molly was flying across the garage to me, her feet bare on the concrete floor.

"Thank you," she said.

And she threw her arms around me. Enveloped me in a hug.

I just stood a moment. Not hugging her back. I wasn't sure what to do with all that emotion. I had never been good with emotion. We hadn't been a huggy family. We hadn't been overtly loving toward one another.

Still, I couldn't bring myself to simply reject this girl who had so little. Who wouldn't have a toothbrush or a change of clothes if I hadn't bought them for her.

I wrapped my arms around her in return.

"You're welcome," I said. "Tomorrow we'll figure out how to get you someplace better."

But it was the wrong thing to say. I could feel it. I could feel her muscles turn to lead. She pulled away from me. Turned her back and shuffled over to the bed. Shoulders slumped. Dejected. She didn't want nicer accommodations. She wanted to be with Etta and me.

I took hold of Etta's hand.

"Good night, Molly," I said.

"Night, Molly," Etta chimed in.

"Good night," she said.

It was clear from her tone that she was hurt.

I took Etta into the house. I left a note on the table for my mother to find in the morning. It said, briefly, that Molly had been invited to sleep in the garage but it was only for one night. And to please, if she was angry about it, resist the temptation to take it out on the girl. To please come take it out on me instead.

I took Etta upstairs and listened carefully. My mother was asleep. And seemed to have stayed asleep through our arrival. And I was thankful for that small favor.

———

It was about one in the morning when I lost it. Etta was still wide awake. Still bouncing off the walls. She wanted stories. She wanted to play. I was exhausted. I was accidentally falling asleep every couple of minutes, only to have her bounce me awake again.

I put her in her toddler bed with the crib sides for just a minute.

"I'll be right back," I said. "I'm just going to check on Molly."

"Molly, Molly, Molly!" she shrieked.

I stood out in the hall for a minute, listening. Waiting to see if she had wakened my mother. When I heard nothing, I crept down to the garage.

I opened the door from the kitchen. Or, actually, the laundry room right off the kitchen. Molly was in bed in the dark, faced away. The garage had a pattern of windows on the top half of its automatic door. Light from the streetlamp on the corner spilled in and fell over her.

"Are you asleep?" I whispered.

"No," she said. At normal volume.

"Did you really mean what you said about looking after Etta?"

"Sure. Bring her in here."

"No, I thought you should come upstairs to watch her."

"What about your mom?"

"She's asleep."

I felt a wash of shame as I said it. I could even feel my face heat up. "We can sneak you in without her noticing" didn't feel like the right statement. I wanted to have said something more like "I'll stand up to her for you." But, beyond its being hard for me to stand up to her, I couldn't tell my mother what she had to tolerate in her own house. That was the problem with my living there.

"Okay," she said.

She either didn't recognize the pathetic nature of the subtext, or she chose to ignore it.

She followed me up to my room.

Etta had climbed out of her toddler crib. Which I had no idea she was able to do.

"Well, that's the end of an era," I said.

I know Molly couldn't have understood my meaning. But she didn't ask me anything about it.

———

A hand on my shoulder woke me up. Or half up, anyway. I struggled up through the depths of a dream I already could not remember.

"Etta's asleep," Molly said.

"Oh. Good. Thank you so much."

"I'm going back down to the garage."

The hand disappeared.

I sat up. Watched her walk to the door in the half dark. The night-light was still on for the baby. She didn't like to sleep in the dark.

"Molly," I said quietly.

She stopped at the door and just waited.

"Thank you. That was a really nice thing to do."

"No problem," she said.

"You're a nice girl. I'm sorry I was so slow figuring that out."

She didn't answer. She just let herself out of the room.

———

I woke in the morning after not nearly enough sleep. Light was pouring through the window and directly into my eyes. I lay awake for a few minutes, wondering why I hadn't bothered to pull the shades. Probably because it had already been dark when we got in. Or because anything I had ever experienced in the way of a life routine seemed to be shattered now.

I sat up.

Etta was still fast asleep in her toddler crib. I wondered how long it would take me to get her back onto some kind of normal sleep schedule.

I dressed quickly and made my way down into the kitchen.

I knew my mother was awake because I smelled coffee brewing. Or having been brewed. It smelled like something that could rescue me.

I stuck my head into the kitchen.

My mother was sitting at the table, reading the morning paper. There was a darkness in her face. Something even darker than usual. I figured she was about to slam me over the information in my note.

Her face came up, and the look in her eyes seemed to confirm that approaching storm. But when she spoke, she kept her words even and calm.

"There's coffee."

That was all she said.

"I have to go check on Molly first."

"Oh, she's long gone."

I just stood there a moment. Trying to process what I had heard. As the words became absorbed into my body, into my cells, they seemed to tingle going through me.

"What do you mean she's gone?"

She offered a twisted frown. "Oh, come now, Brooke. How many different things can that mean?"

I tried to talk around a deep anger that seemed to be rising up in my throat. Like something solid and real, blocking important passages. "Let me put it another way, then. *Why* is she gone?"

"Because she doesn't belong here, and you know it as well as I do. You will *not* be bringing a homeless person into my house. I don't know *what* you were thinking."

"She wasn't in your house. She was only in your garage."

I felt like I was chewing the words as they came out of me. My molars wanted to grind together every chance they got.

"That makes no difference and you know it. It's all my property."

I opened my mouth to blow my stack. To really let loose on her. But that would do no good, and I knew it. She would only match me angry for angry.

I breathed. Counted to ten. Tried to keep my words measured.

"Did you get my note or didn't you?"

"Of course I got it."

"And then you went and did the exact opposite of what I asked you to do."

"I'm not a trained seal, you know. I'll do what I want to in my own home, not what you order me to do in some note."

"Okay," I said. Still working hard on the calm thing. "That's it."

"Meaning what?"

"Meaning Etta and I are out of here. We're moving out. We want nothing to do with you anymore."

She snorted. A derisive sound. "Don't be ridiculous. You have no savings. Where will you go?"

"I don't know. But we're going. She's fast asleep right now. So will you be here in case she wakes up? I have to go out and look for Molly."

She sat back sharply in her chair. I heard the whump of her great bulk hitting the back of it. "Well, that's one impressive announcement," she said. "We're moving out, we can take care of ourselves. We want nothing to do with you ever again. Now please babysit."

I saw her point. I mean, that was one angle from which to look at the thing. From my angle, it didn't seem like too much to ask. Here I was going off to try to fix the mess she had created.

"Fine. I'll go wake her up."

"No, don't do that, Brooke," she called after me. I was already halfway to the stairs. "That's silly to take it out on the baby. Just go."

"Thank you," I said. But they were a tense couple of words.

I grabbed her keys off the shelf near the garage door.

"But you can't take my car," she said. "A man from the automotive paint shop is coming over to get it this morning. Finally."

I sighed deeply. Tried to let go of the rage I was feeling. Tried to let it drain away. It felt like it wanted to hurt somebody. Probably me. That's usually how rage goes.

I set her keys back down on the shelf. Tried to remember where mine even were. Upstairs in my room, in my purse. That's what I finally came up with.

I walked upstairs and quietly let myself back into my bedroom. Grabbed the purse without waking Etta.

As I walked through the kitchen again on my way out the door I said, "Keep an eye out. She can climb out of that bed."

"Oh dear," my mother said. "When did that happen?"

"Life turns on a dime," I said. And spun around to leave again. Then I stopped myself. Turned back to her. "Just how long ago did you throw my guest out of here?"

She snorted again. "*Guest.* Some *guest.*"

"Just answer the question, please."

She glanced at the watch on her massive wrist. "Oh, a good two hours ago, I would say."

I felt all the wind go out of me when she said that. It was a figurative feeling. Nothing really rushed out of me, breath or anything else. Well . . . hope, maybe. I lost most of my hope that I could catch Molly.

She would probably have made her way back to that terrible crate in that terrible neighborhood by now. I could go find her there. Hopefully. But then what? Where would I take her? If I took her to a motel, I would be spending the tiny bit of money I had to find a new place for Etta and me.

Oh, who was I kidding? I had no money to find a new place for Etta and me. But I was going to move all the same. I had really meant it when I said I wanted nothing more to do with my mother.

I had a lot of figuring to do.

—

When I got to the crate, I could tell someone was inside. I walked over and knocked, strangely confident that we would work this out in no time at all. At least the short-range parts of it.

We could all go to a motel for a couple of nights. She could watch the baby while I found a job. I would just tell her that my mother's actions had nothing to do with Molly's welcome with *me*. In *my* life.

An old man stuck his head out of the crate. It startled me a few steps backward. He had a long, wispy gray beard, like the old men in fairy tales, and a brown sweater with holes.

"Yes?" he asked. A bit grandly, as though he were answering an actual door. At an actual house.

"Where's Molly?"

"No idea," he said. He voice was cigarette-rough and raspy. "Nobody I know has seen her for days."

"She didn't come by here this morning?"

"Well, you woke me out of a sound sleep, so it's hard to say."

I rummaged around in my purse and found a pen. I had no real paper to write on, but I had a car insurance bill in there, so I used the envelope. I would have to mail it in using a plain envelope.

I wrote down my first name and phone number.

"When she comes back here, will you please call me?"

I held out the paper to him. He only stared at it. As though it were something alien in his life.

"Yes, of course," he said. "Let me just get out my iPhone 6." His tone of voice rang with sarcasm.

Of course I did not mention that the world had moved quite a way on in iPhone models. That would have been needlessly cruel.

I dug up some change from the bottom of my purse. I had no idea what a pay phone would charge to make a call from the south side to West LA. So I gave him all the quarters I could find. About four dollars' worth.

"Thank you," he said.

He took the money. But I had to wave the phone number under his nose to get him to take that, too.

"If she comes back here, do you even give her this spot back?"

Not that I wanted her to keep needing it. I just couldn't help wondering.

"Finders keepers," he said.

Then he pulled his head back in and closed the end of the crate.

I walked back to my car, wondering.

Wondering how long it would take him to spend those quarters on food. Or cigarettes, or liquor. If he would bother to find a way to call without the benefit of those quarters if he saw her.

If he would ever see her.

Wondering how long it would take me to find Molly if she had to go to some undetermined new place to squat. If she could be anywhere in the city.

If it was even possible to find her if she could be anywhere.

Wondering if I would ever see Molly again. And, if not, if I would ever forgive myself for the careless way in which I had lost her.

Chapter Twenty-Two

Molly: Stupid

It was about two weeks later when I went to see Bodhi—two weeks after Brooke's mother kicked me out.

When the guard led Bodhi into the visiting room, I swear I didn't recognize him. He looked like he'd gained about forty pounds, and almost all of it in his cheeks. The cheeks on his face, I mean.

I tried to think how long it had been since he got put in here, but I could only remember that it was the same night as I found Etta. But I had no idea how long ago that had been, and I couldn't wrap my brain around figuring it out, either. One part of my brain said maybe only a little handful of weeks but it didn't feel like that at all. It felt like something that happened years ago, like maybe in another lifetime or something.

Anyway, the point I'm trying to make, even though I'm doing a terrible job at it, is that I thought he couldn't possibly have been in jail long enough to gain so much weight, but there it was right in front of my eyes. I wondered if they had him on some kind of medication that made him blow up with water weight or if he was going through some other unexpected jail thing like that.

The fact that he wasn't thin as a whip made him seem less Bodhi-like to me, like something so basic had changed that I wasn't sure who he was anymore. Because never eating and constantly moving had been so much the heart of his Bodhi-ness, and I couldn't quite figure out who I had standing in front of me without that clue. It was like a guiding star, like the North Star that the sailors used to use to guide their ships, but after it suddenly winked out and stopped shining.

I guess jail changes a person, but that's only me guessing, because jail was the one terrible thing I'd managed to avoid so far.

Believe it or not, all this was going on in my brain between the time he walked through the door and the time he sat down at the table with me.

He gave me a frown, which also seemed weird, because Bodhi wasn't much of a frowner. It seemed like maybe I was witnessing the one time since I'd known him that everything didn't seem funny to him.

"Why did you run away from that lady's house?" he asked me. "And who took over our crate while you were back in Utah?"

I know it sounds weird to say, but the one obvious explanation for how he could know all that just really didn't occur to me at first, and I don't even know why not. It just didn't click into my brain. All I could think—or I guess really it was more like a feeling—was that he somehow had powers he shouldn't have, and had never had before. Maybe it was because it seemed like he'd changed so much.

"How do you *know* all that?" I asked him, and I think my eyes were wide. They felt really wide.

"That lady came around looking for you. Well, not looking for you here at the jail. She knew you weren't here. But she was looking for you and she came to ask me if I knew anything about where you'd gone. And this was a while ago now. Like, almost two weeks, I think. So all this time I've been worried about you."

"Sorry," I said.

Then I didn't say more because I couldn't think of what else to say.

"I can't think of her name, though. But you know who I mean."

"Brooke."

"Right. Brooke. Why did you run away from her? I think she really cares about you."

I snorted, and it came out through my nose, and it felt weird. I wanted to be really sure he knew I didn't believe what he'd just said, but somewhere deep down I really *wanted* to believe it, but I was trying to blow that wanting out of me, too, because I was tired of believing good things and then getting let down.

"She doesn't care about me," I said. "She just doesn't want to have to feel guilty."

"She wants to help get you into a foster home or something."

"Right, exactly. She wants to turn me back over to my social worker so they can put me in that awful home, or if I'm super lucky maybe another home, and then if it's someplace terrible again she won't have to worry or feel bad about it, because she will have washed her hands of me by then."

"I don't know," he said. "She seemed really worried. Maybe you should let her help."

We both just sat there for a minute, and I was trying to get used to the fact that these were all some pretty un-Bodhi-like things to say. In the old days he would have said Brooke was the establishment, and my social worker was the establishment, and we could get by just fine on our own without all their crap. He would've said, "Never go to people like that when they say they want to help you, because they have no idea what real help even looks like, and they'll only find a way to make it worse."

"You *want* me to go into a foster home?" I asked him.

I wanted to ask a lot more, like did they have him on some kind of drug, or was he getting some on his own in there, or was there some other reason why it seemed like he'd changed? But I didn't want to seem like I was criticizing him, so I just asked the one thing about the foster homes.

I was still thinking he'd be out pretty soon and then we'd go back to making our own way, just like we always had. It wasn't what you might call great, what we had, but we managed, and in some ways it was better than what I'd had since. At least with him nobody ever locked me into a closet or anything, and nobody ever got my hopes way up and then dropped me all the way down to rock bottom again. Every day was pretty much what I expected it would be, and there's something to be said for that.

"Might be worth a try," he said.

"But what about us? You'll be out soon, and—"

He didn't even let me finish the sentence. He jumped right in and said, "I'm going to Kentucky when I get out."

"Oh. Okay. Can I go to Kentucky, too?"

I could tell by the look on his face that the answer was no, but I didn't know why yet. But that was when the buzzing-and-tingling thing started, all through the bones and muscles in my arms and legs and then into my belly. I felt like I was falling down a well, and I mean I actually felt the falling in my body even though I was sitting on a chair.

I always figured at least I had Bodhi.

"Here's the thing about that," he said, and then he made me wait a really long time to hear what the thing about that was. Or it seemed like a long time, anyway. Then he raised his hands and spread them wide and did this sort of gesture with them, like he had just stepped onto a Broadway stage and was about to start singing a show tune. "I have a boyfriend!" he said, and his voice was energetic and came up to a high note at the end, and just in that second he seemed Bodhi-like again. "Isn't that just the best thing? For me, I mean. I realize it's not so great for you, but I hope you'll still be happy for me. I mean, we both knew this would happen sooner or later, right? One of us was bound to meet someone."

It had never in a million years occurred to me to think like that. Not that I thought neither one of us would ever meet anybody as long as we lived, but I thought we were friends and would keep being friends no matter what. I didn't know a new person would be the end of everything for Bodhi and me.

"You met him in here?" I asked.

"Yup. He got out yesterday and I might get out in three weeks even though that would be an early release, and then we're going. So that's why I felt so much better that you had this Brooke person. I really think you might be fine with Brooke. Give it another try."

I just sat a minute, still feeling like I was falling. Or maybe I was feeling it again—it was hard to tell the difference. I wasn't thinking about falling while he was talking, but if I'd been doing it that whole time, then that was one deep-ass well, let me tell you.

"What's in Kentucky?" I asked after a while.

"His uncle has a horse farm there and we can go work. And there are apartments over the barns. And the air is really clean and the grass is greener than anything you ever see in LA."

"Sounds nice," I said.

Then we just sat for a really long time. I mean, seriously, it might have been three or four whole minutes. We were mostly looking away from each other, like down at the table, and it was starting to get awkward.

"So where've you been sleeping for the last couple of weeks?"

I was so not thinking he was about to talk again, and so when he did I jumped out of my seat. Only a couple of inches, but I actually jumped, like enough that anybody could see it, and that was pretty embarrassing.

"Oh. That. I found a camp. There's like a whole big camp of homeless people between the freeway and the river. Well, you know, what they call the river but really it's just a big concrete trench. Some people have tents, but I don't have a tent, but there are some older ladies there and they sort of look after me, and one of them gave me a tarp. And I strung it up so it's sort of like a tent."

"You never told me who stole our spot."

"That old guy with the superlong beard who used to live on the other side of the hole in the freeway fence."

"Oh," he said. "Edward."

And that was a pretty Bodhi-like thing, too. We both lived in that neighborhood the same amount of time—or actually I was there a few days longer after he got arrested and went to jail—and he knew the names of all the other people who lived there and I just knew stuff like their beards and where they slept.

I didn't answer, because I was busy thinking about that, and how different it made us. Maybe we were always too different all along, and maybe I should have seen this coming.

I hadn't, though.

"You don't want his spot," he said.

"No. I don't. I don't know how he managed with all that noise and all those exhaust fumes, and anyway it's better at the camp. A couple of the older ladies look after me."

I know I'd said that already, but I said it again. I have no idea why.

"You should go see that Brooke lady. Tell her you're okay at least. See what she has in mind to help you."

"But once you let somebody get started helping you like that, you kind of get thrown into a situation, and then you just lose control of the whole thing. You know, because you're a kid and all. I learned that already." *I learned it from you,* I thought, but I didn't say that. "And then it can be a bad situation and you can't back out again. And that lady, she just wants to feel like she's a good person, but once they send me off she'll forget all about me. I tried to think once that she would actually care about me but I'm not getting let down again."

He raised one eyebrow, and that was also a very Bodhi thing to do. Which made me sad, because if the real Bodhi was here now, then I knew how much I would miss him when he was gone.

"I don't know," he said. "She came into a jail to find you. Twice. You know how much people hate to go into jails? If there's any chance she cares enough to help you, then I think you need to at least go see for sure."

"Maybe," I said. "Maybe I will." But it was making me sick to my stomach to think about it. "I need to go now," I said.

Which was a really stupid thing to say, because what did I want him to think? That I had an important appointment or something? But it was just too hard to be there with him, and that was what I was really trying to say.

I stood up and he stood up, and he looked really sad, so I stopped looking.

"We okay?" he asked.

"Sure," I said.

But we weren't, and he wasn't a stupid guy, so I'm sure he knew it.

"Come see me one more time before I go?"

"Yeah, okay."

But I didn't really mean it and I didn't plan to do it.

"Promise," he said.

It wasn't a question, like "Do you promise?" It was more like an order, like "I want you to make me that promise right now."

I sighed. Because now I would have to do it.

But maybe I had to anyway, I don't know, because after all it was Bodhi, and even though we were coming apart now, we had a lot of friend history from while we were together.

"Fine," I said. "I'll come one more time. I promise."

But I still wasn't sure. On the one hand, it wasn't like me to promise a thing if I wasn't sure I was going to do it. But then this other part of me was like, *Everybody lets everybody down, so why can't I?*

It was changing me, getting let down so much.

—

After I left the jail I made a really stupid decision, and I mean stupid even for me. I decided I would go out to Brooke's mother's house and give Brooke one more chance to care about me for real.

It was stupid for a couple of reasons, one on top of the other. First of all, getting from the jail to West LA was not a simple thing. People who go everywhere in cars just have no idea how hard a thing like that can be. I couldn't just sit down in a nice bucket seat and turn a key, or press a button with a smart key in my pocket. I couldn't just shift into drive and fly all over the place at sixty miles an hour.

First I had to panhandle to get money for the bus, and it took me the whole rest of the morning, because people just brushed by me and wouldn't listen.

I was on the boulevard, a few blocks down from where I used to walk around looking for bottles and cans, and there were some office buildings there, so there were plenty of people on the street. And I was trying to tell them that I was stranded here and I needed to get all the way to West LA on the bus before I could be okay, but most of them had already made up their minds not to listen to me. I guess I'd gotten pretty dirty again, and even though I still had the hairbrush and I'd used it that morning, I think my new jeans and sweatshirt looked pretty bad. Anyway, my point is, they knew before I even opened my mouth that I was on the street, so they knew it was about money and they didn't want to hear a word of it.

It took me two hours to raise ninety-five cents. I knew it was two hours because I was standing in front of an office building with big, high windows and a clock in the lobby. And then a youngish guy in a nice suit came out and actually listened to me, and opened his wallet and gave me a five-dollar bill.

I thanked him a lot, and my eyes kind of stuck on him after he walked away, and I couldn't stop watching him go, because that doesn't happen every day—you know, finding somebody who wants to be help-ful and nice. But anyway, he was already mostly gone, so there was no point just standing there staring.

So then I could do the second stupid part, which was riding all those buses all over the city, and getting all those transfers, and getting on the wrong bus and getting lost once.

Except, the whole time I was riding there I was thinking those hadn't been the stupid parts at all. I figured the real stupid part was thinking maybe I'd find something good there, at Brooke's mother's house.

Then I had to get off the bus about a mile from where they lived, and walk the rest of the way. It was late afternoon by then, and I was thinking I'd spent most of a whole day on this, and that what she had to say had better be good.

But then when I saw the house I got scared and almost didn't go up to it, because I knew if I knocked on the door her mother might answer. I really never wanted to see her mother again after all the things she said to me that morning when she threw me out. She was not a nice lady, and that's putting it mildly. But I'd come so far to get there, so I just stood on the sidewalk on their block and thought about it.

I decided she wasn't really that much worse than everybody else, because even though she'd said some very bad things about me because I lived on the street, I knew everybody else felt the same way but didn't say it. I could see it in their eyes anyway so what's the difference?

So I walked up to the house and I knocked, and while I was waiting for somebody to answer I was thinking, *Please let it be Brooke,* over and over and over in my head.

Brooke's terrible mother answered the door.

She had this look on her face when the door first swung open, like she was okay with whoever was knocking, but then she saw me and that look disappeared. And then she looked like she'd just taken the lid off the trash can and gotten a whiff of some fish that had been in there a few days.

"I thought I'd made myself perfectly clear," she said.

"I just want to talk to Brooke. We can go talk someplace else, okay? I just need you to tell her I'm here."

She said something I wasn't expecting at all. I mean, I really never once saw this thing coming.

She said, "Brooke doesn't live here anymore."

"Oh," I said. And right away I felt really tired because now I would have to go look for her someplace else, and that was just so much work. "Where does she live now?"

"I'm sure I wouldn't know," she said.

I thought it was a very strange way to say a thing, and, also, I didn't really believe her.

"I know you know," I said, and it was a little bit like standing up to her, so it made my heart thump really hard in my chest and in my ears.

"I really, honestly do not know where Brooke is. Apparently I'm such a terrible person that I don't deserve to know. Apparently Brooke and my granddaughter want nothing to do with me ever again. Now if you'll excuse me . . ."

But she never finished the sentence. She just slammed the door in my face. Or maybe she finished the sentence by slamming the door in my face. It's one of those things that I guess depends on how you look at it.

And then I had to start all over to get back to where I'd been staying. The walking and then the panhandling and then all the buses, because my stuff was there, and I actually had a little bit of stuff now, and it was too much to walk away from. And anyway it was mostly all from Brooke and that made me not want to walk away from it, even though I would've denied that if somebody tried to make me say it out loud.

And besides, those ladies looked after me. I wanted to tell them how stupid I'd been to try to go all the way out there to West LA like maybe somebody in that house really cared about me.

I was hoping maybe they could teach me to be smarter next time.

———

Phyllis was there waiting for me when I got back. Usually she went to sleep early, so that's how I knew she was waiting up for me. I don't know what time it was, but it took me forever to get home, so more or less the middle of the night.

Other than Phyllis there were just a few middle-aged guys standing around a trash can with a fire in it, just like you see in movies with homeless people or hoboes. I think that's what you call a cliché, but it's also what was happening. Everybody else had gone to sleep.

Phyllis was something like the queen of that place. Or maybe "queen" is the wrong word. Maybe she was almost more like an elder, except I know you're not supposed to borrow words like that because they belong to Native Americans and I try not to be disrespectful. Just, right now I can't think of a better word.

"Where you been?" she asked me.

I couldn't really see her face in the dark, but then this big web of lightning lit up the sky and then I saw her, and she didn't look mad. So I relaxed some. A big wind was coming up, and you could feel the energy of a storm. It was one of those nights that's a really good time to have four walls and a door to close.

She had a couple of teeth missing and the ones she had didn't look so good, but otherwise she kept herself clean and looked pretty okay. I think she was older than sixty.

"I went to see Bodhi," I said.

"All day?"

"And then I went to see that lady I was telling you about. To see if she actually cares anything about me."

"And does she?"

"I don't know. She moved away and even her mother doesn't know where she is."

"Oh. Well, I guess that's that, then."

"Yeah, I guess so."

Just then the thunderclap caught up from that big thing of lightning. That was a pretty long time later, which meant it was far away, which was fine with me.

I sat down just inside her real tent. It had the flap end propped up so you could see the concrete river and the storm blowing our way. The river had some water starting to flow. I could barely see it but I could hear it, so it must have been raining pretty good, you know, farther upstream.

Phyllis was sitting cross-legged with her hands on her knees, palms up, which made it look like she was meditating or something.

"I saved you a can of soup," she said.

"Where did we get cans of soup?"

"Willie brought a couple dozen."

"Did he steal them?"

I was trying to decide if I could eat them if they were stolen.

"I don't think so. The cans are dented and they've got no labels. So I don't think they can sell them in that shape."

"So they were giving them away to him?"

She snorted in a way that sounded half like laughing. "They don't give nothing away to us or anybody else," she said. "They throw it all in the dumpster and Willie goes diving."

"Got it," I said. "I'd like some soup. Thanks for saving it. What kind of soup is it?"

"Surprise soup," she said. "Because it's got no labels."

She pulled a can out of the pocket of her sweater and started open-ing it with this really vicious-looking can opener. It didn't have a little wheel. It had something more like a hooked blade that kept scooping in and tearing the tin of the lid. I'd actually seen it before but I swear I thought it was for self-defense.

She carried the open can over to the guys by the fire, and they heated it up for me by holding it out over the flames with this thing that looked like a wire hanger twisted into a long handle.

While they were heating it up she came back and sat with me.

"Thing is," I said, "now I'll always wonder."

"No, you'll know when they bring the can back what kind it is."

I laughed, and it felt good to laugh about something. "No, not that. I meant I'll always wonder if that Brooke lady cared about me at all."

We watched the dark clouds roll in for a minute, looking kind of scary. A good storm always looks safer and better through a double-pane window.

"Maybe she *wants* to care about you," she said.

"Yeah. Maybe. That's kind of how it seemed when I was with her."

"People like that don't mean no harm, hon. There's just so many of us, and they each figure there's only one of them. They get over-whelmed. Don't take it personal."

"I don't," I said.

But I kind of had, until she said that.

Then I saw the guy who was warming up my soup pull the can back in and touch the sides of it real carefully, and then he waved to me.

"You run and get that," Phyllis said. "We'll talk more in the morn-ing if you like."

I took the soup from the man, and he gave me a rag to hold it with because it was hot. I told him thanks, and he had a hat on, and he tipped it to me. It made me feel like I was in a really old movie or something, but also it was nice.

"Mind the edges," he said, because the can was raggedy where the top had come off, and it's not like we had spoons.

I sat on the dirt under my tarp, and the rain just let go. Just all at once like that. Like somebody opened a trapdoor in the sky and all this water fell at the same time.

My tarp tent didn't have a bottom to it, so right away the mud started to flow, so I squatted on my sneakers and let it roll right under me. I drank the soup and it was really hot, and even though it was only vegetable, it was good.

I squatted there and sipped at it and watched the lightning and listened to the thunder, and when the lightning lit up the world, I could see how much water was flowing down the river, and it was scary because there was so much.

I didn't sleep that night, but I was grateful, because the world looked beautiful in that big storm, and because I knew that somewhere in the world there was somebody who didn't have a can of hot soup, and I did.

You'd think I'd be feeling sorry for myself, but somehow that just wasn't the kind of night it was and I couldn't even tell you why.

Chapter Twenty-Three

Brooke: Where Molly?

Etta and I had moved, quite temporarily, to the home of that friend I'd been telling Molly about. Caroline. And the irony just drips off this next piece of information: our accommodations were in Caroline's garage. At least it had access to a close bathroom, just off the laundry room on the other side of the kitchen door. But it was still hard to avoid the feeling that the universe was having a laugh at my expense.

Caroline stuck her head in through the door into the garage. From the kitchen.

"You're back," she said.

"I am."

"Did you find her?"

"No."

She sighed. Then she came in and sat on the cot next to me. She reached for Etta, and I let Etta go to her. She bounced the baby on her lap as she stared at me. I sensed a lecture coming. I'm not sure how I was able to sense that. She had never lectured me before.

"I think it might be time to give up looking for her. It's like a needle in a haystack in this massive city. Shouldn't you be looking for an apartment instead?"

I took it as a shot to the gut. Like someone had slammed a rifle butt into my midsection. Well. Not someone. Caroline.

I had found an apartment that morning. I had no idea how to afford it, but I had it. Meanwhile I hadn't known I was wearing out my welcome so fast.

"I found one," I said. "This morning. Before I ever started looking for Molly."

Etta interrupted. "Where Molly?" she asked. Insistently. Piercingly. She'd been asking it a lot lately. I was no closer to an answer for her.

"I'm sorry, honey," I told my little girl, "but I don't know right now. But I'm still trying." Then, to Caroline, "I can move in next week. The first is next week. But if it's really a problem having us here, I understand. We can go to a motel for these last few days."

We didn't really have the money for a motel. But we didn't really have the money for any of the things I had planned. It was all a matter of sinking deeper and deeper into debt.

Still, if we weren't wanted . . .

"Oh, no, honey," she said. "Brooke, I'm sorry. I didn't mean it like that. I just want to see you get your life back together."

"I'm working on it," I said.

"Well, I should say so!"

I thought we'd leave it at that. Even though what she'd just said didn't feel entirely true. She wanted me to get my life together, but she also wanted her garage back. So she meant it in a number of different ways. At least, that's what my gut was telling me. She just didn't want me to take it badly. She didn't want my reaction to her subtext to come up for discussion. She didn't want to have to feel bad because of what she really meant. Which was just human, I guess, but it still hurt a little.

She'd just come from the hair salon, and her hair was shockingly short. Stylish, but short. She could pull it off. I couldn't have. But it reminded me of Grace Beatty. It made me think maybe I should call

Grace or drop in to see her. Maybe she could be some help in my search for Molly. Probably not, actually. But it couldn't hurt to ask.

Meanwhile I wasn't keeping up my end of the conversation with Caroline. So she plunged back in.

"What kind of job did you get?"

"Nothing very good. Just retail sales like last time. Standing on my feet all day in a department store. Making sure no one takes more than three items into the changing room. Mundane stuff."

"Still, though. It's still good. I mean, you start your new job on Monday, and you can move into your own place on the first. Sounds like you're all set."

"But I'm not, Caroline. I'm not set at all. Because the job will cover rent and food and gas but it won't cover childcare. Why do you think I'm trying so hard to figure out where Molly is? If I have to take Etta back to day care—and I *will* have to, if I want to actually show up at this job—then I'll fall into a pit of debt, and in just a couple of months it will bury me."

"Maybe you could get some more from your mother," she said.

It was a reference to an envelope that had turned up in her foyer. Slid under her front door. It was a note from my mother, saying something to the effect that her granddaughter needed to eat. With a check enclosed.

I guess Caroline had no idea how bad I'd felt about taking that money. I felt like accepting it from my mom should have come with forgiving her, but I couldn't forgive her, so I felt like I shouldn't have taken it. But it was my first and last months' rent, and security deposit. I had no idea how to get by without it. So I'd pushed my feelings of guilt down into a sort of indigestion in my gut. And I'd cashed the check. But I sure as hell wasn't going back to her and asking for more, then walking away and offering nothing in return. Not even a softening of my feelings.

I had reached the end of my patience with Caroline, even though I recognized her good intentions. I have a sore spot—I'm not big on people who want to wrap up all your problems neatly with their simple suggestions. How do people like that think anything became a problem in the first place if its solution was so simple?

Why can't people just listen and then say something like "Yeah, that's hard" in response? Why do they have to try to fix you before they can walk away?

I wanted to ask Caroline, "And then after those first couple of months, what? Go beg off her again? And then again? The idea was to stop leaning on her."

But Etta and I were guests in her home. And it was kind of her to let us stay. So I said nothing.

"Besides," Caroline added, "it's not really fair to ask this Molly to babysit."

"Where Molly?" Etta asked.

"She adores Etta," I said to Caroline. Shamefully ignoring the actual Etta.

"But she'd need to go to school."

It's not as though I hadn't thought of that.

"I was thinking I could use evenings to help her study for her GED."

"A GED is not as good as a high school diploma."

"Well . . . it's almost as good. It's a hell of a lot better than what she's doing now."

"Well, anyway," she said, "she's gone. So you'll just have to make your plans without her."

"Etta and I are going to relax and have a little playtime," I said. "I hope you don't mind. It's been a long day. We'll be out of your hair soon."

"No problem. Don't worry." She handed the baby back to me. Etta looked relieved. She might have had her doubts about the conversation, too. "Sounds like you have everything pretty well worked out."

Which was a stunningly out-of-touch statement after what I'd just told her. But I tried to just stick with the idea that she saw me as fixed because she wanted that for me.

I didn't challenge it. I just let her walk away.

I only responded within myself, by vowing never to live in anybody else's house again.

I was a grown woman. I had to get my life into my own hands. Possibly for the first time ever.

—

In the morning I went to see that odd boy again. In prison. For what I figured would be the last time.

I didn't really believe it would be helpful. But I was running out of time. By Monday I would be working all day. And my actual physical search for Molly—which mostly entailed talking to homeless people who might have seen her—had been a fool's errand anyway.

I had to take one last shot.

When an armed guard walked Denver Patterson into the visiting room, I almost thought he'd brought me the wrong guy. He looked so different. His cheeks were full and soft. He wasn't as thin and agile as a whippet anymore. His eyes looked calm and not particularly searching. He no longer seemed interested in conquering the world.

"Oh," he said, and sat down across from me at the table. "You. I guess Molly was wrong about you."

He reached out to Etta. In a lazy way. She was sitting on my lap, and he just extended a finger and waved it up and down. She smiled and grabbed at it.

"Where Molly?" Etta asked.

I had no attention to spare, so I held her closer as a substitute for answering her.

"Wrong about me? About what? What did she say about me? You've seen her since last time I was here?"

"Yeah. She came in once."

"Did she say where she was living?"

"More or less. But not in a whole lot of detail. She just said it was between the freeway and the river that's not really a river. You know. They call it the LA River, but it's usually just a dry concrete . . . what do you call that? Like a spillway."

He wiped his nose on the back of his hand. Or scratched it. I'm not sure which. The movement seemed oddly slow. Like I was watching a sloth move its limbs. I wondered if the prison people had him sedated. Or if he'd found a way to do it on his own.

"That might help," I said.

"Well, good luck with that. Because there are quite a few miles of river. And quite a few miles of freeway."

I felt all the air come out of me. I felt like a punctured tire.

He was right. She had disappeared into the fabric of the city. I was a fool to think I'd ever see her again.

Etta noticed the drop in my mood and fidgeted on my lap. Just on the edge of crying. I held her even more closely in the hope I could prevent it.

"So what did she say about me?" I asked.

I figured it would hurt. But I still needed to know.

"Say about you?" He asked it almost sleepily. As if he'd dozed off for a second. Forgotten we were talking.

"You said she was wrong about me. Wrong about what?"

"Oh. That. Yeah. She said you don't really care about her. You just don't want to feel guilty."

I was right. It hurt.

He must have seen that on my face, because he rushed to soften the message.

"I mean, she didn't say it like you were a bad person or anything. I think she figures you *want* to care about her, but your caring only goes just so far. You know? Like you'll get her back in foster care and then walk away and figure she'll be fine. But maybe she won't be, but you'll be out of the picture by then. I hope you know what I mean."

I sighed. For a minute I didn't answer.

I not only knew what he meant—and what Molly had meant—but she wasn't far enough from wrong. The last night she'd seen me, I wasn't utterly far from the place of caring he had described. Not far enough for my tastes, anyway.

"So how will you meet up with her when you get out?" I asked.

Because, despite what they both thought about me, I really, honestly cared about Molly's welfare by that time. Maybe it had been a surprise to me, too. I just knew I was utterly haunted by not knowing where she was. By not knowing if she would be okay. By not being able to help her be okay.

I had promised I'd help her be okay.

"I won't," he said.

I couldn't help noticing that he averted his eyes on that conversational note. A dose of shame, from the look of it.

"What do you mean you won't?"

"I'm going to Kentucky when I get out."

"And she's not free to come along?"

"Well, I can't really bring her." For an uncomfortable length of time, he didn't say why not. Then he leaned over the table. Almost conspiratorially. "It's a relationship thing," he said in a soft voice. As though he'd just told me a secret.

"You're abandoning her for a relationship?"

It came out sharp. And accusing.

He sat back hard in his chair. I'd probably had no right to say it to him. How many friendships had I let drop when I'd married David? Then again, that hadn't left any of those friends out on the street alone.

"You're a fine one to talk!" he shot back.

"*Me?* What did *I* do?"

"Your mother threw her out of the garage."

"Well, I'm not my mother. And I've put my mother out of my life over that. And I'm trying to find Molly so I can make it up to her."

Etta, who was quite sensitive to disagreements, notably did not ask "Where Molly?" at the mention of that familiar name. She had fallen into her Quiet Girl mode.

His anger seemed to abandon him. And that abandonment left him noticeably deflated. He rubbed his eyes in a manner that hid them from my view. He was no longer sitting across the table from a person who had treated Molly as selfishly as he had. I could see the effect that was having on his mood.

"We both knew it would happen," he said. His voice sounded mouse-tiny. He did not uncover his eyes. He had a conscience regarding the situation. He just wasn't about to let it get in his way. "I mean, one of us was bound to meet someone."

"And you think she knew that would be the end of your friendship?"

"She must've known," he said.

He dropped the hand that had been rubbing his eyes. There's only just so long you can pretend you need to rub your eyes. He kept his gaze averted. Looked down at the table.

"It just happened," he said. "I didn't know I was about to meet someone. Especially not in *here*. It was a total surprise. These things just happen."

"A second ago you told me it was always inevitable and you both knew to expect it."

"This is getting us nowhere," he said.

I had to agree. But I agreed silently.

I rummaged around in my purse. Etta tried to help me. I tried to avoid her help. Tried to keep the purse out of her reach without being unkind. Otherwise I'd never find what I was looking for.

I had nothing to write on, so I tore a deposit slip out of my check-book. Then I tore off the account number, because I didn't want him to have it. I dug for a pen. Found only a pencil instead.

I wrote down the address at Caroline's. Then the address of my new apartment. I carefully noted that the apartment address was only good after the first of the month. Which was coming up fast.

"In case you see her again," I said.

And I slid it across the table to him.

He picked it up and stared at it for a long time. Like it might say any number of things. Like it was full of complex messages he needed time to decipher.

"Think you'll see her again?" I asked.

"Not sure."

His voice sounded cool. Calm and emotionally detached. I had made an enemy of him with my words. Put him on the defensive. Now I was unsure that I could count on him even to do this simple favor for Molly. Because it was also a favor for me.

"I tried to get her to promise she'd come see me one more time," he added.

"But she wouldn't promise?"

"No. She did."

"But you have a reason to think she'll break that promise?"

"Just something about the way she said it."

"I don't know her as well as you do. But she doesn't seem like the sort of person who promises something if she has no intention of doing it."

His eyes came up to mine. For the first time in a very long time. Maybe even the first time for that visit. They drilled into me. It made me distinctly ill at ease.

"Thing is," he said, "there's only just so many times people can break their promises to you before you start figuring everybody does it."

That just sat on the table between us for a long time. Neither one of us seemed to want to touch it.

"Well, anyway," I said. "If you do see her, please give her a message for me. Please tell her I need her."

His eyes flickered up to mine again. Differently this time. As if he were chasing something that had recently eluded him.

"Wait," he said. "Let me get this straight."

"It's a pretty simple message."

"I'm trying to be sure I know who the 'I' is, and who the 'her' is. So if I see her, you want me to say, 'Brooke says she needs you.'"

"Yes. Exactly."

"Need her how?"

"Just send her to one of those two addresses," I said. "Depending on the date. And I'll work that out with her directly."

Then I caught the guard's eye, and nodded. And he nodded back. And he let me out.

I figured I'd never see Denver Patterson again. And that was more than fine with me.

It was whether I'd ever see Molly again that concerned me. And I was no closer to an answer regarding that question. And Etta would ask again. And again. And again.

"Where Molly?"

I had no idea how long it would take her to forget to ask. I had no idea what to tell her.

———

I dropped Etta off at her day care, knowing it would cost me. Knowing I was falling more deeply into debt. It seemed to be a spiral with no end.

It was only an hour or two after going to see that boy in jail. I had to check out what he'd told me. I had to see how many people had set up camp between a piece of freeway and a piece of the LA River.

I couldn't free myself from the feeling of having to try.

I had no map, and my car was too old and cheap to come equipped with navigation. So I just drove to a part of the city that I knew for a fact had the concrete river running through it.

I pulled over and stopped on the shoulder, despite knowing it was blatantly illegal to do so. I put on my flashers. That way, in case a cop came by, it might give the impression that it was an emergency stop.

With the wind and the din of cars racing behind me, I stared down at the "river," running my eyes along its length until it faded to a pinpoint in the gray distance. It was still flowing with the last runoff of water from the recent rain. It went on forever. Or anyway, it seemed to.

The freeway didn't parallel it everywhere, but off in the distance there were other freeways. Some ran at an angle to its concrete banks, crossing over it as overpasses. So many freeways. So much river.

I breathed out a long breath that I guess I hadn't known I'd been holding.

I wasn't down there. So I had no idea how much room there would be in these various places for homeless encampments.

I would *go* down there.

But I knew now, in my gut, that it wouldn't do much good. Even armed with my new information, this strip of city was still one large haystack. And Molly was still one small needle.

———

The first place I stopped seemed to have people living directly under the freeway. And, oddly, it had something like an entrance. Stacks and stacks of pallets and wooden crates had been used to build a sort of wall around the camp. There seemed to be only one opening. Only one way in.

Beside that opening sat a man in his forties, his back inside a small, open tent. He smoked lazily, his eyes closed. The hazy sun burned down onto his bald scalp, which appeared sunburned.

He seemed to be something like a guard at the gate, though that might have been an accidental effect. It made me think of the mirror opposite of Saint Peter. Tending the gate to a place where, in this iteration, nobody wanted to go.

"Excuse me," I said.

He opened his eyes. Fixed me with a gaze that was not aggressive. It was also not curious. Looking back, I'm not sure it was much of anything. He just noticed me there, standing over him. And seemed to accept it.

"I'm looking for a girl. Teenage girl. Reddish hair. Well, if it's clean, it looks reddish. Sixteen. Goes by Molly."

He squinted his eyes at me. It might have indicated something about his opinion of me and my question. It might have been that the sun was at my back.

"You a reporter?" he asked.

His voice sounded surprisingly high and clear. Like the voice of a boy in a choir.

"No. I'm not a reporter. Why would I be a reporter?"

He shrugged. He still seemed only half-interested in my presence.

"No idea," he said. "But whenever somebody like you comes around here asking questions, it turns out they're a reporter."

"No. Not me. I just know this girl. And I'm trying to find her."

"To give her a better life," he said.

It struck me as an odd thing to say.

"Well . . . yes."

"So same general idea as a reporter."

"If you don't mind," I said, "I realize you don't owe me anything, including information. But if you could just tell me if there's a girl that age here . . ."

"Nope," he said.

"Nope there's no girl here, or nope you won't tell me?"

"Little of both," he said.

"Can I just go in and look around?"

"I wouldn't. Everybody who's here now is still trying to sleep."

I glanced at my watch, vaguely wishing I hadn't worn it. It had been a college graduation present from my mother. It had been expensive.

"It's after eleven in the morning," I said.

He shrugged again. "Don't know what to tell you."

I started to walk in. Look around for myself. Despite a cold hammering of fear all through my chest and gut.

He stopped me with words.

"She's not here," he said. "Youngest people here are like twenty, but anyway, we're all boys. But for a dollar I'll show you where the really big camp is."

I dug a dollar out of my pants pocket. I was careful to make it seem like the only bill I had in there. I had purposely left my purse locked in the trunk. Because once I came down here and made it clear I had a little money, what was to stop someone from taking it all?

"That's the ticket," he said, and took the money from me.

He picked up a stick. I thought it was a bad sign, despite its being a fairly small stick. But I was wrong. It was just a writing tool for him.

He proceeded to use it to draw me a map in the gravelly dirt.

———

When I'd parked again and walked to the big camp, I saw it was more of a sprawl. A miniature city. It had no makeshift walls like the last city. It just spread itself out from underneath the freeway, through the vacant lots that sloped down to the concrete bed of the river.

Here, it seemed everybody was awake.

An old man was hanging hand-washed clothes on a rope strung between two long sticks he'd managed to embed in the hard ground. A younger man had a fire going in a pit and looked as though he was trying to make coffee.

A woman walked across my path. Then she stopped suddenly. Her eyes flew wide at the sight of me, as if she had seen a ghost. But, if so, the ghost was me.

"Phyllis!" she shouted. As though calling to somebody. Not as though she thought that was my name.

Then she ran away.

A woman came rolling out of her tent, sighed, and struggled to her feet. She located me with a sweep of her eyes, then moved in my direction with slow but sure steps. She looked to be about sixty, or maybe in her fifties but worn down. She was wearing a sweat suit in an alarming shade of pink.

She walked right up to me. And I mean right up. Way into my personal space. I could smell her breath. When she opened her mouth to speak, I could see she was missing two front teeth. The rest, the ones she still had, didn't look any too good.

"Cop?" she asked.

"No, ma'am," I said.

Which was interesting. The "ma'am" part, I mean. She commanded respect. I gave it without thought or question.

"Reporter?"

"I'm getting asked that a lot today."

"Which is a yes or a no?"

"No. Not a reporter."

"Looking for somebody in particular?"

"Yeah. A girl named Molly."

"She's not here."

Then she turned to walk away.

"Wait," I called to her retreating back. "What if she *was* here? Would you tell me?"

She didn't stop or turn. Just shot a single word back over her shoulder to me.

"No."

Something broke in me. I shouted. Literally shouted. My frustration boiled over and everything just came flying out.

"Wait!"

She stopped. Turned to face me. She did not move closer. Just waited. Waited to see what else I was inclined to shout about, I suppose.

"I don't understand this!" I called to her across the considerable distance. In my peripheral vision I saw at least two dozen people staring at me. "Why would you not help me? Why would anybody not tell me where Molly is if they know? I just want to help her. I'm just trying to help!"

Then I stood, silent. Feeling foolish. And she stood still, just waiting. Maybe waiting to be certain I had it all out of my system.

"Sure," she said after a pause. "Everybody wants to help. People come down here from time to time, wanting to help. Problem is, they never do help. They're just never any help. Look. Lady. When someone disappears into this city, they're gone. If we wanted to find the people we left behind, we would. Give it up, okay?"

Then she turned away again. Marched back to her tent.

I got into my car and drove away.

—

I showed up at the police station at seven o'clock the following morning. I was hoping I could time my visit just so. I was hoping Grace Beatty would be just about to go off duty.

As I walked up to her desk, she was standing. Not on the phone. Not with anyone. Just standing there, looking down. Riffling through some paperwork. It did give the impression that she might have been on her way out.

She looked up at me, and her eyes changed. Reflected her recognition of me. And it was a good change. A good recognition. I breathed a sigh of relief. I hadn't been sure. I might have been nothing but a thorn in her side all along. How was I to know?

"Hey, you," she said.

I said, "Hi."

But it felt weird. And difficult. I was suddenly overcome with emotion. Maybe it was being back there. Maybe I was reliving the worst night of my life just by stepping into that place. Or maybe I really did care about what I'd come to say.

"Where's your little one?"

"I dropped her at day care. I didn't want her to be here when I talked to you about Molly. She understands a lot. And she's pretty upset about Molly being gone."

Grace Beatty just stood a moment. Her eyes remained on my face, but not looking into my eyes directly. She seemed to be waiting. To see if I was done. It reminded me of Phyllis at the homeless camp. All these people just standing there. Staring at me. Waiting to see if I was done. I didn't know exactly what it meant, but I took it as a comment on my current emotional state. A lot of explosive stuff seemed to need to get out of me. People seemed inclined to stay out of the way.

"Well," she said, and paused. "I'm off shift now. Want to go get a bite?"

"Sure. But maybe not at that same place."

We walked out the front door of the station together. Down the steps. Into the cool morning.

"Food not so good?" she asked as we walked.

"No, it's not that. It was fine. Or . . . actually . . . I don't really know how it was. I was so upset I couldn't taste anything. It was probably fine.

I'm just not doing well with all the memories from that twenty-four hours."

"Got it," she said.

We walked in silence for a time. Then she stopped in front of a little storefront tavern. Which, to my surprise, seemed to be open and serving drinks at that odd hour.

"Want to knock back a few?" she asked me. One of her eyebrows arched up. It made her face look mischievous.

"It's seven o'clock in the morning."

"Seven o'clock in the morning is my version of after hours. But if it doesn't work for you, no problem. I understand."

"I have to pick Etta up at day care soon," I said. "But I could knock back one."

———

We sat at the bar together. I was staring at the image of the two of us in the mirror. Running my hand over the cold wetness of my beer bottle. Noting how confident she looked. And how lost I looked. Wondering why everybody seemed to have this life thing down to a science except me.

"I made such a mess of everything," I said to her. Breaking a long silence.

"In what way?" She ran one hand back along her closely cropped hair as she spoke. As though it needed smoothing down.

"With Molly."

"Oh. Right. That."

"I owe her *so much*. I mean, think how different my world might be right now if she hadn't been there for me that night. And then I went and let her down. I made her a promise, Grace."

"When did you make her any promises?"

"Oh," I said. "That's right. You don't know."

So I gently unraveled the story. Brought her up to date. The trip back to Utah. Waking in the morning to find my mother had put her off the property. My efforts to locate her since.

Then I fell into silence, wondering if I had just put myself in any legal jeopardy. If I knew where this runaway teen was, which at one time I did, had it been my job to report it? Tell her social worker? I had no idea.

I waited, my heart thumping.

She ran her hand over her hair again. Let out a deep sigh.

"I think you're being too hard on yourself," she said.

I felt myself relax some. My heart slowed to a more normal pace.

"I don't think I am. I think I let her down."

"Well, I'm not saying there's no way you could have handled it that would have been better. But you're human, Brooke. You were trying, anyway. You met her at the worst time of your life. Your emotions were going every direction at once."

"And after that?"

"After that, you had your baby daughter to think about. It's counter-intuitive to throw open your door for a relative stranger off the street."

"I would have thrown my door open for her," I said. "After I knew her a little. Problem was, I didn't have a door. I only had somebody else's door. It helps to have a door of your own."

She smiled. But it was a sad-looking thing.

"If you came here to be absolved, you got it," she said. "You meant her no harm."

"Actually . . . I was hoping you might be some help in finding her."

She shook her head. Without pause.

"Not really. She's not wanted for any crime. If she were a younger child, she'd be seen as a danger to herself, and then the police could get involved. But she's sixteen. Old enough to be an emancipated minor. But . . . more to the point . . . we don't know where she is, either, Brooke. I mean, we find people based on things like credit card trails.

You know. Living-on-the-grid kinds of things. The best I can really do here is let you know if she gets arrested."

"She won't get arrested."

"What makes you say that?"

I took a sip of my beer before answering. I had said it so quickly. And so glibly. Now I had to decide how much I should stand behind what I'd said.

"She's just a basically honest person."

"Yeah. I get that. But need does things to a person. Makes them do things they never thought they would do."

I drank my beer for a long time in silence. I was trying to decide if she was right. And if I wanted her to be.

I never could decide.

———

Two days later, on the last day I could before starting my new job, I strapped Etta into her car seat and took another trip to the jail. To make a liar of myself by seeing that Denver Patterson boy one more time. Because I had to know if Molly had gotten my message.

The only person behind the desk was the woman with the braided hair. She knew who I was. She knew who I'd come to see.

"He's gone," she said.

"Gone?"

I felt as though she'd wakened me out of sleep. I couldn't seem to put a meaning to her simple words.

"Released."

"Oh," I said. "Released. Off to Kentucky."

"Yep. Off to Kentucky."

She rolled her eyes in a way that seemed to indicate she had heard about the Kentucky plans far too many times for her liking.

It struck me then. That I would never know.

Etta fussed on my shoulder, feeling the change in my mood.

I turned to walk out. But I stopped again. I couldn't leave it alone. I had to know.

"Did he get another visit from his friend before he got out? That girl?"

"I'm sorry to have to say . . . ," she began.

And, in her pause, I thought she was telling me Molly had not come. And I wondered how many times I'd have to hit the **END** sign on this dead-end street before I got it. Before I gave up and went home, both literally and figuratively.

But the finish to the sentence was not what I expected.

". . . I'm not allowed to give out that information."

"Got it," I said. "So I'll just never know."

"Never know what?"

"I gave him my address to give to her. But now I'll never know if she got it."

"Sorry," she said.

"It's okay. You're just doing your job."

Then I went home. Both literally and figuratively.

———

I was walking down the hallway of my new apartment building when Etta started in on me about Molly again.

"Molly, Molly, Molly," she chanted.

I realized it was time to stop avoiding the issue and tell her the damn truth.

"Listen," I said. Gently. "There's something I need to tell you."

I stopped in the hallway. We stood in a spill of light from a window in the little nook between our new apartment and the one next door. It lit Etta up from behind like a halo. Made her look like the chosen one. Like pure light.

"Etta, I have to be honest with you about Molly. She's gone. And I don't know how to find her for you. And I don't know how to find her for me. I just don't know where she is and there's really no way to find out. And I'm sorry. But the truth is, I don't think we're going to see Molly again."

"Molly," she said.

And, this time, she pointed.

I spun around.

There she was at the end of the hall, leaning one shoulder against the flowered wallpaper. Just watching me. As though she might decide to stay or she might decide to run.

"Molly," I said. It came out breathy. As though I were noting a thing beyond belief.

"What do you *mean* you need me? What does that even *mean*? You need me *how?*"

I felt a little tug at the corners of my mouth. Upward. And it had been a while, I can say that for a fact.

"Why don't you come in?" I asked her. "And I'll tell you all about it."

Instead she took a step backward.

"Why should I come in? I mean . . . what's in it for me?"

Her voice had moved into full-on defense mode. If she could have donned a suit of armor, I think she might have felt better. And I'm pretty sure she would have done it.

"Well . . . are you hungry? I could order pizza."

At first, nothing.

Then, in a quiet voice, she asked, "What kind of pizza?"

"What kind of pizza do you like?"

"Anything but pineapple," she said. And, much to my relief, she took a step in my direction. "Or anchovies," she added.

Chapter Twenty-Four

Molly: Crazy like Family

I wasn't really liking how the talking was going and I wasn't really feeling like she cared about me the way I wanted her to, but I was really liking the pepperoni pizza and I think that's why I stayed.

We were sitting on the floor because nothing was really set up to be an apartment that somebody lived in yet—just more like a big pile of boxes. There was a couch, but it was covered in more piles of boxes, and it felt like too much trouble to fix that. So we were sitting cross-legged on the carpet, and I was thinking about carpet in general, and how amazing a thing it is when you're used to concrete and dirt. Funny how you can take a thing like carpet for granted if you've always had it and you figure you always will.

The baby was chewing on a piece of crust that she was holding really tight in her amazingly tiny, wonderful little fist. She was so beautiful and sweet that I almost wanted to say yes to what Brooke had asked me—the whole babysitting for free because she couldn't afford day care thing—even though that plan was obviously everything for them and nothing for me.

I wasn't expecting Brooke to talk, so when she did I jumped a little.

"So you did go see Denver one more time."

"No," I said, thinking she was talking some kind of nonsense. "I've never been to Denver in my life."

"Denver the boy," she said.

"Oh. Bodhi."

"Right. Bodhi. I mean, obviously he gave you my new address. When did you go see him?"

For some reason, the question made me nervous. Well, not even the question really, but I think more just talking about Bodhi made me feel weird. It made my stomach stop and think twice about whether it was willing to digest any more pizza.

"I'm not sure," I told her. "It might've been four days ago or it might've been five."

She frowned, but she didn't say anything. And I don't really like frowns, so I just kept talking.

"I sort of didn't want to go see him, because I'm mad at him and he hurt my feelings. And I'm getting tired of doing stuff for people when I know they wouldn't do that much for me. You know what I mean?"

I didn't really plan to wait and get an answer on that, but I didn't know what to say next, so a space came into my talking and she used it to answer me.

"Yeah," she said, "I think I do. But then you went anyway."

"I figured a promise is a promise."

I looked away from my slice of pizza and up at her face, and she was looking at me with this weird look in her eyes, like she'd just found out I was an angel with wings or a superhero or something. It made me nervous, so I looked away again.

"Why did you wait so long to come find me?" she asked.

"Did it seem long?"

"Well, yeah. It seemed like forever. But what I mean is, if you had the address for four or five days . . ."

I set down my pizza slice. There were about two bites left before I hit the crust, which I'd also intended to eat, but the conversation was getting serious again, and it started ruining my appetite.

I snuck a really quick look at her face, but she was staring at me, so I looked away again.

"I wasn't sure you really cared about me," I said.

And it was more honest than I meant to be, so it made my face get all hot, so I figured it was turning red, and I knew she could see that. So it was a pretty humiliating moment.

"What changed your mind?" she asked.

It hit me that she was talking to me really quietly and gently, like I was super fragile or something. Like I was one of those blown eggs you make for Easter that're only the shell and you have to handle them just so. Then after a minute I started wondering if she was right about me. About that. If I was holding myself together in a way that was dicier than I'd been pretending to myself and everybody else.

I said, "Phyllis told me you came looking for me, so that seemed like maybe a good sign."

"So she *did* know where you were!"

It came out loud and scared me a little.

"Yeah. She knew."

"Well, why didn't she tell me?"

I was still looking down at the carpet, and my face still felt red. I was beginning to worry that that red thing might never go away again in my whole life.

"She sort of has this rule," I said. "Sort of everybody who lives down there has this rule. You don't answer any questions about anybody else. If the law comes asking, or their family comes asking after them, you don't give anybody away. You always let it be up to them if they want to see somebody or not. You never let somebody get ambushed."

"But if you hadn't gone to see that boy and gotten my new address . . . she could have blown it completely by letting me walk away."

"She knew I had your new address," I said, and I swear my face got even hotter. "I told her."

"Oh."

I could tell she was embarrassed now, too, even though she didn't say anything. I mean, after the "Oh" she didn't say anything. But in the quiet I could sort of feel her embarrassment. I can't really explain it any better than that.

It wasn't really like me to stand up for myself in a conversation, but I figured it was going to have to be—you know, like, going forward I was going to have to change that. So I took a big, deep breath and I told her what I thought about her babysitting deal. It was hard, but I just did it anyway.

"Here's the thing," I said. And then I had to stop and breathe again. "I really love Etta, and I know you need somebody to take care of her, and I get that you can't afford to pay somebody, but it isn't really fair to ask me to do it for free."

I stopped and breathed some more, and thought about all the other parts of it I needed to say, and tried to figure out how I would say them.

I mean, where could I possibly even sleep in this neighborhood? And would I have to walk to her house every day, or would I need to take the bus because I had to sleep far away? And who was going to pay for all that bus fare? And then I might be sleeping in a place where I was all alone, and I wouldn't have people like Phyllis and the middle-aged guys looking after me, and that was a scary thought.

But then I started thinking maybe at least while I was here during the day I could take showers and eat food out of her refrigerator, and that was something. But maybe she couldn't afford to have me eating all that food, and I couldn't figure out how to ask if that was allowed.

So all those thoughts were making it hard for me to talk again, so I picked up that mostly eaten piece of pizza again and took a big bite, just to have something to do. And while I was doing that, she talked.

"I wasn't thinking of you doing it for free, exactly. I was thinking of it in return for room and board."

The pizza wasn't nearly chewed yet, but I stopped chewing it, because I didn't know what she meant. And I really, really wanted to know what she meant, the sooner the better, but I couldn't talk around all that pizza, and it just sort of turned into this big dead lump that kept me from doing anything I wanted to do.

Then I made myself chew it up and swallow it, fast, because all that stalling was getting me nowhere.

"What room and board?" I said after I managed to swallow that half-chewed bite. It hurt going down. "Room and board where?"

"Here. Room and board here. I thought you knew."

"How could I know that?"

"I'm sorry. I guess I wasn't making myself clear. I thought you knew. I meant you would live here and babysit during the day. What did you think I meant when I said I would help you study for your GED in the evenings?"

"Well. I guess I just thought . . . you know. We'd study. And then you'd walk me to the door and say goodbye."

I looked up quick at her face, then away again. It was really fast, so I'd already looked away again before I could really think about what I saw there, but she looked kind of hurt and sad, like she couldn't believe I'd think that about her.

"I wouldn't be able to offer you your own room," she said. "There's only one bedroom, and I thought Etta and I could share it. The couch folds out, so that would be your bed here in the living room. I know it's not much, but there's a half bathroom right there." She pointed to a door. "So you wouldn't have to come through the bedroom at night if you needed to use the restroom. But you *would* have to share that main bathroom with me anytime you wanted to take a bath or a shower. And you'd have to fold the bed back into the couch every morning. I know it's not much. But it's what I have to offer you right now. You'd eat normally every day. And if the GED doesn't sound good enough, I totally understand. We could do better if you want. I'll quit my job and get a night job and then you could go to school during the day. It'll be hard, but . . ."

Then she just stopped talking, and it sort of seemed like she might never start again.

We just sat there, not looking at each other. Almost like we were afraid to look at each other, and I was thinking it was weird to think of two people living together when they were afraid to look at each other. But I figured I would do it anyway, because we could probably learn to look at each other if you gave us enough time, and anyway I had to at least see if I was right. And besides, I figured we could both look at Etta in the meantime, and that was something. We had that little girl kind of tying us together in a way that just might work.

I opened my mouth to talk, and I had this long, achy pain all of a sudden, all down through my chest, but it wasn't really a bad pain. I know that probably sounds weird, but it's the truth. It was like what was happening, or at least what I thought was happening, was so big it made my heart stretch until it hurt.

"So you're actually asking me to live here . . . you know . . . like I was . . ." It was a hard thing to say, but I knew I had to spit it out, because if I was wrong about it I needed to know that right away. "Like I was your family," I said when I could make myself say it.

"Yeah," she said. "That's what I'm offering. If you'll accept it."

"Starting when?"

"As far as I'm concerned, starting when you walked through the door an hour ago."

I felt the skin on my forehead wrinkle down. "I have to go back and get my stuff."

"No," she said. "Don't even go back there. Please. I don't want to risk losing you again. It's not that much stuff."

"But it's the stuff you bought for me," I said, which was embarrassing, because I was totally letting on that the stuff meant more to me because it was from her. Too late, though. That cat was out of the bag.

"I'll buy it for you again," she said.

"But you said you hardly have any money."

"I don't have money for childcare," she said. "I have money for a sweatshirt and a hairbrush. Now, come on. Eat another slice of pizza. Everybody in this house gets enough to eat. Then I'll show you how this couch folds out."

———

I knew it was almost midnight because I could see the clock on the microwave in the kitchen from my bed. It was a good bed. Comfortable and soft, but not soft enough to give a person a backache. Just sort of welcoming soft.

I was lying there on my back, with my hands behind my head, in a huge, long T-shirt that Brooke gave me to sleep in, but I wasn't sleeping at all. The moon was nearly full, and the light from it was pouring in through the window because I hadn't pulled the curtains shut. We were on the third floor, and there was nobody to see in, so I hadn't bothered. I could have gotten up and closed them to make it darker, but I sort of liked the light from the moon. It made shadows of the mountains of boxes in the middle of the room, like real mountains and valleys but with straighter edges.

The door to the bedroom was open, and I thought it was nice that Brooke had left it that way, because it made me feel like she trusted me, or at least like she was willing to try. I'd sort of thought she would lock me out of her room every night or something like that.

So I guess it seemed like we were off to a pretty okay start.

I could hear Etta snoring, which was funny. It always made me laugh, or almost laugh, that a girl so little could have a snore so big. I couldn't hear Brooke snoring, so I didn't know if she was asleep or not.

I said her name. "Brooke." I said it just loud enough, or at least I hoped it was just loud enough—not so loud that it would wake the baby, but I hoped it would be something she could hear if she was awake. "You asleep?"

"No," she said. And it was just that same right amount of loudness.

"I'm worried about something."

"Okay," she said. "Talk to me about it."

"What if I get on your nerves?"

"So what if you do? *I* might get on *your* nerves, too."

"So . . . wouldn't that be bad?"

I heard her sigh a big sigh. It must have been big, because I could hear it from the next room.

A minute later she came out and sat on the edge of the couch bed with me. I could hear the springs creak under her when she sat down, and I liked the sound of it, because I think it sounded to me like not being all by myself.

She said, "Remember when I told you about how I wanted two kids and I wanted them in my early twenties?"

I said, "Yeah."

Because I remembered pretty much everything she'd said to me and everything I'd said to her, ever, probably because it all seemed important.

"So if I'd gotten my wish on that, as you pointed out at the time, I'd have a teenager just about your age right now. And don't you think she'd get on my nerves? Of course she would. I know lots of people my age with teenagers, and they drive each other crazy. Most of the time. Any time you live with another person there's always some level of driving each other crazy. I mean, I hear what you're saying. You're worried we won't get along. But when you have a child, there's no guarantee you'll get along."

"But they're blood family."

"Not necessarily. One family that I know, the boy is adopted."

"But I'm not adopted by you," I said.

I think I was trying to get closer to the thing that was worrying me, even though I didn't really want to go all the way there.

As it turned out, though, she went there *for* me, so then I didn't have to, which I thought was nice.

"So, the fear is . . . what? That if things get tough between us and we're not getting along, I'll just dump you again?"

"Yeah," I said. "That."

She sighed again, and it sounded extra loud from this close. Also I could see the shape of her making a shadow in the light from the moon, and it was nice because it looked like the shape of somebody I knew.

"Tell you what," she said. "I don't have a crystal ball and I can't predict the future, but I'll promise this much. I'll make you a solid commitment. No matter what happens, and no matter how we get along, you can stay for two years. Until you're eighteen. And then, if we both think we're better off apart, I'll help you get a job and a place of your own. I'll even put that in writing if you want me to."

"No, that's okay, I believe you," I said, because I really did believe her, because I knew she wouldn't offer to write it down if she didn't mean it.

Or that was part of why anyway.

The other part of it was that sometimes you just have to take a chance on something, because otherwise you definitely end up with nothing. You just have to be a brave girl sometimes, like I told the baby a thousand times that night.

"Good. Now stop worrying and get some sleep."

And she got up to go, but before she walked away she gave me a kiss on the forehead, like mothers do with their very own kids.

Before she could get back to her room, I said something to Brooke I'd been meaning to say. "You have to promise me you'll call your mother. Maybe not right away but sometime."

She stopped in the doorway and looked back at me, and I couldn't really see her face all that well, but I knew she was a little bit confused, because I could feel it.

"Why would you want me to do that?"

"Because she's not the worst mother in the world."

"She's not the best."

"No, she's not, I get that, but she's not the worst, and I know you know what I mean."

She just stood a minute, and then she opened her mouth to talk. I thought she was going to tell me to mind my own business, so what she said really surprised me.

"Okay, I promise. Now stop worrying about everything in the world and get some sleep."

I mostly stopped worrying. For the time being, anyway. Later I would worry some more, but life is just like that and nobody can exactly save you from it.

I didn't really get much sleep because I was busy lying there and memorizing the ceiling in my new home, and the way the silence felt, and feeling the place where her lips pressed down on my forehead.

It was all like something I didn't really want to sleep through.

But then I opened my eyes and it was morning, my very first morning in my new home, so I guess I really did get a little sleep after all.

BOOK CLUB QUESTIONS

1. The title *Brave Girl, Quiet Girl* references some poignant scenes throughout the book. In what way is this literary phrase used as a central theme?

2. The love between mother and daughter is highlighted in the three main relationships, each one fraught with its own challenges to finding love and acceptance. What are the commonalities that each relationship struggles with?

3. Early in the book, Brooke says the following: "Well, you know how it is. We either grow up to be our mother or we make a solemn vow to the universe to be her polar opposite." Do you believe this to be true? How does Brooke's attitude color her relationship with her own mother?

4. When Brooke plans to drive to the movie theater with her daughter, Etta, Brooke's mother begs her to use her car for safety. However, it's because Brooke has the Mercedes that the car is stolen. Do you believe that it was either woman's fault that this happened, and could it have been prevented?

5. Both Brooke's mother and Molly's mother have very ingrained beliefs about life. In referring to her daughter, Molly's mother says, "There's no welcome in my home for the devil," while Brooke's mother believes the

whole world is a dangerous place. What do you think is the underlying emotion driving both of these women's viewpoints?

6. When Bodhi takes off to find food for Molly and Etta while they're in hiding, he's arrested for stealing about seven dollars' worth of food. How does this reflect on the legal system and the problem of teen homelessness in the US? In what other ways did this book shine a light on this issue?

7. What does it reveal about Molly's character when, despite the risks and having everything to lose, she puts herself in harm's way to help a lost child?

8. After Brooke does what she considers the right thing with Molly, bringing her to her mother's home, Molly spends the night in the garage. Brooke wakes, only to find that her mother has thrown the homeless teen out, and now Molly is missing. How does this pivotal point trigger a transformation in Brooke's character?

9. What do you think finally changed Brooke's mind about allowing Molly to move in with them and become part of her family? Do you think it was the most beneficial decision for all involved?

ABOUT THE AUTHOR

Catherine Ryan Hyde is the author of more than thirty-five published and forthcoming books. An avid hiker, traveler, equestrian, and amateur photographer, she has released her first book of photos, *365 Days of Gratitude: Photos from a Beautiful World.*

Her novel *Pay It Forward* was adapted into a major motion picture, chosen by the American Library Association for its Best Books for Young Adults list, and translated into more than twenty-three languages for distribution in over thirty countries. Both *Becoming Chloe* and *Jumpstart the World* were included on the ALA Rainbow List, and *Jumpstart the World* was a finalist for two Lambda Literary Awards. *Where We Belong* won two Rainbow Awards in 2013, and *The Language of Hoofbeats* won a Rainbow Award in 2015.

More than fifty of her short stories have been published in the *Antioch Review*, *Michigan Quarterly Review*, *Virginia Quarterly Review*, *Ploughshares*, *Glimmer Train*, and many other journals; in the anthologies *Santa Barbara Stories* and *California Shorts*; and in the bestselling anthology *Dog Is My Co-Pilot*. Her stories have been honored in the Raymond Carver Short Story Contest and by the Tobias Wolff Award and nominated for Best American Short Stories, the O. Henry Award, and the Pushcart Prize. Three have been cited in *Best American Short Stories*.

She is founder and former president (2000–2009) of the Pay It Forward Foundation and still serves on its board of directors. As a professional public speaker, she has addressed the National Conference on Education, twice spoken at Cornell University, met with AmeriCorps members at the White House, and shared a dais with Bill Clinton.

For more information, please visit the author at www.catherineryan-hyde.com.